A FLYING FISH WHISPERED

ALSO BY ELMA NAPIER

Fiction (as Elizabeth Garner)
Duet in Discord (1936)

Memoir
Youth is a Blunder (1948)
Winter in July (1949)
Black and White Sands: A Bohemian Life in the Colonial Caribbean
(ed. Polly Patullo, 2009)

Travel
Nothing So Blue (1927)

A FLYING FISH WHISPERED

ELMA NAPIER

PEEPAL TREE

First published by Arthur Barker
in Great Britain in 1938
This new edition published in 2011 by
Peepal Tree Press Ltd
17 King's Avenue
Leeds LS6 1QS
England

ISBN13: 978 1 84523 102 6

Supported by
ARTS COUNCIL
ENGLAND

CONTENTS

To Patricia

EVELYN O'CALLAGHAN

PLOT AND PLANTATION: ELMA NAPIER'S ECOLOGICAL VISION IN *A FLYING FISH WHISPERED*

Introduction
Published in 1938 under the pseudonym Elizabeth Garner, Elma Napier's *A Flying Fish Whispered* might, initially, be dismissed as a steamy romance with an exotic setting catering to a British audience with a taste for tropical risqué. It is far more. Even as the female protagonist indulges in the clichés of the popular romance, the narrative acknowledges her level-headed awareness of self-delusion. Like the other (much better known) Dominican women writers Jean Rhys and Phyllis Shand Allfrey, Napier lovingly details the island's spectacularly beautiful landscape, which has enchanted travel writers since the nineteenth century. But Napier's novel is also far more than an excuse for a travelogue. It embodies and promotes a different kind of relationship to the land than that of the tourist, however, and savagely critiques the human and environmental consequences of British colonization. *A Flying Fish Whispered* constitutes a pioneering attempt, way ahead of its time, to engage with feminist and ecological discourses. Written by a British woman who settled in Dominica, the novel demonstrates how rapidly Napier came to see with a Caribbean eye and with astute insights into the nature of the local colonial order. The text brings to life the physical and social contours of the island, and the contested political dynamics at a crucial period of its social transformation. By turns stylistically uneven, magically evocative, passionately proselytising, both radical and of its time, *A Flying Fish Whispered* properly belongs within the Dominican and postcolonial Caribbean literary tradition, and its reissue is a real achievement.

7

Elma Napier

Elma Napier (1892-1973) was born in Scotland, the daughter of wealthy aristocrat Sir William Gordon Cumming, who came to be the subject of a famous scandal: he was accused of cheating while playing cards with the Prince of Wales. Elma herself was hardly conventional, falling in love with a married man at the age of 18. With her first husband, Maurice Gibbs, an upper-class Englishman, she emigrated to Australia in 1914 where she lived for nine years – for part of the time, on a sheep ranch in the outback – and where she began to write. She first met Lennox Napier (1891-1940) in Honolulu in 1919. A cultured English businessman with progressive ideas, Lennox was born in Singapore where his father was Attorney General of the colony. They fell in love and she left her husband in 1923 and subsequently divorced him but at a cost: the court required that she leave the two children of the marriage in the custody of their father. Her daughter Daphne eventually rejoined her mother at the age of 20 and married a Dominican friend, Percy Agar.[1] Elma and Lennox were married in Rangoon in 1924 and spent their honeymoon in Saigon. Both before and after her marriage to Napier, Elma toured extensively, spending time in Japan, India, the United States, Melanesia, South Africa as well as Europe and South America, where she acknowledged that she was finally weary of moving around with two small children: "Thank God, I have never been one to walk through the fields in gloves, a fat white woman whom nobody loves; but it was all too much and too much."[2] In the West Indies, she finally found a place to settle down, and there she happily spent the rest of her life.

Introducing her edition of Napier's autobiographical *Black and White Sands*, Polly Patullo explains that the Napiers "discovered" Dominica on a Caribbean cruise which they had "taken on account of Lennox's fragile health – and [Elma writes] 'fell in love at first sight'".[3] The family settled in 1932 on the (then) remote north coast of the island and built a home, known as Pointe Baptiste, at Calibishie. Their son Michael explains that there "were no roads to the south of the island so journeys to Roseau involved driving to Portsmouth and then a three hour boat journey along the leeward coast, stopping at villages on the way".[4]

As if Pointe Baptiste were not remote enough, Elma and her family later built a "second home" at Chaudière, deep in the rainforest (now reclaimed by the bush). A place where two rivers join, Michael Napier notes that getting there involved following a footpath and crossing a river six times! Progressive and rather bohemian in outlook – the beaches being secluded, bathing suits were often dispensed with – the couple became deeply involved in the life of the community in particular and Dominica in general. White, British and privileged they were; yet they could not have been more different from the rest of Dominica's tiny white expatriate society, mostly colonial officials. "While the other wives baked cakes and gossiped about the servants, Elma wrote articles for the *Manchester Guardian*, talked to men about politics and learned about the landscape and culture of her adopted island" (Patullo, pp. v-vi).

In 1937, Lennox Napier was elected representative for the North Eastern District stretching from Pennville to Morne Jaune. Notable among his achievements was his fight for boat landing and sea shore rights for the villagers of Woodford Hill and Wesley, which led to the legal guarantee of the right of Dominicans to access their beaches. The incident is fictionalized in *A Flying Fish Whispered*. Lennox was also valued by his constituents for his representation of Dominica's needs to the Colonial Secretary in London in 1932, prior to the Moyne Commission visit of 1939. After his early death from tuberculosis in 1940, Elma – who had become a leading literary and political personality on the island[5] – was persuaded to become the first woman elected to a Caribbean parliament in 1940 and the first to serve in Dominica's Legislative Assembly. She was the representative for the North Eastern District for some ten years. She also pioneered cooperative efforts, encouraged the formation of village boards and self-help programmes, and campaigned (along with Lionel Laville) for the construction the Transinsular Road which connected the north to the south of the mountainous island for the first time. She died in 1973 at the age of 81 and was buried in the forest on her land at Calibishie.[6]

What the flying fish whispered
The novel charts a doomed love affair between a married white creole man, a would-be planter from Parham Island (Antigua) and a long-term resident Englishwoman in the mountainous and forested St. Celia (Dominica). The initial passionate attraction fizzles out as his insistence on exclusive ownership and exploitation of the land for profit clashes with the needs of the locals, ultimately repulsing Napier's protagonist, Teresa Craddock, who sees in her would-be lover a similar colonizing attitude to herself. In *A Flying Fish Whispered*, Derek Morell threatens the natural order with the reimposition of colonial and plantation economies on landscape and peasantry, paralleled by his bullying and increasingly vindictive attempts to own and control the female body. The souring of the romance culminates in legal confrontation between Teresa, her brother and the villagers on the one hand and Derek and his wife on the other. Linking the woman's resistance of male control with an anti-colonial protest against the imperial commodification of nature, and deeply concerned for the preservation of the island's flora and fauna, Napier's text represents an early example of Caribbean feminist and postcolonial ecocriticism.

The text announces itself as a romance from the first page. In the capital city, Teresa encounters a stranger: "their eyes met, in which moment a flame was kindled that later blazed into fire" (p. 37; page references to this edition). And so they proceed to flirting on the long boat journey up the coast. "Does it mean anything to you… All this loveliness?" asks Teresa. "St. Celia is giving you of her best" (p. 41). To which the intriguing newcomer murmurs, " 'It isn't the island I'm going to love… but you.' And said it so softly that she though she must have dreamed he said it; thought that a flying fish had whispered" (p. 41). We are in familiar territory here, and expect the formulaic outcome. However, in Napier's atypical version, the object of Teresa's desire soon turns out to have feet of clay; more prosaically, on their second meeting Teresa cannot help noticing with a shudder "the lumpy bones of his ankles and the damp black hairs above them" (p. 52). She revels in the reawakening of her sexuality (delicately referred to as "Nature's urge to reproduction", p. 85) after years of mourning the death of her true love, but is aware of her need "to bring love in; to complicate the issue; dream herself into a mental union before she could envisage a physical one" (p. 86). Lust idealized as love: *A Flying Fish Whispered* testifies to the resilience of this romantic fantasy among women, even one as intelligent and "liberated" as Teresa. Well aware of the "foolishness" in her heart, she chooses to let

> this tide sweep her beyond the breakers. Sweep her to – what? But that night she would not consider "what". There might be calm water ahead, or rocks, or dangerous currents, but to-night she would think only of the intoxicating look on a man's face, of the whisper of his voice. To-night he and she would be alone together in a world of her own dreams. (p. 60)

Napier's awareness that these delicious feelings *do* constitute foolishness undercuts the fantasy:

> …Teresa had no illusions about heartaches, knowing that they followed upon indulgence as inevitably as liver attacks. But if one should permanently avoid these one would have lived emptily. How colourless would be one's old age if there were no purple patches to remember, no roses and raptures. (p. 59).

Anyone who has experienced a heady if inappropriate passion will sympathize with Teresa's dilemma, as she weighs scruples against desire in a more considered – and protracted – fashion than usually applies in a romance. Yet we are drawn to her *joi de vivre*. A sensual, passionate, uninhibited woman who does not care much for respectability, Teresa is generous and kind, and never takes herself too seriously. There is a bracing humour in her self-mockery even as she confesses her erotic enthralment: "I'm all fluid, slopping like a cup of tea in a railway train. My mind is a mustard-coloured mess" (p. 72). Love is figured here as disintegration of the self leading to rapture, "a passionate fever bringing in its train light-headedness and delirious dreams" (p. 106). But like cups of tea and liver attacks, reality is always around the corner.

A domestic tragedy sends Teresa for an interlude to Parham Island, Derek's flat, arid home where conditions have hardly changed since the days of slavery and "the landscape, as well as the life of the island, was dominated… by the twin steel chimneys of the sugar factory" (p. 132). Her desire for him cools as she realizes her infatuation is with an illusion, and that her passion has blinded her to the heartless and rigid planter ideology which Derek has imported into her beloved island. Teresa links herself with the land he plans to use, fearing his determination to bend nature and people to his will in pursuit of his goal: "If he found what he wanted... then the axe would follow, and the cutlass, and a burnt desolation" (p. 69). Deeply committed to the island and its people, she parallels the imposition of power on human and natural destinies when she wonders whether "he was not big enough to love this wild scenery, wanted it tamed? And if some day take her into possession would he want ruthlessly to cut down and tame her, to reduce her to the level monotony of flat cane-fields?" (p. 75).

"The lust of possession"
For Derek Morell has come to St. Celia from Parham Island,[7] a place known for its brutal plantocracy. And indeed he and his island are associated with slavery: "I was heir to a house three hundred years old," he tells Teresa, "one of those heavy stone mansions that still had slaves' quarters" (p. 72). He wants to turn his land in St. Celia into a sugar plantation, with – it is implied – a similar attitude to labour as his slave-owning forbears. Such an attitude is referred to in the text as "Parham Island ways", alluding to conditions reminiscent of slavery which still operate there: "they're still practising slavery" (p.152). Visiting the island, Teresa observes landless peasants totally in the power of "the planters, the factory manager, [and] the merchants", the new masters who control wages and even determine where workers must spend their paltry wage (p. 135). The very landscape is haunted "by the ghost of black men of long ago, who built the house and the catchment and the sugar mill, and who were never, technically, free" (p. 141). A clear connection is made between the callousness of the past slave masters and that of the of current British administration toward its once-valued possession. Surveying the ruined wharves and fortifications of the port, a colonial official comments, "'So much these islands mattered to us once,' the General said. 'And now so little'" (p. 142).

12

Sylvia Wynter's seminal article "Novel and History, Plot and Plantation" provides a dialectical model for the ways land came to be viewed in Caribbean society: either as slave *plot* (small tracts of land, vital resources on which the enslaved grew food and sold/bartered any excess) or master's *plantation* (a system for efficient exploitation of natural and human resources in the service of profit). For Wynter, the Caribbean was "'planted' with people, not in order to form societies, but to carry on plantations whose aim was to produce single crops for the market".[8] In other words, Caribbean people came into being as adjuncts to the product (sugar) which they produced. In Wynter's formula, the plot prioritizes *use value* in which human needs dominate what is produced; the plantation is organized according to *exchange value*, where the product – in response to market demand – is more important than human needs. The commodification of land by the plantation economy alienated those who were forced to work it, yet traditional West African notions of land as sacred were retained in the value placed on slave plots/gardens. The relevance of the distinction to *A Flying Fish Whispered* is obvious. The Parham Island ethos constructs land and labour as commodities to be used; St. Celia is configured as a place where there is an *interrelationship* between living beings and their surroundings, a mutual connection between people and their place.

Derek's attempts to manage the plantation he has bought cheaply according to "Parham Island ways" clashes with established communally-minded local conceptions of land rights and ownership. With his stereotypically frugal Scottish wife, the intention is to "succeed financially as planters" whatever the cost to themselves or others. He gives tenants notice and destroys their gardens (plots) to clear the land for cane, grudges fallen coconuts to the peasantry and threatens to close access to the beach. But, asks Teresa, "How would the people get their fish?" Derek's wife speaks for him: "That, Miss Craddock, would be their business, not ours" (p. 80). The same woman who complained at the lax standards of justice in the island cannot recognize her own immorality when confronted with the fact that people will starve if the beach is closed.

Napier's *Black and White Sands* recounts similar sentiments expressed by an American about his failed estate: "it is hard to get a jelly-nut for my own use because the people still pilfer. They don't reckon it is stealing to take a nut or a fig from the old estate. It is as though it were still our business to feed them" (p. 138). The reference to a now abandoned paternalism on the part of "us" for "the people" directly alludes to the slave past. For Teresa, "stolen coconuts mean no more to her than blackberries… picked from high road hedges" (p. 79). But the Morells are wedded to the principle of ownership – what Teresa calls "the lust of possession" – in their relationship to the land (p. 57). She points out that of the "fifteen hundred acres of Neva" plantation, only about "a hundred were planted in coconuts" so Derek has far more land than he needs for his planned canefields; but, he counters, "I might need these some day. Anyway, it's the principle of the thing" (p. 65). And it is the planter's language of ownership and property rights that he enlists, rather than any concept of mutuality and interdependence. The latter perspective is articulated by locals such like the old priest: "is it not so that when one buys or inherits a property one acquires at the same time certain responsibilities, the duty of administering the land for the greatest good of the greatest number?" (p. 174). "For years," the coloured Council member tells colonial officials, the peasants have "been allowed to help themselves to the Neva coconuts" (p. 90). Teresa learns that "Derek himself had gone sour when, eighteen years ago, he had been turned off his garden" (p. 80). Yet, now he turns peasants off theirs and parsimoniously resents them taking *his* (unused) coconuts from *his* property. And the disappearance of one of his cattle serves to harden the determination to prevent anyone but *himself* and *his* labourers having access to *his* beach, *his* portion of the sea, *his* property. If such thinking is permitted, Teresa feels, St. Celia will become like Parham Island, sucked dry and abandoned to poverty and dereliction.

Napier's own distaste for the Morell's capitalist politics might be suggested by the similarity of their surname to "morel" (a kind of mushroom) and is reminiscent of Frances Lanaghan's account of *Antigua and the Antiguans* (1844).[9] Itemizing the classes which make up Antiguan society, Lanaghan scathingly refers to ill-bred whites who aspire to social rank as pale mushrooms (*"fungi"*) which spring up overnight from muck. Similarly, Teresa images the inbred "poor whites" of the islands of the Saintes, with their "pale flesh peeping through rags" as having the "bleached unnatural look of things grown in the dark or kept in cellars" (p. 173). Like a fungus, Derek and his wife spread the infection of their Parham Island thinking. The planter ethos locates Derek's dream of canefields squarely within the discourse of his slaveholding predecessors: making money, whatever the consequences, is all that matters, and land or people are simply resources to be exploited to this end. In the novel, matters come to a head. The events which follow mirror Dominican history.

"Ominous murmurings reach us from the Northern District," reads the *Dominica Tribune* of January 8, 1938.[10] "The villagers of Wesley are asking why the Government has done nothing to restore them the right, which they believe is theirs by user [rights] from time immemorial, to beach their fishing boats on the foreshore at Cariboa Bay." A Captain Stebbings, whose estates occupied almost eight miles of foreshore, is reported as giving notice to fishermen who land their crafts here, the only safe landing spot on this rough stretch of coastline. The subsistence fishermen are informed that they would no longer be permitted to access the bays, as Stebbings suspected one or more of them for the theft of coconuts and a cow from his property, which he suspected, had been exported for profit to Guadeloupe. Moreover, no one could wash clothes in the river that ran through his land, nor was anyone permitted right of way to or from the beach without his permission. Two fishermen failed to remove their boats; they were prosecuted and fined three pounds (an outrageous sum at the time) which they could not pay. Since they could not fish, they had no income. "As a result of these fines the villagers of Woodford Hill and Wesley approached Mr. L.P. Napier, the elected member of the Legislative Council for the district, and asked him to prepare a petition to the government for the restoration of what they honestly believed to be their rights."

The presentation of their case to the Legislative Council led to the formation of a committee by the Governor to investigate the matter and as a result, Stebbings was made to allow the villagers "the use of a small strip of the Woodford Hill beach" and access to the river mouth for laundry purposes. However, he would not compromise with regard to Cariboa Bay, forbidding access to the Wesley fishermen. "Mr. Napier pointed out that times were changing, that it was now recognised that landlords had obligations as well as rights" and that it was grossly unfair to penalize the fishermen of Wesley – who had paid license fees for their boats – and to deprive the village of supplies of fresh fish for the supposed theft of some coconuts and a cow. In view "of the serious disturbances which have recently occurred in other British West Indian islands", the *Tribune* warns the Government of the "grave risks involved in delaying action on this matter" since infringing on "not only their legal rights but also of their rights as human beings" could result in "a very ugly mood".

When Teresa proves unwilling to consummate the affair with Derek, he shows a much uglier side: "he wanted, nakedly but furtively, to go to bed with her. Wanted her body, and not her friendship" (p. 179). Enraged at her rejection, Derek abandons any scruples regarding his duties to the land or the community. Teresa begs him to cease his "petty persecution" of fishermen and small farmers "who live on the verge of starvation; for whom there is no work" as a result of his actions (p. 215). Coldly, he responds that he will only consider granting such a request should she become his mistress (p. 216). Her heartache cured, Teresa nonetheless resents "how unfair life was to women… Tommy could sleep with Georgette and suffer no nerve storms nor spasms", whereas her change of heart has led to the suffering of an entire village (p. 209). Like the newspaper report previously cited, the novel ends before legal changes forced landowners in Dominica to recognize that national resources were, at a fundamental level, held in common; and that environmental justice necessitates that *all* citizens have access to the earth, the rivers and the sea. Elma Napier's fiction nonetheless insists on the integrity of this position by placing her characters on either side of the debate and empathizing with the passionate insistence of her feisty heroine that the needs of the poor majority outweigh the landlords' capitalist/planter ethic.

Early ecocriticism

Polly Patullo asserts that Napier was an "early environmentalist [who] fought to preserve the island's great forest ranges, and describes its ecology with an eager eye" (p. vi). Indeed, the novel shows Napier, through her protagonist, expressing an ecological awareness far in advance of her time. Teresa abhors the wanton destruction of the forest for short-sighted agricultural ventures, be they large scale, as in the logging for the Canadian market (p. 231), or small, as in Nicholas's slash-and-burn peasant tactics for land clearance with the resultant soil erosion (p. 167). Her didactic tone sometimes grates, however true the sentiment: "men have cut forests that they might snatch food from the soil; and now the soil flees from them, washed by rain from the rock surfaces to thicken the rivers and to stain the seas" (p. 73). Such moralizing is out of kilter with the novel's lively narrative voice, but is driven by Teresa/Napier's horror of what the island faces, in human as much as natural terms, from the planter mentality of Morell: "Drink to our success here," Derek said, "to the ultimate downfall of the forest" (p. 79). Deeply saddened by what is lost – "the little trees… the orchids that would perish in flames… the peasants' gardens" – Teresa romantically puts her faith in Caribbean nature, which will resist and outlast human destruction: "the red cliffs would remain, and the sea. The most determined planter could never tamper with those" (p. 74). Indeed, she thinks, Derek does not know what he has taken on, for "St. Celia had more tricks up her sleeve than a peasantry careless about the rights of property" (p. 80). The woman identifies with the subversive power of tropical nature which will not be bound by the hubris of male will to power.

In effect, Napier's angry indictment of the clash of values between "Parham Island ways" and those of St. Celia with regard to environmental, social and economic justice, draws attention to two very different representations of the Caribbean space and also anticipates the fundamental ideological and ecological conflict embedded in Wynter's paradigm of plot and plantation which became central to the critical vocabularies of West Indian literary studies from the late 1960s. Ironically, theorists like Wynter would have probably dismissed such prescience by someone like Napier, who at the time would be relegated to the peripheral category of elite expatriate observer. In Parham, Napier mourns the degradation of the Caribbean environment as "to white-sanded beaches there drifted the refuse of the Atlantic" (p. 132). Back in her own island, Teresa reflects on a similarly careless disregard for ecological issues on the part of the British government representative charged with important decisions. After all, "he would never see the island again, nor care, after his departure, if it were networked with concrete highways, or left in pristine innocence" (p. 224).

Expatriates and creoles, colonials and anti-colonials
The novel is ahead of its time in ecological awareness, but it also radically critiques colonial rule and its racist matrix: Teresa disassociates herself from the ill-manners of the colonial Administrator who recoils "at a coloured man calling a white woman by her Christian name" (p. 90). Keenly aware of racial inequities and the impotence of colonial dependency, the novel occasionally sparks with rage at imperial exploitation of the West Indies and its people. *A Flying Fish Whispered* mocks the pusillanimous yet pompous refusal of the colonial Governor to address the moral crisis of human versus property rights: "No, no, Craddock, this is a question of right and wrong, not of administration" (p. 224). Teresa puts the blame squarely on "the Home Government" which, she and Tommy know, "would do nothing" (p. 238). This impasse will continue as long as "the Government" consists of expatriate officials whose whole term of office is spent in longing for its completion, at which time they depart St. Celia, "shaking the dust of it from their feet, [and] straightaway forgot the island; and were themselves forgotten" (p. 227).

British-born Teresa clearly allies herself with the local population, black and white, against the management of the island by such colonial expatriates, the kind of "Englishmen whose slogan is 'the Empire for the English'" (p. 158). She is disparaging about "English women in the West Indies [who] do their own cooking to economize on ingredients" but "keep servants for the sake of being able to write home with pride in their number" (p. 53). With her brother, she unapologetically prefers "Creole cooking"

18

to the insipid English food served at Government House (p. 88), and dispenses with sentimental English traditions: "thank God for no plum pudding, no snow, and no robins" (p. 108). Unperturbed by her brother's coloured mistress, Teresa herself acknowledges that mixed-race West Indians have a right to be suspicious of "the impertinence of whites" (p. 88). Given the history of English racism and exploitation of blacks in the colonies, she understands such distrust; likewise, she despises expatriates and colonial officials who have no real interest in or commitment to the island. In Napier's memoir *Black and White Sands*, she reflects that like her heroine,

> we had made our entrance in Dominica at the end of an act, when the orchestra was already playing a new one… Gloves and stockings, silver salt cellars and tea equipages, the White Man's Burden and the prestige of the Master Race… This attitude was rigidly maintained until the tide of democracy and commonsense, to say nothing of war conditions, swept it away. (p. 92)

The disregard of the Mother Country for the welfare and long term development of her West Indian colonies and their people fostered a deep hostility among many of the supposedly loyal subjects of empire.

Teresa might even be a proto-nationalist, passionately loyal to her adopted island and those who live there and resentful of colonial condescension. As privileged as she clearly was, Napier's acknowledgement of the need for social change and push toward self-government (Lennox Napier's name appears on a petition for Dominican self-government in the mid-Thirties) marks both author and protagonist as pretty revolutionary for their time.

Whispers of *A Flying Fish* in *Wide Sargasso Sea*

The mutual misunderstanding and distrust of West Indian creole and English expatriate is a theme that dominates *Wide Sargasso Sea* by Dominican Jean Rhys.[11] In fact, *A Flying Fish Whispered* plays out several of the conflicts which feature in the later novel and it is tempting to make intertextual links. The evocation of the wild landscape beloved of the female protagonist but antithetical to the colonizing male, the fraught romance of people from different cultures, even similar place names, all remind Napier's readers of Rhys's better known story. "Neva" (p. 37), for example evokes Geneva, the family estate on which Rhys bases her fictional Coulibri, itself echoing Napier's "Colibri" (p. 40). Elaine Campbell notes parallels in the two texts, although Napier wrote to Alec Waugh in 1949 asking, "Who is Jean Rhys? I must try and read her... None of us have ever heard of her."[12] Rhys left Dominica around 1907, while Napier only arrived in the 1930s. However the two *did* meet, as Sue Thomas notes, on Rhys's only return trip to the island in 1936.[13] Rhys records the contact somewhat caustically in her letters: "The Calibishee lady is by way of being literary" and appeared to be more interested in getting to know Rhys's husband, the publisher Leslie Tilden-Smith.[14] Napier may not have remembered Rhys, but Rhys more than likely knew Napier's work. For example, both Elaine Campbell and Veronica Gregg have commented on Rhys's use of the title which Napier gave her collection of travel sketches (*Nothing So Blue*) in her short story "The Insect World". [15]

Certain incidents in *A Flying Fish Whispered* are echoed in Rhys's more crafted novel: a female protagonist traumatised by a tragic fire; frustrated sexual desire turning to revenge and hatred; a man from another culture seeking to possess and control the land/woman. Further, Campbell itemizes images central to *Wide Sargasso Sea* appearing first in Napier's text: a woman in a red dress on fire (p. 117), the mirroring of white woman in the black (p. 120), the reclamation by the forest of a house associated with white privilege (p. 124), and the depiction of a wild tropical landscape beloved of the female protagonist but distrusted by her lover who prefers "a tamed and ordered Nature" (p. 65). Typically, Rhys reversed the national markers. Napier's Teresa, the passionate woman who identifies utterly with topical nature, is British, though long settled in the island, while Rhys's Antoinette is a creole. Derek, the coldly materialistic planter who is blind to the island's beauty and wants only to use its resources, is a West Indian creole. Rhys's unnamed husband is an English fortune hunter and Antoinette is objectified by him. But in Napier's novel it is the West Indian man who resents what he perceives as the Englishwoman's patronage:

> You think I'm too uncivilized to control myself? A savage West
> Indian who doesn't know how to behave? Oh, half the time I
> know you're looking down on us. Not really thinking we're
> your equals. (p. 109)

And though she denies it, Teresa *is* irritated by "the "assumption
of inferiority" (p. 116). Subsequent to her change of heart and his
taunts, "You met me more than half way", her response reflects
the class difference that separates them: "There was a touch in her
manner of – who is this clerk turned planter that he should throw
my former condescension in my teeth" (p. 180). Passion turns to
coldness, and when Derek tells Teresa, "Your love didn't amount
to much, whereas my bitterness is strong" (p. 214), it recalls the
husband's unspoken words to Antoinette in *Wide Sargasso Sea*:
"My hate is colder, stronger" (p. 136). Whether or not Rhys read
Napier's novel, the love affair ending in distrust and hatred in
both works directly points to the failure of communication
between colony and metropole.

Feminist intimations
If Napier was ahead of her time in working environmental and
anti-colonial concerns into her fiction, I suggest that the novel *also*
expresses sentiments that might be termed proto-feminist. Teresa's
mother, we are told, was a suffragette who fought for the rights of
women, as her daughter now fights "for the rights of negro
fishermen" (p. 225). She is stunned that "men anywhere, men one
knew, could still be debating as to whether women were, or were
not, fit to sit on juries" (p. 165). And she has profound objections
to becoming "the pleasure of this man who had a sense of property,
who might seek to own [her]" (p. 109). *A Flying Fish Whispered*
explicitly exposes the double sexual standards of white men like
Derek, who is of "pre-War vintage" and believes "that there was
one sauce for the goose and another for the gander" (p. 71). And
Teresa resents the fact that "certain phases of life were made
unjustly easy for the other sex, who were less subtle in their
requirements" (p. 86). So her brother Tommy openly has a
coloured mistress, but a similar arrangement is socially forbidden
her.

More daringly, perhaps, the novel also acknowledges double sexual standards for black and white women. Teresa, like her cook Tilly, is open about female sexual desire, frankly admitting that she wants "to go to bed with" a man (p. 84). Similarly, Tilly states that "I must have a man every fortnight... else I am ill" (p. 44). However, the white woman is rather more delicate in expressing her needs; and the text portrays black women as more in tune with nature and their own natures while white bodies look out of place in the tropics. Only belatedly does Teresa realize that her feelings for Derek were not love, but "mere lust shorn of its tinsel" (p. 120); black women are under no such illusions. Teresa "floated on air" as a result of "stolen meetings, stolen kisses" while Norah has her baby alone in her servant's room, "got up from her bed and went about her work again" (p. 106). Sex "for servants and livestock" is "an ever-recurring feature of existence" (p. 45), but Teresa has scruples about being termed a "loose woman" (p. 71). The difference between sexual mores for black and white women is inviolable. "Tilly was among her own people and their ways were not hers," acknowledges Teresa (p. 122). So while "illegitimate babies were not treated as sins" among black women, even the most liberal of white ladies find that "it was still not easy to have a child without a husband" (p. 61).

Such attitudes are of their time; the novel was, after all, published in 1938 and set somewhat earlier. Napier's own social status and her character's self-positioning in relation to the place and the people among whom she lived (and clearly loved) is complex and needs to be contextualized within its period. *A Flying Fish Whispered* opens with a harbour scene where men on the jetty "jabbered, hoisted, sweated" as Teresa notices a "man she had never seen before" wearing "a white suit like everyone else's" and waits on news from "beautiful young men" sorting mail in the Post Office (p. 37). Race and class markers are ostensibly absent, but it is obvious that some kind of men jabber, hoist and sweat while others perform important clerical jobs and still others wait for public transport in white suits. The first actual mention of race comes onboard this transport, when Teresa and the stranger are described as "two white faces among black ones" (p. 39). For sympathetic as Teresa and her brother may be to their black

Dominican neighbours, like the Morells they are still distinctly other. This is evident in the kind of essentializing remarks made by Tommy: "You know what these people are. They spend it all on a spree in town, or they go to law with their neighbours. Then there's nothing left" (p. 43). As for feminist solidarity across race – a concept not even articulated at the time of the novel, of course – the white Teresa accepts her privileged status without interrogation. However vividly drawn, none of the black women in the novel ever transcend their status as servants. Even the most lively and central of these is described on her deathbed as preoccupied with her domestic responsibilities: "Miss T'resa, de cauliflowers is on de stove. De cauliflowers is still on de stove" (p. 119). Such jarring indicators of entrenched difference epitomize Napier's awkward yet honest evocation of gender, race and class relations of the period, which applied, it seems, even in the most enlightened and intimate social circles.

Plotting the local world

The contrast between local and expatriate is most pronounced in the novel's responses to St. Celia's natural environment. Like other Caribbean women writers preoccupied with pastoral and botanical imagery (Jamaica Kincaid's gardening essays, the poetry of Olive Senior and Lorna Goodison, Oonya Kempadoo's and Shani Mootoo's corrupted Edens), Napier's writing is notable for its clearly informed depiction of an exquisite Dominican landscape in all its seasonal variation. The intimacy of the protagonist with the beloved place is evident in her eye for nuances of colour and light: a roof is "rusted to the pale red colour of mango flowers" (p. 46); moonlight is "spread like white butter on the flat broad leaves of the banana trees" (p. 232). This lyrical evocation of the island's visual beauty suggests a painter's sensibility:

> Sea and sky were flooded with palest pink, and where the sun had been there remained great wedges of yellow light divided by streaks of egg-shell blue. Light lingered still on the mountain tops, gilding the forest and the wisps of cloud that streamered from a jagged peak. (p. 41)

Trees, flowers, plants and creatures of all kinds intimately *belong* in their natural world. Until, that is, human agency disturbs the relationship: so the Ça Ira river sensuously lingers

> ...for awhile in a dark gully where the siffleur montagne nests under black cliffs; ripples through sweet smelling ginger in a twilight of dasheen and tannia leaves; and finds deep shade among cocoa trees whose purple and golden and red pods hang upon black twisted trunks. But close to the village women wash clothes in its smoother reaches; its waters are clouded with soap-suds. (p. 46)

Like the rivers and streams that carve the landscape, motion informs Napier's peripatetic narrative. It follows her characters as they walk, swim, plant, drive or sail on and around the island, mapping and bringing it to life for readers.

Teresa's easy acceptance of the environment contrasts with that of Derek's uneasy wife who projects her own fantasies and fears onto the Caribbean space. For the nervous Janet, a "palm tree quivered as though with fever" (p. 76), and the river in flood is red "as though it carried blood to the sea" (p. 78). The only space she considers non-threatening is the orchard she has planted, constructed and viewed through a familiar British frame of reference. On the other hand, she anthropomorphizes the forest as "a dark sinister woman, ready to crush her, ready to steal" (p. 74).[16] Like her husband, Janet distrusts the tropical excess of St. Celia and prefers the flat, tamed and cultivated landscape of Parham Island. Both women acknowledge that nature in the West Indies can be destructive: floods and landslides, blight and disease take their toll. But while the expatriate rails against what she perceives as a hostile force, the locally identified Teresa observes a healthy respect for the island's climatic and geographical vagaries and loves it "without fear" (p. 94).

A Flying Fish Whispers draws on Napier's life, and there is a hint to this effect when Teresa avers that "knowing a writer's fiction, one afterwards read his biography, finding there the raw material from which he had drawn his creations" (p. 132). Reading Napier's memoirs, the parallels with the fiction are striking: like Lennox Napier (probably as a result of injuries sustained during the First World War) Teresa is instructed by doctors that for health reasons "she must live in a warm climate" (p. 86). Her memories of snowy childhood Christmases (p. 107) and the "last night in London before we came out here for the first time" (p. 91) correspond with similar observations in her autobiographical accounts. The architecture and topography of Ça Ira (Pointe Baptiste) and its surrounds are fleshed out in *Black and White Sands*. Multiple references to people, incidents, anecdotes and even dialogue encountered in this memoir are familiar from the fiction. For example, in *Black and White Sands*, May the cook asserts "that she must have a man every fortnight, else she was ill" (p. 49), and perishes "horribly by fire... so, in grief and terror, we learned that a negro's colour is only skin deep and never to the ending of my life shall I forget the white patches on her body" (p. 128). Almost word for word, the autobiography rehearses the novel's ironic account of the wrecking of the jetty in the main port. *Black and White Sands* testifies to the development of Napier's skill and/or editorial acumen in that it is sparer and more crafted than the novel, though equally riveting.[17]

Yet however informed by experience, the novel is a clearly structured piece of writing. It is divided into sections which track the path of Teresa's sexual intoxication, breakdown, reflection and insight, and the consequences of her change of heart in the social and personal spheres. As Elaine Campbell notes, the text neatly unfolds into two parts: "Fever and Flame" and "Coconuts and a Cattle", with a twenty-page "Interlude" in the centre of the book ("An Expatriate", p. 86). The several chapters which make up "Interlude" are pivotal in signalling the binary oppositions set up in the novel: between Teresa in and out of love; the social order of colonial/Parham Island and creole/St. Celia; relationships between the sexes and between humans and the land. Moving from strange and magical St. Celia to a more quotidian space jumpstarts the revision of the differences which Teresa has vainly attempted to underplay in her affair with Derek Morell. Her enlightenment as to Derek's true nature is prefigured in the depiction of Parham Island's illusory charms:

> Parham Island is as unlike St. Celia as one island can be to another. Seen from the sea it has a prettiness of pale green cane-fields, of purple shadows lying on burnt hills. But when you

come close to it and touch it you find that it is dry and dusty, and that the prettiness is only an illusion contrived by the sunlight and the clear air. (p. 131)

After the interlude, the romance plot is relegated to the past and the text foregrounds the struggle for workers' rights at a key time in West Indian history. Campbell observes the juxtaposition of "issues of sexual and racial social imbalance" and praises Napier's narrative control which "preserve[s] the novel from deteriorating into a polemical tract" ("An Expatriate, p. 91).

At the same time, it has to be admitted that the work is stylistically uneven. It is occasionally bathetic and the tone can be rather shrill and disapproving, as in the diatribe against West Indians' love of litigation as a legacy of "slave mentality" (p. 160). Sometimes there are lapses of taste, as in the unfortunate reflection that, "A cook had been burnt, but the world had to go on" (p. 171). There are perhaps too many "purple passages" and a portentous overuse of motifs such as "torn pieces hanging to the telephone posts like broken kites" (pp. 105, 116, 131). Napier may be unconsciously acknowledging her own occasional overwriting when she has Teresa humorously object to an excess of mismatched metaphor (p. 67); certainly the author shares her character's sense of the ridiculous and an ability to laugh at herself. The telling does sometimes ramble away from the tale, and the novel's chronology is fluid. So we are told about an event and then wryly informed that "the sequel came three weeks later, but the telling of it belongs here" (p. 196). For instance, Ma Nolette's deathbed scene triggers Teresa's memory of Rosalie Nolette's infected finger and her abortive trip to hospital, then meanders on to the death of Ma Nolette herself and her prophesy of a connection between her son and Teresa. It is somewhat awkward and roundabout way of foretelling the linked destinies of the two families. These interpolated anecdotes are sometimes puzzling, sometimes bizarre, but always fascinating. Staying with a friend in the mountains, Teresa happens to leave behind "pink silk panties" which are appropriated by the yardman. Returning a year later, she asks what he has done with the garment.

"I wear them in bed," Harrigan said, adding: "When I am in bed I read the Bible." And showed them his book with an ace of spades marking his place in the Old Testament, and a joker that in the New. (p. 230)

While the novel could have benefited from pruning, Teresa's quilting provides a useful trope for Napier's stitching together of event and memory into the fabric of her text. "The fabric of memory is woven of scraps and patches," she affirms in *Black and White Sands* (p. 236). More sprawling and less technically proficient than Rhys's evocation of Dominica, Napier nonetheless reflects a similar immersion in the texture of the place. The prose photographically captures the colour and shape and the names of plants, and the nuances of climate. Napier is adept at catching light and sound as she describes, for instance, the appearance of the sky with rain approaching, the quality of light under wild banana trees or the sudden quieting of the surf pounding the cliffside as one moves inland into the windless tunnel of scrub.

I may have given the impression that the text prioritizes the depiction of a lovely place, with people of secondary interest. However, just as each place is associated with a certain kind of light, climate or vegetation, so too it is associated with particular characters. Indeed *A Flying Fish Whispered* is crammed with human interest. True, some characters are barely sketched and little more than types or caricatures, but Napier has a knack for creating memorable snapshots, even for those who play only peripheral roles. The "eccentric and undependable" Dr Crew, for example, is "tall and skeleton-like, a Buddhist, a Welshman, and a believer in Social Credit" but is far more concerned with finishing his paper for a medical journal than attending to a seriously ill woman (p. 111). Formal occasions and official spaces are linked with types rather than personalities, such as the General (p. 133) and the Governor who serve as stereotypes of colonial officiousness. By contrast, domestic and outdoor spaces provide a stage for servants, neighbours, fishermen, and peasant farmers, vividly individualized with all their particular idiosyncrasies faithfully rendered. The garden at Ça Ira is the province of Henry the groundsman, and the house is that of Tilly and her sister Norah, polar opposites. Tilly is vivid, expressive, attractive, cheeky and a flirt. Shortly before her death, Teresa comments: "Never had she looked prettier, more full of the joy of living, more radiant... a lovely laughing girl in a red dress" (p. 106). By contrast, Nora is lugubrious, silent, upright and discreet.

Teresa's world is full of personalities, named people, many of whom have their own back stories: the gardener, for instance, who quotes the opinions of one "Partridge deceased on every problem, horticultural or otherwise" (p. 99). The combined effect is, again, a stitching together of disparate characters into a community; people who have duties and responsibilities to each other, each according to their means. Thus, Teresa and her brother lend money and provide transport for medical attention and Français the carpenter does not charge for making a neighbour's coffin since "It is the custom ... to give help when a friend has a dead" (p. 49).

Narrative location
Sometimes intrusive and polemical, Napier's narrator can also efface herself, and demonstrates linguistic facility with code-switching between English and Dominican creole when point of view shifts from the consciousness of the protagonist. In fact, chapter three is set entirely among Rosalie's family and neighbours and Teresa appears as a character in *their* narrative, mentioned only in passing. Elsewhere the reader is given access to the conversation and thoughts of the unemployed in Parham Island in their own words (p. 135). Rendering such local speech patterns, Napier proves herself an astute observer of the sociolinguistic behaviour of bilingual Dominicans: "'And wherefore,' said the policeman in the stilted English of one who would be more at home in patois, but feared to speak it, lest by doing so he should infringe the dignity of an officer of the law, 'do you walk into Town?'" (p. 47). Napier's writing reveals a real ear for the translation of Dominican creole into quaintly formal English: "that girl Tilly, she say things behind my back that if she repeat to my face I will not answer for the consequences" (p. 93). As the author observes, "[i]n Dominica, it seems that English is better for being a 'learned' language, and it is often curiously old-

fashioned; it is the language, in fact, of Shakespeare and the Bible" (*Black and White Sands*, p. 103). The narrative follows the twists and turns of linguistic differences, what is said and not said on specific occasions, such as Norah's euphemism for why visitors cannot be taken to Teresa as she sunbathes naked by the water: "I tell them the way to the river is hard" (p. 61).

Napier and the Caribbean literary canon

Campbell credits the writer Stephen Haweis, who came to Dominica in the early twentieth century and stayed for the rest of his life, for shifting "literature about Dominica away from the detached report of the literature of colonization and away from the romantic picture-painting of nineteenth-century commentators. It moves the literature about Dominica towards a literature of concern about Dominica by Dominicans."[18]

She locates Elma Napier's work in the same category, making a space for her in the postcolonial canon. "Her family is now in its third generation in Dominica... [and] Napier's forty-one years in Dominica combine literary and political activity" ("Literature and Transnational Politics", p. 357). Is this kind of evidence really necessary to justify attention to an early Caribbean novel by someone who happened to be born out of the region? In the relatively recent history of Caribbean women's writing, there have indeed been periods when authors have been excised from the literary record. Thus, Campbell (1982) asks why the critic Sylvia Wynter names Ada Quayle as the first West Indian woman novelist, to the exclusion of Elma Napier, Jean Rhys and Phyllis Shand Allfrey, all of whom produced novels much earlier. Alison Donnell also queries the critical disavowal of some early West Indian poetry by women whose work was ignored or dismissed as "embarrassing and undesirable, often imitative and usually dependant on colonial forms and ideologies".[19]

It is a fact that writers have been marginalized or excluded by critics of West Indian literature. This has to do with the perceived quality of their work, or the author's race/class/politics, place of birth or subject matter. As Donnell explains, the current literary and political context determines who is in and who is out; but luckily the verdict is subject to interrogation and revision by later readers. So, after decades of debate, no one now queries Rhys's contribution, and her novels and stories, along with those of Allfrey, are republished and taught at schools and colleges in the region and internationally. Articles, reviews and books have been written about their work. Yet Elma Napier's fictions will be new to many readers. Napier herself experienced literary marginalization in her own time. In *Black and White Sands* she comments that her second novel "was published during the Munich crisis and sank like a stone"; still, she is delighted (if amused) when a tourist tells her that "Your *Flying Fish Whispered* is the best book ever written about the West Indies" (p. 168).

The tourist's claim may be somewhat inflated, but I do think the novel's time has come. It is informative, amusing, gripping, lyrical and evocative. More specifically, *A Flying Fish Whispered* offers fertile ground for ecocritical analysis. DeLoughrey *et al* suggest that "literature can play a vital role in reshaping human attitudes toward the natural world and that the natural world bears the marks of the best and worst of human behavior."[20] One of their key concerns is with "how Caribbean texts inscribe the environmental impact of colonial and plantation economies" (p. 2). Clearly Napier's novel captures the dramatic and pervasive impact of human activity – good and bad – on the Dominican environment. In *A Flying Fish Whispered*, she seeks to co-opt literature as an ally in the defence of a natural world threatened by the reimposition of "colonial and plantation economies". The "extraordinarily beautiful island" of Dominica has been celebrated, Campbell points out, precisely "because it had not been successfully exploited by the planters who ravaged other West Indian islands" ("Literature and Transnational Politics", p. 355). It is writers like Napier who dramatically remind us of the need to be aware of this, now more than ever.

University of the West Indies, Cave Hill, Barbados

1. Her first son was killed over Canterbury, England during a German raid in 1942.
2. Elma Napier, *Winter is in July* (London: Jonathan Cape, 1949), p. 230.
3. Polly Patullo, "Before Dominica: a portrait of Elma Napier," Introduction to Elma Napier, *Black and White Sands: A Bohemian Life in the Colonial Caribbean*, ed. Polly Patullo (London and Roseau: Papillote Press, 2009), p. iv.
4. Michael Napier, "History of Pointe Baptiste", <http://www.pointebaptiste.com/history.html>.
5. Elma Napier had written two memoirs, *Youth is a Blunder* (London: Jonathan Cape, 1948) and *Winter is in July* (1949) before she came to Dominica, as well as a volume of travel sketches, *Nothing so Blue* (Kensington: Cayme Press, 1927). She published a variety of articles and short stories in magazines whilst in Australia and Britain, and finished the third part of her autobiography, *Calibishie Chronicle*, in Dominica in 1962 (now published as *Black and White Sands*, Polly Patullo ed., 2009). By then she had also written two novels set in the island, *Duet in Discord* (London: Arthur Baker, 1936) and *A Flying Fish Whispered* (London: Arthur Baker, 1938), both published under the pseudonym Elizabeth Garner (possibly because of their frank sexual content). She contributed articles to the local press, the regional literary journals *Bim* and *The West Indian Review* in the 1950s and 1960s, and wrote columns about her life in Dominica for the *Manchester Guardian* and *Blackwood's Magazine*.
6. For this biographical sketch, I have drawn on Polly Patullo's introduction to her edition of Napier's autobiographical *Black and White Sands*; Virginia Blain, Patricia Clements and Isobel Grundy, eds., *The Feminist Companion to Literature in English* (London: B.T. Batsford,1990), p. 786); and Lennox Honeychurch's online *A to Z of Dominica Heritage* at <http://www.lennoxhonychurch.com/heritage.cfm? Id=121>.
7. Some critics have seen Barbados as the original of Parham Island, but Teresa clearly distinguishes between the two:

"I've never been to Parham Island, but I hate Barbados, with its green glaring flatness. I love the forest, you see" (p. 73). Furthermore, Parham was the first English settlement in Antigua, and the island's first port.

8. Sylvia Wynter, "Novel and History, Plot and Plantation," *Savacou* 5 (1971), p. 95.

9. Frances Lanaghan, *Antigua and the Antiguans: A Full Account of the Colony and its Inhabitants*, Vol. 2 (London: Macmillan, 1991), p. 193; first published in London by Saunders and Otley (1844).

10. Anon, "Cariboa Bay: An Appeal for Action", *The Dominica Tribune*, Saturday, January 8, 1938, n.p. The newspaper clipping to which I refer was kindly supplied by Napier's grandson, Lennox Honeychurch (Dominica's foremost historian/ writer/ anthropologist/ environmentalist), to whom I and countless others owe a debt of gratitude for his generous guidance through the literary, geographical and cultural riches of his homeland.

11. Jean Rhys, *Wide Sargasso Sea* (London: Penguin, 1968).

12. Elaine Campbell, "An Expatriate at Home: Dominica's Elma Napier", *Kunanipi* 4: 1 (1982), p. 92.

13. Sue Thomas, "Conflicted Textual Affiliations: Jean Rhys's 'The Insect' and 'Heat'", in Hena Maes-Jelinek, ed., *A Talent(ed) Digger: Creations, Cameos and Essays in Honour of Anna Rutherford* (Amsterdam: Rodopi, 1996), p. 287.

14. *Jean Rhys: Letters 1931-1966*, ed. Francis Wyndham and Diana Melly (London: Andre Deutsch, 1984), p. 29.

15. Veronica Marie Gregg, *Jean Rhys's Historical Imagination: Reading and Writing the Creole* (Chapel Hill: University of North Carolina Press, 1995), pp. 174-177.

16. The image is echoed by the British husband in *Wide Sargasso Sea*, who considers "the forest… a dangerous place. And… the dark forest always wins" (p. 137).

17. Some wonderful images of the Napier house at Pointe Baptiste and surrounding views can be accessed at <http:// www.adventuringsouth.com/2011/05/black-and-white-sands-of-pointe.html>.

18. Elaine Campbell, "Literature and Transnational Politics in Dominica", *Journal of Postcolonial Writing* 24: 2 (1984), p. 356.
19. Alison Donnell, "Difficult Subjects: Women's Writing in the Caribbean pre-1970", paper to Sixth International Conference of Caribbean Women Writers and Scholars, Grande Anse, Grenada, May 18-22, 1998, p.1.
20. Elizabeth M. DeLoughrey, Renée Gosson, and George Handley, eds., *Caribbean Literature and the Environment: Between Nature and Culture* (Charlottesville: University of Virginia Press, 2005), p. 28.

PART ONE

FEVER AND FLAME

I

The launch, tied up alongside the broken jetty, lurched heavily, sickeningly, to the swell of the Caribbean. Men jabbered, hoisted, sweated. Sun blazed from a cloudless sky. Only under the jetty – where brilliant fish swam between wooden piles encrusted with sea-urchins and waving seaweeds – was there shade. As each sack of flour or case of gasolene was flung on board, the launch shuddered, as though her overweighted body could bear no further burden.

"Do we start on time?" Teresa asked. And the clerk in charge of loading shrugged his shoulders. "That will depend on the mails," he said.

A man she had never seen before was leaning against the barrier, looking at the crumpled end of the jetty that a tramp steamer had rammed. He was a tall man wearing a white suit like everyone else's, but Teresa knew at once that the man himself was different; and as he turned at the sound of her voice their eyes met, in which moment a flame was kindled that later blazed into fire. Because a stranger in Capesterre is a rare thing, she guessed that this was Derek Morell, who had bought Neva.

She looked at her watch. Then walked along the sea front to the post office where beautiful young men stood in rapt contemplation of three rows of pigeonholes.

"Is the Grande Anse mailbag made up yet?" she asked.

"We're making it now," one answered, adding casually: "Perhaps you could tell us the time?"

Teresa knew that the post office clock faced outwards and was set so high on the building that only from a hundred yards at sea could the time be told. "It's ten minutes to three," she said. And then, delaying the mystic rite of making up the mail by another half minute, she extracted her own newspapers before going back on to the jetty. Quarter of an hour later the mailbags followed on a handcart.

If the passengers sit closely and if some of them are children the motor launch *Petrea*'s first-class accommodation can seat sixteen. That day Teresa counted fifteen, and one was a child. To keep out the sun a canvas curtain had been drawn across the horizon. Beyond the uncovered engine, from which issued not only noise but oily smells, second-class passengers sat in a colourful half-circle. Opposite Teresa, so that their knees touched, there was Derek Morell.

"Can this island have held us both for a month?" he was thinking, "and I not have seen her, not known that she was waiting for me in this place?"

"Are you Craddock's sister?" he said aloud. "I was at Ça Ira the other day but you were not there."

Teresa nodded and said: "I've met your wife, in Grande Anse." And remembered a tight-mouthed sour woman, queerly mated to this man, whose deep-set eyes seemed already to be caressing her; whose skin was drawn so tightly over his bones that his head looked like a skull; whose mouth spoke thrilling practised words that denied his thin lips and the rigid line of his jaw. It was only afterwards that she knew his lips were thin and his jaw hard. Then she saw only his eyes, heard music in his voice.

Janet had said of Teresa, and Teresa knew it: "I have seen Miss Craddock once and once was enough. She was nearly naked in Grande Anse." It seemed that she had been wearing no stockings and a frock without sleeves. Derek's mouth twitched, and she knew that the remark was in his mind also, and she smiled at him, making that really the beginning, the first smile rather than the first words. "This frock," she said, "hasn't a back either."

Her back was invisible now, pressed against a white-painted board, but her legs were smooth and thin, tanned to the same colour as her arms. Through openwork sandals he could see toenails matching the crimson of her finger tips. Her black hair was drawn off her face and coiled into a knot, but a few wisps had escaped on to her forehead and heat had tightened them. She was embarrassed by his scrutiny – for the sun had been very fierce on the jetty, and she was tired. She opened her bag and extracted powder, afraid lest her nose should be providing a mirror for his own countenance. "The picture is perfect," he said. "Don't paint perfection."

Impertinence from a stranger? She hadn't taken it so. They two, wedged like matches in a box, were yet alone; two white faces among black ones; two sharing a joke unshared by others. "I'm going to dust the picture," she said, "not paint it." But her mirror assured her that her nose had not been emulating its qualities, and she put her puff away again, conscious that in seeking it she had prodded her neighbour's ribs.

Slowly, majestically, the coast unfolded itself; grey cliffs edging hills that rose into blue peaks; brown houses huddled in valleys; a church gleaming white against a green background. Sometimes the smoothness of the sea was broken by little fish that, rising to the surface, stuttered along the water on their tails.

At the end of an hour two men who had been eating oranges defied the brazen heat by going on to the forward deck, leaving behind them a general loosening of muscles, a rearranging of feet, a spreading of cramped limbs that revealed, with string invitingly slack, a bundle of magazines from the Capesterre library. One of the crew opened it, handed to his mate copies of the *Sketch* and *Tatler*. Barefooted coloured boys, their clothes so patched that none could tell where the original garment began or ended, they balanced themselves on a rail above a stinking spluttering engine to read the *Tatler*. Teresa remembered, from faraway and long ago, a dowager impeccably "county". "I never," she had said, "let the lower classes see those papers. They might not understand."

Off little villages, wedged in between the mountains and the sea, where fishing nets were spread to dry, and coconut palms overhung grey sand and shingle, a warning bell was sounded, and canoes came slowly from the shore to exchange, loquaciously, passengers and bags and baskets. Once there was a scream of: "Stop the launch," and some braced themselves for a collision, while others looked to see who had fallen overboard. Thirty feet astern Teresa saw a flash of silver and rainbow drops glittering on a string. A man perched on the roof had caught a fish and was fearful lest his line should break. Here and there upon the sea were pieces of bamboo – serving as floats for fish-traps – whereon sea-birds rested.

As the heat lessened Teresa climbed also on to the forward deck. Here there was neither sound nor smell of engine, only the slight heave of the sea and mountains towering darkly above her. She sat on a kerosene case beside the sentry box wherein the captain stood to steer the ship, and there Derek Morell joined her, wishful, so it would seem, to avoid discussion of the Spanish war. "Are we not fortunate," Mr. Golightly's voice boomed from below, "that God in His mercy should have let Henry the Eighth sever our dear England from the Church of Rome?"

Mr. Golightly's skin was black as that of a negro impersonator's polished with boot blacking, but John Bull himself was not more English. "Shakespeare," he had said once, "is as much my Shakespeare as yours." A travelled person, he had been to New York and Paris. "Paris," he told Teresa, "is a city of light." And she, to whom that place was anathema, agreed with him for quietness' sake.

"What happened to the Capesterre jetty?" Derek asked. And she said: "It seems that the *Branka*'s captain rang down 'full-steam astern', and the engineer thought he must mean 'full-steam ahead'. The sort of simple mistake that anyone might make. That was a year ago, and quite soon now they're going to rebuild it. Once the Grande Anse jetty broke its back under a load of bone manure that my brother had ordered. We thought that the fertilizer would produce fantastic seaweed, but nothing happened."

"Probably the fish ate it," Derek said. "Were there fantastic fish?"

At Colibri the doctor joined them, handing up from the canoe his walking-stick, his bag, his helmet, and a series of gin and whisky bottles labelled with the names of drugs. Ignoring the labels, Teresa chose to be facetious about his luggage; for a pennyweight of joke goes a long way in the launch towards evening, when eyes and hearts are weary, and the sea gods hang upon the keel to hold it back. Young lime trees were landed, planted in bamboo sections instead of pots; and a black pig – desperately squalling until flung on to the ballast stones of the boat and thereafter mute, with tears welling from tiny eyes.

The sun had vanished now, vouchsafing a clear clean sunset and a sight of the final flash of green known as the emerald drop. Sea and sky were flooded with palest pink, and where sun had been there remained great wedges of yellow light divided by streaks of eggshell blue. Light lingered also on the mountain tops, gilding the forest and the wisp of cloud that streamered from a jagged peak. Morell was at Teresa's side, gazing not at the mountain but at her.

"Does it mean anything to you?" she asked. "All this loveliness? St. Celia is giving you of her best."

He turned from her to the slow moving coast, to the clear deep water – bottle green – shadowed under cliffs. "You must teach me to love it," he said. "To me, it's very new country. It's gates are still barred."

They two were alone together, enclosed in a little circle of their own intimacy. A strange stillness lay on land and sea as though the world held its breath for the coming of night. "It isn't the island I'm going to love," he said, "but you." And said it so softly that she thought she must have dreamed he said it; thought that a flying fish had whispered, or a turtle, rising to the surface to breathe.

Later she knew that Derek hated the island, but not as Janet his wife hated it, who was afraid. "It takes big people to love mountains," Tommy had said once. Derek's heart was rooted among cane-fields through which the wind rippled, billowing them like the sea; and in mangrove swamps that were neither quite sea nor quite land, but only grey mud spread with a film of water. For him night's purple shadows fell on dry bare hills patched with cotton bushes. But Janet dreamed of stacked corn and turnip fields; of curlews following the plough to the heather's edge.

As they rounded the last corner and came into King Charles' Bay they saw, shining like a mirrored star, the one light on the Grande Anse jetty. Morne Collat, frowning on the town, looked naked and cold as though it were bare rock only and not covered with forest at all. But now and then against the skyline there were outlined little feathery trees like the hairs on a man's arm.

"At Elder's on Twenty-third Street," Mr. Golightly was saying, "you can get the best pigs' trotters in New York."

41

II

"A most exciting man," Teresa told Tommy, who was her brother. "I thought he was going to kiss me right there on the deck of the *Petrea* under the noses of old Golightly and the doctor."

Tommy said: "What a pity he didn't. The island needs a new scandal. Puss Borrowdale's baby has been overdone. But as a matter of fact I don't like all I hear of Morell, though he's pleasant enough to talk to."

"Tell me the worst," she said. "If he's going to love me I must know every dark secret." She had been able – then – to joke about love, knowing that fire raged behind the smoke of that man's warm appraising glances, fire with which it might be amusing to play. But she was not at all, at the beginning, afraid of burning her own fingers. For Teresa love had been buried long ago in a grave in Paris. Sometimes its ghost walked, but not here. Not in the West Indies. Here you lay sleepily on verandas looking down on to a sea that was spread before you like blue glass, having pale streaks on it and a white edging. Here you walked with your dog in the forest and swam in deep green pools sprinkled with white pois-doux blossoms or blue petrea. You made orchids grow and tomatoes. But before Derek came love never interfered at all with the business of living.

"Morell comes from Parham Island," Tommy was saying, "and the ideas he has brought with him are not ours. Neither has he been here long enough to start putting them into practice."

"Such as?"

"Turning people off their gardens."

Plantations of tannias and dasheens and bananas; yams twining their foliage around thin stakes; sweet potatoes spreading

42

theirs flatly over furrows; pumpkins and pigeon peas, a little sugar or maize. "They'll squat on Crown land instead," Teresa said. "And he's paying compensation."

"Compensation is no good against a garden," Tommy answered. "A man clears land and plants provisions hoping to reap for a year. What's the use of ten shillings or a pound, cash down? You know what these people are. They spend it on a spree in town, or they go to law with their neighbours. Then there's nothing left. No pound, no garden."

She knew Tommy was right, but she had to defend a man who had looked at her as though she were lovely. "After all," she said, "he's bought Neva. The land is his to do what he likes with."

Tommy said: "I never pretended it wasn't. He's within his rights. It's a *manque de tacte*, that's all. Anyway, Neva was no place for a stranger to buy."

They had been to Neva, often. It was on the other side of the island, on the Atlantic coast. The place had been deserted for years, had become overgrown. Only the foundations of the old house were still standing. Once Teresa had traced a stone aqueduct leading to a tumbled heap of rubble and some rusted machinery buried in convolvulus vines. The Morells were living in what had been the overseer's house, a three-roomed shack a mile or two up river. They hadn't even a telephone. But in the fields there were old lime trees still bearing fruit, and between the beach and the road the coconut palms were choked with sprouting nuts. The beach was a mile long, its sweep of white sand the only safe resting-place for boats on all that rocky shore. Rafts and canoes were drawn up under the almond trees, and Caribs came in there with cargoes of boards or baskets or oranges.

"I wonder why he bought it," Teresa said. "Why they came here at all." She had wondered before, but much more so now that she had met him. He didn't look like a planter, nor a man suited to the wilderness.

"It was going for a song," Tommy said. "But if you've made a conquest, Teresa, for God's sake be his guiding star. Before long he'll be needing a soft shoulder to cry on. His wife's are bony. A Parham Island man must go slow with those Ville Rousse people, and if they do pick up a coconut now and then it'll pay to ignore

43

the fact. He came here the other day, grumbling about theft, and I don't want any trouble in my district."

Tommy was round and red and easy-going, an elected member of the Legislative Council. His heart was as large as his frontispiece, and there had never been trouble in his district. The people were poor, but a joke from their member enriched them, and he had that priceless asset – time in his pocket, which he put at their disposal.

"We must fight for the soul of Derek Morell," Teresa said next morning; and Tommy wondered how much of his soul she wanted, knowing that women were always self-deceivers. Teresa had been dreaming all night of those deep-set eyes, or thought she had been dreaming because she remembered them so early. "There's a bad influence at the back of him," she said, "and Mrs. Morell will be a tough coconut to husk." That remark about her nakedness had not endeared Janet to Miss Craddock. "A sourminded female," she said, "who wears stockings because she has ugly legs."

"It's obvious you don't feel that way about your own," Tommy suggested fraternally, looking at the long bare limbs that protruded from his sister's shorts. "But meanwhile come and see the rabbits. That new buck might be a hermaphrodite for all the use he's being."

Tilly the cook was singing a song with the refrain of – "I wish I were back in my mother's womb."

"Do you really?" Tommy said. "A pretty grim place, I should have thought," and Tilly giggled. She never understood much of what he said, but she was very pretty and a good cook.

"I must have a man every fortnight," she told Tommy once, "else I am ill."

"An invitation to the dance?" Teresa questioned.

"Probably, but there's nothing doing. A landowner," he pronounced sententiously, "should never foul his own nest."

Tilly was with them five years. When she died she was twentyone and a mother. Teresa had a picture of her as the plump child who had come to them first, not as cook but as messenger, standing at the top of the hill and holding under one arm a hen, and in the other hand a string of fish, silver and scarlet and gold. On her head there was a basket, from which protruded the necks of three soda-water bottles, and these gave her a strangely coquettish look, as though she wore an old-fashioned toque with rakish feathers trimming it. "I back, Miss T'resa," she had said, "I back." Now, she would never come back. It didn't seem possible that the house could stand without Tilly.

It appeared that the buck rabbit was fouling nobody's nest but his own. Teresa seldom visited the little hutches that were set up on stilts under the pois-doux trees, because from the first she had said "There must be no fraternization with rabbits lest we become too sentimental to eat them." Their first pair had been established on a platform in the chicken run, and a cock had flown up and pecked a newborn litter to death. Some aspects of life, Teresa decided, did not bear thinking about. She had always disliked fowls, and since then hated them. Now, she stroked the nose of the impotent and offending buck, but her mind was not fixed on rabbits, and as soon as possible she went back into the house. Servants and livestock made sex an ever-recurring feature of existence, but it struck her suddenly as indecent and horrible that a man's whispered tribute, the look in his eyes, should be part of this crude coupling, this everlasting reproduction of species. She sat down at her desk and looked out upon a clump of bay trees blown into reverse by the wind; and she thought – how tiring to be a tree, harried and twisted at the whim of any breeze. "Swayed by our own emotions," she said to herself, "we have at least the illusion of controlling them." Then she wrote to Mrs. Morell, asking her and her husband to come over to lunch on the following Sunday.

Janet made some excuse, and it was many days before Teresa saw Derek again. His whispered, incredible words ran about her mind like a flickering flame, the smoke of which was no more than a haze blurring the horizon. No open fire broke through to give warning of danger. Life followed its even tenor, bringing that daily freight of laughter and little heartaches that Teresa likened to fragments of torn kites blown by the wind and caught upon telephone wires to hang by the roadside; things of no importance, that one remembered.

III

The Ça Ira River rises on the lower slopes of Morne Collat and hurries incontinently towards the final oblivion of the sea. It lingers for a while in a dark gully where the siffleur montagne nests under black cliffs; ripples through sweet smelling ginger in a twilight of dasheen and tannia leaves; and finds deep shade among cocoa trees, whose purple and golden and red pods hang upon black twisted trunks. But close to the village women wash clothes in its smoother reaches; its waters are clouded with soapsuds; and tattered garments – blue or cream-coloured, or orange – are spread on its sun-warmed boulders. And it seeps at last into the Caribbean through rounded pebbles, among which lean black pigs rootle for filth.

On the outskirts of the village, where the slow dragging sound of surf on shingle blends with the swift murmur of the river, Ma Nolette lay sick. Ma Nolette's house had stone foundations and three worn steps leading to the door, old weathered stones taken from the ruined buildings that once stood upon the seashore. Its roof was rusted to the pale red colour of mango flowers, and its wooden walls were lined with newspapers, and here and there a holy picture or a series of cigarette cards. It was said in the village that Ma Nolette was a soucouyant, that when night fell she shed her human skin and, transformed into a huge firefly, entered the house of her victims to suck their blood. Now, on her deathbed, she lay in a mahogany four-poster, and her face was shrunken and grey. When the doctor came he had to shuffle into the room sideways and put his hat under the bed.

Teresa had a strange affection for this old reprobate who had been wont to squat immobile by the side of the valley road, frightening people with her eyes and laughing at them in her heart. "Miss T'resa have fire in her soul," she had said once; and Teresa remembered that now, when the warmth of an unseen flame was creeping into a heart which, for a long time, had been cold and dead. She sat beside the dying woman, and wondered what life would be like at the very end of it.

Rosalie, Ma Nolette's daughter, did the Ça Ira washing, and Teresa noticed that the girl's finger had a sore angry place on it that was paining her. "That is a bad finger," she said. "I will speak to Doctor Packer about it." And the doctor said: "You must come to me at the hospital tomorrow and I will cut it that you may have relief."

That night Rosalie put a poultice of soursop leaves and candle-grease on to her finger, but in the morning it was swollen to the size of a ripe plantain, and the pain ran up her arm and throbbed in her armpit. "You must go to the hospital," Ma Nolette said. So Rosalie put on her yellow and white striped dress, placed a straw hat above her Madras, and carried in her hands her black kid shoes with high heels.

Once upon a time the village at the mouth of the river had been itself a town, and all along the seashore there were stone houses about which vines and creepers had woven a green shroud. From out of their roofless walls coconut palms grew and breadfruit.

A gang of prisoners were repairing the road, and Rosalie talked for a while to the khaki-clad policeman in charge of them. One of the prisoners had once been Rosalie's boy, but he had left her for another girl, and had broken into a house and stolen earrings for her. Rosalie made an elaboration of ignoring him.

"And wherefore," said the policeman in the stilted English of one who would be more at home in patois, but feared to speak it, lest by so doing he should infringe the dignity of an officer of the law, "do you walk into Town?"

Rosalie told him how she had poisoned her finger with a thorn, and that the doctor was going to cut it at the hospital. "Why, gal, that is just perfectly foolish," he said. "At the hospital they will half kill you before they let go of your finger. When they opened my leg it took four men to hold me still."

Rosalie walked on more slowly, pretending to herself that the pain in her finger had grown less. There was a man sculling across the bay in a canoe piled high with coconuts, and the boat's wake made a trace on the water that was like a scar. Nagging waves pulled at the stones under the palm trees and fell back with hissing sucking noises. When Rosalie came into town she put on her shoes, and they creaked as she walked past the fishmarket. Two girls from her own village, one carrying a tray of avocado pears on her head and the other dangling a string of red fish, asked her where she was going. She told them that she was going to the hospital to obtain ease for her finger.

"To do that you must be clean crazy," they said. And one added: "When I go to hospital the pain tease me so they put me to sleep before they cut me."

Rosalie wavered and turned back. To be threatened with pain so bad as to be put to sleep was intolerable indeed. She hurried along the road by the sea-coast, her face grey with terror, dust settling on her hat and shoes, her arm throbbing as though devils hammered it.

Next day it was swollen like a young palm tree, and the pain was so great that she lay on the ground all day. The women stopped their chattering by the wash-pool to brew teas of wild ginger and lemon grass to calm her fever, and Ma Nolette made a charm of crossed sticks tied with blue thread. Teresa sent word that next day she would herself take Rosalie to hospital.

As night fell, Ma Nolette's son, Robert, beached his boat on the shore and blew his shell to make known that he had fish. Robert lived on the other side of the island and kept his boat on Neva Beach. But that night he had come to Ça Ira village to visit his sick mother, and when he saw Rosalie's finger, he said: "It would seem that that limb should be cut." And Rosalie answered dully: "It should be cut."

The sun had fallen into the sea behind a rampart of grey clouds, whose edges were touched with silver. Fire blazed from under the cook-pots, and in the smooth lower reaches of the river water ran clear and the moon faced its own unbroken reflection, for soapsuds had floated away and mud had settled where drinking cattle had trampled it. Robert fumbled in his pocket, and brought out a razor blade that was only a little rusty. Mr. Morell, he said, had given it to him out of a Gold Flake cigarette tin. He called to his friends, and they laid Rosalie on the floor. While one man sat on her chest, others held her feet and her arms, and Robert slashed the sore place with his blade to let out the poison.

Next morning her finger was better, and she walked up the road to the Big House carrying a tray of clean clothes on her head and singing Hallelujah to God as she walked. But that evening her mother died, and so was joy changed to mourning. To qualified mourning, however, for Ma Nolette would never again frighten people by the roadside; dry up the cows; make the dasheen rot in the ground. And in the hour before she died she whispered to her son Robert: "Stay close to Miss T'resa, for your two lives are crossed like the sticks of a charm." By which saying Robert knew that his mother was passing away in foolishness, for how could the life of a poor peasant be bound to that of Mr. Craddock's sister at Ça Ira?

He borrowed money from Tommy to pay for the boards of the coffin, but Français the carpenter gave his services free. "It is the custom," he said, "to give help when a friend has a dead." Teresa sent down a wreath of frangipani blossoms, because she remembered that in the Pacific these trees were planted in cemeteries. But Tommy, more practical, gave Robert a gallon of rum for the wake.

IV

Derek Morell came to Ça Ira on a day of storm and rain. Wind blew the sea into dark patterns, ruffling its shades of grey; and the faraway whisper of surf, drawn over stones, was drowned by seeping noises of water gurgling into gutters. On Teresa's knee lay the nucleus of a patchwork bedspread, its component parts achieving, by mere continuity, colour effect out of all proportion to their single values. Beside her stood a basketful of prepared pieces cut into hexagonals of every texture and hue; sartorial memories, among which her needle and thread moved with slow monotonous rhythm.

Here was a red and blue check bought in Barbados from a Broad Street store. She remembered a frantic hour's shopping on a Saturday morning; and a half-caste shop-girl, with negroid hair and gold earrings, who served her with a sob in her voice, saying: "I'm so glad you came, so glad. Yesterday there were only fifty cents in my book, and today nothing," so that she had longed to go on buying, if only to put more happiness into that little pale face imprisoned in a shop. Outside in Broad Street, so narrow that two cars could hardly pass, huckster women had pestered her to buy St. Celia oranges; and the pavement had been so crowded with the feet of the people going out from the city to the pale green cane-fields and the golden beaches, that she had taken refuge in one of those musty victorias upon whose box-seats old wizened men droop over broken reins. At the end of the street, beyond Nelson's monument and the little carenage where sloops and schooners tie up, she had seen with relief the open dancing sea and the white steamer that was to take her away.

Under the place where the roof leaked, spreading liquid

threatened to engulf her chair legs and make boats of the scraps of cotton that she had let fall on to the floor. Faintly, she could hear the roar of the river, knew that it was in flood. Picking up a fragment of flowered crêpe her eyes followed the train of thought to red hibiscus blossoms, shrunken and empurpled by wetness; and saw that the alamandas wreathing the veranda posts had been beaten to their knees by the storm. The crêpe had come from the Syrian's store in Capesterre, and reminded her of fat white women having the sad eyes of Armenians; and of white greasy men whose sleek hair fell in wisps over their pockmarked faces. In the street there had been uproar and commotion, for a man slipped on a mango skin while carrying a medicine bottle in his hand. Blood had spurted from a severed artery, making the pavement a shambles; and his life had been saved only by someone's surprising presence of mind, and the speedy adjustment of a tourniquet. Next day a small boy had dogged his footsteps, crying: "Please, Sir, to give me thruppence. Sir, I am the boy who wiped your blood from the doorstep of the Syrian. Please, Sir, a penny to buy bread."

Teresa smiled at the recollection, and Derek saw the smile still on her face as he came up the veranda steps, his clothes wringing, rain pouring from his hair.

"Good Heavens," she cried, "what a day to be out in." And he answered: "I went up river and was caught by the flood. So I climbed over the ridge and came down through the Souffrière valley."

Neva was back to back with Ça Ira. The two places were ten miles apart by road, but not more than four if you climbed over the mountains between them. There was a pass at fifteen hundred feet. "I've been that way," Teresa said. "It's a terrible track in wet weather. You must change at once and have something hot. I'll lend you a suit of Tommy's."

"Where is your brother?"

"In Capesterre. There's a Council meeting." Surely he must have known that. His pretending not to made her self-conscious, aware of their isolation as she would not have been with any other person. The house screamed its emptiness, although there were servants in and around it.

"Here," she said, pulling out of a drawer khaki pants and a shirt. "Get out of those wet things. I've had tea, but I'll tell Norah to bring some more."

From the kitchen there came noises of wordy strife. Norah screamed something in patois, and Tilly's giggle was followed by a smacking sound as though her sister had boxed her ears. Teresa sighed, because for a long time there had been peace in her house, and now there was this strange unexplained tension between the two girls, who for days spoke not at all or only on business, and then broke out suddenly into one of these vivid tropical storms.

"The servants are fighting," she told Morell when he reappeared looking overgrown in her brother's clothes. "But have a drink in the meantime." She couldn't help noticing the lumpy bones of his ankles and the damp black hairs above them. One should never look at latter ends, she thought; they spoil everyone. For a little while his charm worked hardly at all. Then she met his eyes again, saw the thin-lipped mouth that was strangely desirable, and knew that his spell was upon her; that no matter how indifferent and conventional his words might be, nor how ugly his ankles, some indefinable magnetism was drawing her helplessly towards him.

"West Indian servants are the devil," Derek said. "Yours are sisters, aren't they?"

She wondered how he had known that. But her servants had never been devils. Even this frightening incomprehensible feud was carried on tactfully. Her elbows were cushioned. Teresa liked West Indian servants and disliked generalizations, but she did not argue with him because she realized that this conversation was only the preliminary curtseying in a set of lancers. It meant nothing, but was according to rule. Not for a long time had she so suffered from shyness, but the whispered words of that flying fish, or was it a turtle – "It isn't the island I'm going to love, but you," sang very loud in her ears, reddening her cheeks and drying up her savoir faire.

"The fact that they're sisters makes their quarrel all the deeper," she said. "But I don't know what it's about."

"Probably some man."

"I – suppose so." But her assent was given reluctantly, because she did not believe that women quarrelled inevitably about men. Thinking so was a symptom of male complacency. Tilly's baby was nearly a year old, and she had christened him Fitzroy. "How can a child thrive," Norah had said, "bowed down with a name like that?" Perhaps she was jealous of the baby, resented Tilly's keeping it with her.

"We haven't a servant," Derek said. "For some reason they don't get on with Janet."

Teresa knew the reason. She had only seen Janet once, but once was enough. She recognized the type. Janet was too careful, too good a housekeeper. It never paid. Numbering potatoes and counting grains of sugar never got one anywhere, and Janet was the sort of woman who knew to a scraping how much margarine should be used per head per week. Geoffrey Hylton had said once: "English women in the West Indies do their own cooking to economize on ingredients. But they keep servants for the sake of being able to write home with pride in their number." Well, Janet at least did not keep a dog and bark herself.

"It's very clever of your wife to manage without," Teresa said politely. "Everyone here is depressingly efficient. Out of sheer cussedness I maintain my boast that I'm the only woman in the island who can't make a cake."

"And can't you?" He thought she was pulling his leg. In his orbit all women could make cakes.

"I don't know," she said. "I'm like the man who was asked if he could play the violin. I've never tried." She was sure that Janet could make cakes, but thin niggardly ones, lacking the butter of human kindness.

"Have some rum in your tea to keep out the cold," she said to Janet's husband. "And what about quinine?"

"Rum, please, but not quinine. I'll be all right. I'm not here by accident, you know. I came on purpose, prepared to get wet."

She was embarrassed by his candour. To begin with he had implied that flooded rivers had driven him over the pass. Now, it was as though the visiting gentleman in the fourth figure had omitted his bow or prematurely grabbed his lady.

"I'm sorry," she said, "that you couldn't come before. Mrs. Morell said you were still too busy settling in."

"I didn't want to come. I let her refuse that invitation. I couldn't bear to meet you again in a crowd with Janet there, and other people, all playing ladies and gentlemen. I had to see you alone first, to be quite certain that I'd made a fool of myself."

"And – are you certain?"

"Yes," he said. "A man falling in love is always a fool."

Her fingers were trembling as she took a cigarette, fitted it into her long holder. She could hear Henry putting away his tools in the shed under the house. An orange fog blurred the horizon where the sun was setting behind rain. A little grey bird balanced itself on a long stem of grass, forcing down the seeds to within reach of its beak.

"Are you smoking because you want to," Derek said suddenly, "or because you think you look seductive behind that holder?"

She bit on the holder till it nearly broke. "A little of both," she said. And then: "You know, that was very flattering of you."

"Why – flattering?"

"It's flattering of you to notice my effects."

Derek laughed. "I'm not as blind as a puppy, you know, nor as young." There was an irritating complacency in his voice but she ignored that, and Isabel thumped with her tail at the word puppy.

"She's always having them," Teresa explained. "Isabel is a prolific and self-centred little bitch, but unutterably dear."

"Like her mistress?"

"In no way. But I protest at your use of the word think. I don't *think* I look seductive with this holder. I do." It was Teresa who was leading the dance now; advancing, retreating, spun off her feet, a little breathless.

Derek put down his cup and helped himself to a slice of the cake she had not made. "Perhaps so," he said, deliberately withholding the compliment she had invited, teasing her with it as he teased Isabel with a piece of cake held just out of reach. "I've heard it said."

Janet had said it, not meaning it kindly. "Nearly naked in the street. And smoking through a thing like a flute." Janet had never been seductive, but she was a good wife. She looked after a man's pocket and his stomach too.

Teresa wasn't thinking about stomachs. She was wondering if he was going to kiss her; wondering if she could bear it if he did

– or if he didn't. She had always had this queer terror of a first kiss. It was like diving into cold water. You wanted to do it and you daren't. Kissing had always been important to her; it was never the casual happening that it was to some people; the inevitable accompaniment to a taxi ride; the aftermath of a dance. She wanted him to kiss her, this man of whom she knew nothing, yet dreaded it. Which inconsistency was a trick of the nerves, unaccountable. Crushing out her cigarette, she took up her work again.

"What's the idea?" he said, looking at the patches.

"It's a bedspread, made up of old scraps. Scotch blood will out, you know. I love using things up." And because the atmosphere, made heavy by her own imagining, was almost too exciting, too overpowering, she went on talking to relieve tension; knowing that afterwards, when she was alone, she would be sorry that she had pushed opportunity aside, had not dived into the deep cold water.

"I like remembering things connected with each bit that I'm using," she said. "I wore this green linen in Demerara, the day we saw the manatees in the Botanical Gardens. There was a canal covered with lotus leaves as large as round tables, and trees, that I don't know the name of, shed brilliant petals on to the thick water. A man whistled, and grotesque monsters rose to the surface to be fed with the grass that we put into cold slimy mouths, harelipped and slightly whiskered. When the creatures were tired of us, and we of them, they rolled back their huge grey bodies into a muddy flowery privacy."

She hesitated, wondering how much she was boring him. It was hardly raining at all now, and he seemed to be looking at the sea with half-closed eyes, the sea that had no patterns on it any more but only one dull streak of gold, escaped from behind clouds. That was three years ago," she said, "and last summer at the London Zoo I saw them again, the selfsame sea-cows living in a tiled bath, a bath that was offensively hygienic, with a rude light overhead and never a wisp of weed nor a single leaf to hide their ugliness from a stream of staring, shifting people. I asked the keeper if he fed them grass and he jeered at me. "Grass?" he said. "They don't eat grass. Only lettuce leaves.""

Derek laughed. "A difficult diet in Demerara," he said. Then: "I must go now. Janet's alone and she'll be worrying."

Had she driven him away by her futile talking? She longed to cry: "Stay longer. Stay till it's quite dark. We can be alone in the dark." Now that deep water was out of reach she craved to be in it. But all she uttered was: "I'll take you back in the car."

"Nonsense, I couldn't ask that of you, on a night like this."

"Nonsense yourself. On a night like this you couldn't get back, by the Souffrière valley. You'd be found dead next morning, pickled in sulphur. But have a whisky before you go."

"No thanks." And she knew that for some reason he was in a hurry to be gone, and half hated him for it. Something about the party had gone flat, and she blamed the unconscious sea-cows, wallowing in their tiled bath. Under the car's hood she was hurtfully aware of his nearness; wished that it could have taken longer to skim down the hill and across the divide to the Atlantic coast; and yet, perversely, drove as quickly as she could because it was getting late and – Janet would be worrying. Within twenty minutes they might have been in some other island, so rugged was the coast, so fierce the sea. Waves gnawed at the cliffs as though to devour them, and surf thundered on to the strip of sand that was Neva Beach.

"I'm going to be rude and inhospitable," he said, "by not asking you to come in. I'd rather say Good night to you here in the dark." Teresa felt that way too, but couldn't help wondering whether he was afraid of his wife. "Drop me at the old works," he said. "I'll walk up." And as it was not raining she took him at his word and he directed her how to turn in the narrow road. Then stood beside her while she lit a cigarette.

"I don't always smoke for effect," she said. "No one is going to see me now." But he didn't listen to what she said, only caressed the steering wheel with his fingers, making it impossible for her to start.

"I won't kiss you tonight," he said abruptly, "even if you'd let me. It's inevitable that we should some day, but I want to wait a little while. There's something final about a kiss. Once given, we shall never escape from it, nor from its memory. I don't know what you're thinking of me. Hard things, perhaps, although you've been very kind. Either I must seem to you mad or very impertinent. I think the first is true but not the other. I've made use of a few women in my life, Teresa, and loved perhaps one. But I don't kiss casually. Between people like ourselves it's too important."

She had been thinking more or less that not half an hour ago. This – this broken speech – whispered against the sound of frogs singing, of rain dripping off trees, of a river roaring, was sweeter than having your mouth crushed and your senses bruised by someone not in sympathy, who thought a kiss cheap. "Nothing quite like this has happened to me before," he was saying. "St. Celia must be possessed of some intemperate spirit determined to drive a man crazy, that he should fall in love at first sight. Do you know, that first time I saw you, I followed you along the sea front to the post office because I couldn't bear to lose sight of you. I was like a fish drawn by a flare. I asked a complete stranger what your name was."

She hadn't known that. She had met his eyes on the jetty and thought that a flame had seared her. Then he had sat down opposite to her in the launch, and their knees had touched.

"Teresa," he began – "it's the loveliest name. I'm going to use it often. Teresa, will you meet me here tomorrow? Today I've been gauche and stupid, but there are many things I want to say to you. And I want to show you my estate. All my life, ever since I was twenty-two, and that's eighteen years ago, I've worked for other people. You don't know what it means to me to own land for myself."

So that was why he had bought Neva. Driven by the lust of possession, wanting a place of his own. She had wondered what he would make of it, of this wild country and hostile sea; and hovered over his question, his invitation, knowing that she stood where roads branched, and that now, in this wet darkness, was the time of choosing. Was she to tread the path of sweet foolishness that would end in pain, or that of austere wisdom leading to dessication and loneliness? Derek was married, and one had tried through life not to steal. But on the other hand his wife had said: "I have seen Miss Craddock once, and once was enough." Was loyalty owing to the woman who had said that? Then his hand touched hers where it rested on the wheel, and in a moment the choice was made. Doubtless it had already been made long ago, in the womb of time.

"I'd like to see you tomorrow," she said.

He asked if she knew the way up from the beach on to the east end of the cliff. "You climb over the roots of an old fig tree," he said.

She told him that she knew.

V

Teresa drove home that night more slowly than she had come. The road was black and wet with not even stars reflected in it, but only her own lamps whose triangular wedges of light left behind her an unnatural darkness, and made caverns on either side of her between the trees. She drove slowly, not only because the track was slippery and twisted, but because during the last hour she had become more precious to herself than for many years. Suddenly she was of value; valued life. No longer was one day going to slip into another without change, making existence like a polar summer, pleasant but unvaried. Now the contrasts of light and darkness were to be hers again; joy and anxiety would succeed each other like the ribs of a corrugated iron roof; and after excitement there would follow heartache. For Teresa had no illusions about heartaches, knowing that they followed upon indulgence as inevitably as liver attacks. But if one should permanently avoid these one would have lived emptily. How colourless would be one's old age if there were no purple patches to remember, no roses and raptures.

Back on the Ça Ira veranda, she drew Isabel into her arms, kissing the nose so often scratched by cats to whom the dog jealously denied her affections. She was glad that Tommy was away, fearing the telltale light in her own eyes; dreading her brother's calm common sense at the moment when foolishness was in her heart. For she meant to be foolish; meant to let this tide sweep her beyond the breakers. Sweep her to – what? But that night she would not consider "what". There might be calm water ahead, or rocks, or dangerous currents, but tonight she would think only of the intoxicating look on a man's face, of the whisper of his voice. Tonight he and she would be alone together in a world of her own dreams.

She put away her patchwork, picked up her basket, sorted the muddled pieces. The top one was a bit of a yellow striped tablecloth, bought long ago in Martinique. She remembered black-red wine served at sunset; and a bearded chattering priest straying like a goat among the creepered ruins of St. Pierre. In 1902, so he had told her, walking from the town to his own village, he had climbed the cone of Mont Pélé and, looking down into the crater, had seen seething fiery lava bubbling below. Two days later had come the great eruption. "*Et pfui*," he said with a flick of the fingers, "*tout était fini*." Now ground doves cried to each other where streets had been, and the rays of the dying sun fell on the wet bodies of fishermen who beat the water with stones to frighten fish into their nets.

How many lovers, Teresa wondered, had died in that disaster? How many had gone on living, bereft? She had gone on living. It was six years now since her own catastrophe had made a holocaust of her life; had covered the green places with ashes; had shaken faith and hope to their foundations. Where the sea was lay a great darkness; rain dripped tears from the gutters, and she could hear waves sighing softly on to grey stones. But in front of her there was a warm light burning, and Isabel thumped on the floor with her tail. Before she was born thousands had died at St. Pierre in the flash of a second; and now a cloth brought from that place had reminded her, tonight of all nights, of things that were better buried, buried or burnt; so that she snatched up that yellow fragment and crushed it angrily between her fingers. For if grass were pushing through the ashes again, even though it were a rank weed of forbidden love, it must be let sprout and grow strong, and not wither among cold memories, or be nipped in the bud by a pain that was dead. "*Et pfui*," the priest had said, "*tout était fini*." Well, some things were finished, but not all.

Next morning Norah came to Teresa, wriggled herself against the door jamb; tried to say something, and failed.

"What's the matter?" Teresa asked, and the girl wriggled again. "I would wish to speak with you," she began, and then said

60

nothing, so that Teresa looked at her anxiously, dreading inconvenient revelations.

"What is it, Norah?" she said. "You must tell me."

Norah was plain of face and rigid of feature, as unlike Tilly as one sister could be to another, combining a complete lack of humour with a habit of calling unexpectedly upon her Maker. "Oh, God," she cried if she forgot a spoon, or if the cat stole the butter. "Oh, God," she said when the King died, and when the car backed itself into the red bushes, splintering a fence.

"What is it?" Teresa asked again. "Is anything the matter?"

And at last Norah blurted out: "I go to make a baby," and burst into loud tears, covering her head with her apron.

Teresa was enormously relieved. She had feared that Norah was going to give notice, or else accuse Tilly of some crime that would have to be recognized. And yet Norah was so angular, so unbending, so essentially formidable, that the idea of her having a baby, and apparently soon, was altogether fantastic. She wondered how any man had dared. Long ago Norah had come upon her lying naked in the sun after bathing. "A lady and gentleman to see you," she had murmured to the distant summit of Morne Collat. "I tell them the way to the river is hard." Thus Teresa had appreciated that her servant was a woman of tact, even if forbidding. But a woman of tact, not of passion.

She jumped out of her chair, put her arm round Norah, begged her to stop crying. "You should be happy about it," she said. "Babies are nice things." Once Teresa had supposed that some day she would have babies, but now she knew that it could never be so. In her world, unlike Norah's, it was still not easy to have a child without a husband, and the only man she had wanted to marry had been dead six years. She would never have a husband, and therefore never a baby. And in that moment, suddenly and irrationally, she found herself longing to bear Derek Morell's child. Janet, his tight-lipped wife, had never given him that. But as there flashed into her mind a miniature scarlet replica of the face that was so much in her thoughts she realized how singularly inappropriate would be that skull-like head and obstinate jaw to an immature human; and drew back from her vision with a smile that had to be swallowed lest Norah misinterpret it.

"The man's going to help you, I hope." She felt that it would be impertinent, interfering, to ask who he was.

"He help me. I only afraid you turn me away."

"Nonsense, Norah, you know I'd never do that." Teresa couldn't see herself sacking a good servant for a thousand babies. "Soap and water," Tilly had said once when a pup of Isabel's desecrated the Bokhara, "will wash away everything except sin." Here illegitimate babies were not treated as sins, but rather as insurances against a penurious old age. When Tilly had Fitzroy she went to Capesterre and did not come back for three months, saying it would bring misfortune to go on the sea too soon after having a child, and to walk over the mountains would have taken two days. But Norah said she would go to the hospital in Grande Anse and need only be off duty for a month.

"Don't cry," Teresa said, "we'll look after you. Are you feeling sick?"

"Yes, Miss T'resa, I sick." But she wasn't howling any more; had stopped wriggling.

Teresa finished her letters and tied up the mailbag. Then she went out to find Henry the gardener. Once upon a time the lawn at Ça Ira had been a drying ground for coffee, and under the grass and the earth there was still a stone paving. At the edge of the valley huge saman trees, with creepers falling from their branches like hair from a woman's head, threw a shade that was not only cool and dark, but also dignified. Tommy said those trees made him feel like a Lord of the Manor. One thought of immemorial elms and looked instinctively for rooks' nests.

Henry, his umbrella over one arm and a cutlass swinging from the other, met her with a grievance. "Massicot," he said, "is owing the master money, so he tell me not to bring milk any more. He say he will bring milk to pay off the indebtedness."

"But that's absurd," Teresa said. On her desk at that moment there was a letter from Massicot suggesting other means of discharging the debt. "I am now taking this oppertunity," he had written, "to let you know I heard a hint that you want a horse to buy, and will be a good plan, for it will faten the place for you in a few months. If in case it is true, I am offering you a stallion of thirteen years of age, so he is still a young horse, height thirteen hands. The price is only nine pounds, but it can reduice."

Teresa wanted a horse, even "reduiced", no more than she wanted Massicot's milk. "We never told him to bring milk," she said. "Only Henry, I do wish you could let us have it a little earlier."

He said: "I pasture my cow in the Souffrière valley, Miss T'resa. It is one long little distance."

She agreed that it was a long way. The Souffrière valley was right under the crest of the mountain, a place round as a bowl that had been a crater, where nothing grew except grass and low bushes. A stream ran through it, reeking of sulphur. When the wind blew in that direction the smell drifted down the river to Ça Ira. Derek had come to her by that way, a long time ago, or was it only yesterday?

Henry pulled a scrap of paper from his pocket, slowly unrolled it. "I keep this for the master," he said, and handed to Teresa a sliver of bamboo. "That was in my foot, and I cut it out. I want the master to know that my foot was bad."

Solemnly Teresa took the sliver, promised to deliver it to Tommy. Then on a quick impulse said: "Mr. Morell from Neva was here yesterday. How are things going there, Henry? Is it true that the people dislike him?"

"I hear that same. But the people in Ville Rousse are hard people. Mr. Morell must work to keep his produce. Always they have been taking coconuts from that place and now he has forbidden it."

"What do they take them for? To eat?"

"Some they take to eat. But Mr. Morell, he saying they sending them to the French country. He say the smugglers taking them who bring back brandy and wine. Robert Nolette tell me that three days ago the sea is so rough they must jettison a whole cargo, and ten gallons are thrown into the water."

"Is Robert a smuggler?"

"No, Miss, but he beaching his boat alongside some that are."

Teresa felt that to take coconuts to eat was a pardonable offence, but that to steal them for export was immoral. Her argument was inconsistent because the money earned by smuggling might buy food; and she refrained from voicing it to Henry, not wishing the principle to be applied to her own tomatoes. An hour later she talked of that same thing with Derek Morell.

VI

Below them was a mile-long stretch of beach on which lay three boats and a half-dozen rafts. Teresa wondered which was Robert's and which the smugglers'. A naked man walked thigh-deep in water, and when it seemed good to him flung a cast-net into the sea and sometimes drew in nothing and sometimes little silver sprats caught by their gills in string meshes. Waves rolled ponderously on to the sand, bringing pink-lined shells and little cowries to mix with the dead leaves of sea grape and almond trees fringing the shore. From the river's bank there rose the voices of women washing clothes; and beyond its slow waters, bordered by mang trees, themselves smothered in flowering vines, coconut palms grew out of a wilderness of their own sprouting nuts. "Like an overcrowded conservatory," Teresa said, "where aspidistras have run mad."

"I told you this island made things mad," Derek answered. "Today I'm mad as the Americans mean it. Angry. How can I stop people from stealing my nuts?"

At the far end of the beach spray showered to a height of fifty feet against red cliffs, on the rim of which Teresa knew tiny paths to be threading dark bushes blown horizontal by the wind. A mile and a half away she could see the houses of Ville Rousse spotting the hillside as though a handful of grey boulders had been flung to the forest and had there rooted among trees.

"Must you stop them?" she said. "Do you need all those nuts for yourself?" It seemed to her that the people of Ville Rousse would think no more of taking these than she of picking blackberries from an English hedgerow.

He said: "There's a market now both for copra and for whole

64

nuts. I'm hoping to make something out of it. Actually of course, I'm only exporting from the Glebe fields" – Teresa knew that there were fifteen hundred acres of Neva, of which perhaps a hundred were planted in coconuts, undrained, uncleared, although still bearing. "But I might need these some day. Anyway, it's the principle of the thing. The nuts are mine."

Principles. Hard rigid things, rigid as the right of possession. Yet some people could make them flexible as the bark of a mahaut cochon tree, twisted into rope. She herself had twisted the principle of honesty into condoning the theft of Morell's nuts, although admitting that she might be rigid about her own tomatoes. There were, however, a great many nuts and very few tomatoes.

"I shouldn't take it too seriously," she said. "Remember the place has been neglected for a long time. Old Mrs. What's-her-Name in England never expected a penny out of it, and Harvey took the line of least resistance. People get into habits."

"People must get out of habits," he said. And for the first time she saw that his eyes and mouth were hard and his jaw set, while his face strengthened in anger; but soon her sense of the ridiculous swamped all other feeling – for what in Heaven's name, she thought, could a few coconuts matter – and she sang under her breath: "Who's been digging up my nuts?" quoting the little bird in *The Tale of Tommy Tiptoes*, who caused all the trouble. "Who's been digging up my nuts?" she sang, but she didn't sing it out loud lest she cause trouble herself.

"Let's go through here," she said, turning from the contemplation of palm trees. "It's lonelier on the other side, and wilder." Although she guessed already that wildness was not what Derek sought, but rather a tamed and ordered Nature. At the foot of the cliff there was a rusted iron stanchion rooted in coral and traces of stonework where a jetty had once been. On top, hidden in scrubby vegetation, were ruins of houses; square blocks of masonry bound in vines with now and then a stone missing; and among them guava bushes, white spider lilies, and a crop of agaves with saw-edged leaves. People had lived here once, Teresa thought; and caused flowers to grow; and had died. Now, a wilderness was made of the place where they had been. So, too, might the Neva plantations be some day taken back by the forest. Then, coconuts would sprout unhindered and be neither exported nor eaten nor dried for copra, although some would rot in the stagnant river-water, and some be tossed by the sea.

Derek and Teresa passed through the trees into open country, a bare stretch of turf sloping to grey fretted rocks through which the sea shot into the air by means of blowholes and dissolved like steam.

"This place might not be St. Celia at all," Teresa said. "Nor even in the tropics. It reminds me of Brittany. There should be a grey fishing village, with yellow lichen making patches on blue slate roofs. Chicory growing in the long grass; and red sails on the sea."

"I brought Janet here, and she said that it was like Scotland. Her home is in Fife, you know. A hard bleak country."

How queer it was that you could make one place become another, because you wanted to. There was nothing here of the Scotland Teresa knew; of its soft misty outlines, of those enclosed seas calling themselves lochs. And there were people to whom Brittany meant only the flat sandy places in the south; or Carnac, where the old stones were. "But I've never seen blowholes in either," she said. "These little sideways ones make me feel that the sea is spitting contempt at us."

Derek said: "The sea doesn't spit. It's too big to show contempt, even of us. I think it comes here to blow water out of its lungs, like a whale does."

She was liking him again now. She hadn't altogether when they were talking about nuts.

"Will you come home with me later on," he said, "and meet Janet? You see, I'm going to be very sane this morning. I'm not even going to tell you that you're lovely. So we can face my wife with scrubbed consciences."

He had no right to suggest that her conscience was not scrubbed and whitewashed, save by her being there at all, but she let the implication pass. "I can't come," she said. "I'm even nakeder than last time." Her shorts were very short. She had no hat, no sleeves, and wore her hair in two long pigtails.

"Try and think kindly of Janet," he said. "It's not your fault that you've got a wrong impression. I know that silly remark was repeated. But I want you to see her as she is, so strong, so upright. It's a phrase of mine that while I dream noble deeds she does them all day long. Janet's tough and practical; born and bred to be; tempered by the frore winds of her own country."

Teresa tried to think kindly, but his words failed to soften the picture she had made of a woman hard and rigid as a principle; a woman without sweetness and light in her make-up, with no saving grace of humour. "She had a hard childhood," Derek was explaining, "hadn't much love in her life." And Teresa wondered, was that due to cause or effect? Had Janet become unloveable through lack of love, or had her parents' affection beaten helplessly against that rigid austerity as waves might beat against an iron cliff? "When she was a child," Derek said, "the black shadow of poverty was made blacker by her mother's anxiety to keep on the gentry side of the middle-class border. That's given her a prejudice, I think, against the lilies of the field."

"Meaning me as a lily?"

"Do you resent the comparison?"

"I should like the species defined. A madonna? A tiger? A spider lily? Which am I?"

"I shan't tell you," he said. "We're talking about Janet, not you. She's my second cousin, you know. I met her for the first time when I went to stay with my grandmother in Scotland. She was being clever and competent with an incubator, a little mouse-like creature with the determination of an ox."

"Good Heavens, no," Teresa cried. "I can't swallow that metaphor. A lily I may be, and she mouse-like, but there's nothing of the ox about Mrs. Morell." They laughed together as their minds followed lumbering carts drawn through muddy ruts by heavy biscuit-coloured oxen moving slowly, patiently, with flies hanging on their eyelids. "No," he said, "Janet isn't like that."

"I see her rather as a squirrel," Teresa suggested, "little, and quick, and sharp." And he swooped on the suggestion, although sheer politeness only had prevented her from saying – rat, which she thought a far better simile, having sensed cruelty in Janet's sharp eyes, and meanness; which qualities, probably erroneously, she did not attribute to squirrels. "You're dead right," he said. "A squirrel, storing away nuts. She's very saving, you know, luckily for me. If she hadn't saved I wouldn't be here."

It seemed that one couldn't keep nuts out of the conversation. Those symbolical ones were not coconuts but that faraway kind that Timmy Tiptoes had gathered in thickets. "They began to empty the bags," Teresa murmured, "into a hole high up a tree that had belonged to a woodpecker. The nuts rattled down – down – down." But there was nothing in Janet, she decided, of Goody Tiptoes, who was a fat and comfortable little squirrel.

"Have you ever been along the top of those red cliffs?" she asked, nodding with her head at the distant showering spray.

"I didn't know one could."

"Let's go," she said. "I'm glad there's something you don't know about your own estate. The paths aren't easy to find, but I've learnt them." And as they turned their backs on the sea – Isabel being noisily thankful that they were moving again – she added: "You know, Neva has been more or less public property. Tommy and I have trespassed all over it. We've stolen guavas, and flamboyant and cassia seedlings, and I don't know what else from the garden of the Old House."

"Please go on stealing them. You have a life permit."

It had never occurred to Teresa that Neva was not everybody's to walk over as they pleased; nor the fruits of the earth hers to pick as she chose. Guavas and seedling trees had only a little less value than superfluous coconuts, but it seemed that the theory governing them was the same. This was a principle – flexible where a pretty woman was concerned, but rigidly maintained against negroes already suffering from malnutrition. Here – she thought bitterly – we have life in a nutshell, and almost she turned away from this man who fascinated her. Almost she turned, but not quite.

Near the mouth of the river there was a heap of coconut husks, shelled by a cutlass. "Those were my nuts," Derek said.

VII

She had left her car under a white cedar tree from which a dozen
pink blossoms, spiralling like miniature parachutes, had drifted
in under the hood. Hermit crabs tumbled among the fallen fruit
of the sea grape trees, and beneath these there were little red
mushrooms, rooted in sand. They drove in silence along the
metalled track lying behind the beach; but this wound further and
further inland so that when she stopped beside a breadfruit tree,
a weary giant long since struck by lightning, the noise of the surf
was only a distant murmur, no louder than bees on a summer day.
All around them there was the silence of trees, not the trees of the
forest, but a scrubby secondary growth, here and there cleared for
peasants' gardens. And because, six weeks ago, Morell had given
his tenants notice, these places had already an untended look.
Wild eggplant and razor grass were choking the ground provisions; vines strangling the bananas.

"This soil is not good enough for bananas," Derek said. "If I
can find what I want I mean to clear forest in the Neva valley and
grow them there."

If he found what he wanted, rich alluvial soil, sticky and black,
then the axe would follow, and the cutlass, and a burnt desolation.
Chatagniers, gommiers, bois rivières, would lie – not in the dust,
because on Neva there was no dust – but in mud; or else in the
river, blocking and damming it until a flood came to carry the
felled timber to the sea.

Sighing for the doomed forest Teresa said, pointing to the little
trees: "In summer many of these have the loveliest flowers:
especially the bois tan, and another the people call wild orange,
though it's labelled schwartzia in the Capesterre gardens."

"How wise of the people. Schwartzia is a horrible word. Is the
tree like an orange?"

"Only in its smell. And the flowers are yellow. All this land was planted in sugar once. That's why there's no real forest."

"If God spare – as my overseer says – it'll be in sugar again."

She swung round, staring her surprise. "In sugar? Are you going to plant sugar?"

"Why not?"

"I don't know why not. But why? I thought only peasants grew it on this side of the island for their mountain dew."

"I'm not going to make mountain dew," he said. "But take me to the edge of the cliff, Teresa, as you promised. Perhaps with the wind blowing and the ocean in sight, I shall be able to make you see things as I see them. Tell me, my sweet, do you always look so fierce and defensive if a tree is threatened, even a scrubby secondary tree?"

She led him down a path that he had thought was a drain from the road. Bushes laden with yesterday's rain soaked them as they passed, and there were little pools of water collected in the hollows of red slippery clay. Isabel vainly pursued a yellow and black land crab that defied her, open-clawed. "In February and March," Teresa said, "these woods are full of white orchids." Soon there was no undergrowth any more, only windblown shrubs making a roof over a carpet of leaves; and the noise of the surf was loud again, a continuous roar unbroken by the soft hissing of sea on sand. They came out on to a high promontory and looked back across Neva Bay to where, half an hour before, they had talked beside blowholes.

"Have you a head for heights?" Teresa asked. "It's frightening."

"I have for myself but not for others. If you go too close I'll get the jitters." And making her imaginary danger an excuse he caught hold of her arm.

"I thought you were sane this morning," she protested, although his touch pleased her so that she longed to be a nervous woman, clinging to him for support. Whereupon he loosed her arm again, saying: "If I were quite sane I should throw you over that precipice and be quit of you. You're fated to bring trouble on me, Teresa, and I know it. Take me away from this place."

There were fishermen's tracks along the whole length of that coast, sometimes edging the cliff and sometimes disappearing under dark trees. Where a landslide had been, or the sea had encroached, the path made a detour inland. Where a gully was it came down almost to sea level and there was lost to all but the initiate. You sought for a notch cut in the clay, or for a scraping of gravel where a foot had rested. Here and there were lookouts from which a man could see straight down into deep water and signal to another where to throw his net.

"Am I exhausting you?" Teresa said as they climbed from a pebbly beach to two hundred feet again. "It's not much farther to the finest view of all."

"Your question is an impertinence, Miss Craddock. Do you imagine you can tire me out? I'm not more than ten years your senior, when all's said and done."

"Just about, if you're forty. In three months I shall be thirty, and definitely a spinster. One is at thirty. That's why so many people stay twenty-nine." A funny word – spinster. When they read the banns in church they always said "spinster of this parish" even if the lady in question were an infant of eighteen. Yet, the word seemed to picture a withered woman turning a wheel, or a long thin one knitting with steel pins in a lonely room.

"Do you know the old definition of spinster?" she asked. "What my dictionary calls 'obs.'? It's a 'woman of loose character, fit for the spinning house'."

"And are you a loose woman, Teresa?"

"I don't know yet. I'll tell you in three months' time." How could you define loose? It meant different things to different people. Janet's standards, for instance, would be tighter than her own. And what would be Derek's, she wondered. He was of pre-War vintage; would believe, perhaps, that there was one sauce for the goose and another for the gander.

They stood on a red platform surrounded on three sides by a sea blue as the eyes in a peacock's tail, edged with a trimming of white foam. "Almost the national colours," Derek said, "but in fancy shades." The coast was spun out for miles on either hand, an endless series of broken cliffs, with on the south one blue peak shaped like the eye-tooth of a dog. The mountains behind them were blocked out by the vegetation through which they had come, and the cliff at their feet was so sheer that they could see fish swimming in the water – emerald green monsters browsing on seaweed – and coral growths that were like brown toadstools.

"I'm frightened for Isabel on the tops of cliffs," Teresa said, "although she's more surefooted than I."

"Looking at you, Teresa, and thinking about you, is very like being on the edge of a precipice. If once I let go of myself, I shall fall to unknown depths. And yet" – he didn't look at her as he spoke, but stared down into the sea – "I long to throw myself over and know what lies in the depths, whether sweetness or pain."

He shouldn't talk that way if they were going to see Janet afterwards. "If not a loose-liver I'm loose-minded," she said to herself. "Either this man must intrigue me enough for his wife to mean nothing; or else I must ignore him, snub him, nip this absurdity with the cold wind of common sense. As it is I'm all fluid, slopping like a cup of tea in a railway train. My mind is a mustard-coloured mess, growing cold in a saucer."

"We came here to talk sugar," she said severely. "I still want to know – why sugar? Surely you're not one of those visionaries who prattle of a sugar factory in Grande Anse?"

"A vision, I admit," he said. "But to me beautiful, a dream that might come true. I've got sugar in my heart and in my brain, Teresa. I'm going to cut down all that scrub – yes, I know what you're thinking, all those pretty trees – and have cane-fields there. I want to hear the wind swishing through the trash and ruffling the feathery arrows. I want to look down the aisles for the little red weeds that hang there like swinging bells. I used to watch them when I was a child, and I haven't been able to since. Teresa, I'm going to bore you to death telling you all this, but I want you to understand. I was brought up to be very rich, you know. My father had huge estates. I can remember what are called the good old days; carriages and horses, fine wines and high living. I was heir to a house three hundred years old, one of those heavy stone mansions that still had slaves' quarters, and a mill with an immense stone chimney. That's all that is left of it now, the chimney. I was at school in England, and in France for the last year of the War. I came back to find my father a bankrupt. There had been folly to the point of crime." Teresa saw his hand shaking above the little pile of gravel that he had been gathering unconsciously. "He died soon afterwards, and the estates were sold, sold for some damned land settlement scheme. Oh, yes, the canefields are there still, speckled with date-palms and made scrubby and untidy with patches of cotton among them. But they aren't my canes. The house has fallen to pieces, you know how easily that happens in the tropics. The peasants took away stones as they wanted them. I got a job in a Government office, sat for eighteen years at a desk, a Civil Servant. And all my life I've wanted land, land to grow sugar on."

Here was the dreamer speaking, the dreamer that she learned to love. And often she wondered, afterwards, how he could be reconciled with the Derek that he became; and supposed that she was too prejudiced, or too psychologically ignorant, to see where the two men dovetailed, to understand how a sense of property might make nightmares of dreams.

"So it doesn't matter, really," she said, "if you don't make a profit out of it. You just want to have sugar there, to see it, hear it, grow."

"You do understand, Teresa."

"I understand with my head, not with my heart. I mean, sugar means nothing to me. I've never been to Parham Island, but I hate Barbados, with its green glaring flatness. I love the forest, you see, and the mystery of never knowing what's round the next corner."

"There were forests in Barbados once," he said. "Wasn't it named for the bearded trees? But men have to grow things and live."

Everywhere, the world over, men have cut forests that they might snatch food from the soil; and now the soil flees from them, washed by rain from the rock surfaces to thicken the rivers and to stain the seas, so that men begin to trust in the forest again, planting trees that their roots may hold the soil for them.

"We're lucky in the West Indies," she said, "that crops are so good to look at. Bananas, coconuts, oranges."

"Bananas and citrus, also – with permission of the local populace – coconuts, should give us a living," Derek went on. "Sugar is to be my toy, my gambling game, with a factory on the far horizon and the hope of inspiring others. Meanwhile, I aim higher than mountain dew, but I'll probably only break even.

There's a little capital left of the money we've saved, with which I can get the land cleared."

She was sorry for the little trees, for the orchids that would perish in flames, for the peasants' gardens. But the red cliffs would remain, and the sea. The most determined planter could never tamper with those.

"Have you ever wondered," she said irrelevantly, "why people who are elsewhere called farmers, or agriculturists, are known only as planters in 'these promiscuous parts'?"

"I've never wondered; but it's because they plant and never reap, I suppose."

"A pessimistic supposition on which to start a new venture." She had encroached on his heap of gravel, was absent-mindedly throwing one pebble after another into the sea. "But, Derek" – she hadn't used his name before, although it came so naturally that neither noticed it – "Derek, you've told me so much, you must forgive my asking. Where does your wife come in on all this? Does she also crave to see cane-fields billowing in the breeze?" Surely Janet was no dreamer, no gambler.

He didn't answer for a moment, and when his words came they were no answer. She counted seven long waves rolling out of space towards her before he spoke again. "Janet hates the forest," he said abruptly. "She's afraid of it with a fear amounting almost to mania. She's a queerly imaginative person in her Scotch way, and she says that the forest at Neva Ford is like a dark sinister woman, ready to crush her, ready to steal."

A dark sinister woman. Here there were sunshine and a wide sea, yet the same thought struck them together. "I hope she's not thinking of me," Teresa said, and her laugh was a little forced. "I'm dark, but surely not sinister. And I don't crush." How awful to have a love affair with a man whose wife had second sight. Or even a morbid imagination.

"Janet would like to live in Scotland," Derek said. "When we had saved enough money to get me out of bondage she wanted to buy a farm in Fife and grow turnips, acres of blue-leaved turnips. But I could not do that. Do you know that country? I should die of it."

She was with him in this. One couldn't, having known sunshine, go back into the dark.

"Coming to St. Celia was something of a compromise. Places in Parham Island, even if for sale, were in any case too expensive. Neva makes a new beginning for both of us, something fresh to tackle. And being here leaves both of us homesick, she for her turnips and I for my canes."

"But you're getting your canes."

"And she's got two or three turnips. Janet's planning to grow vegetables on a grand scale."

Teresa found them suddenly pathetic, these two wanting to be in different places and compromising on a third that neither liked. "But you *are* going to love this island," she said. "You can't help it. It's so beautiful."

"You're beautiful, Teresa. I'm going to love it through you." He wouldn't bow down to her island, wouldn't worship the mountain tops and the dark forest. Could it be true, she wondered, that he was not big enough to love this wild scenery, wanted it tamed? And if he should some day take her into possession would he want ruthlessly to cut down and tame her, to reduce her to the level monotony of flat cane-fields?

With that thought still in her mind she felt his hands gripping her shoulders. It would be easy not to struggle to let herself slip over the precipice into the rough waters of love. A dozen times that morning she had longed for the touch of him, for his kiss. Yet he had said: "Today I shall be sane," and where kisses were there lay madness. If she yielded to him now she would be aptly symbolized by the forest, a dark sinister woman ready to steal with the predatory fingers of lush parasites, and to hold what she had stolen with lianas that bind one tree to another. Thoughts are swifter than the touch of fingers, than the meeting of lips. She twisted herself free of him, whistled to her dog.

"St. Celia is beautiful," she insisted, "and Isabel the most beautiful thing in it. But we must go now; it's going to rain." And indeed the sea was not blue any more, but grey.

Among the trees again, with the waves and the wind cut off, it was so quiet that they could hear dead twigs scrunched under their feet, and lizards rustling. Teresa tore a leaf from a bay seedling and bruised it between her fingers for the sake of the bitter smell of it, that was also sweet.

VIII

The house at Neva Ford stands on a rock where two rivers meet. Among the eastern ridges Janet Morell could see coming rain hanging like a mist of steam, and the fronds of a palm tree quivered as though with fever. Tree trunks shone whitely against the darkened undergrowth. Between the rivers and on the further bank of the main stream virgin forest was still clothing steep hillsides that were spurs of mountain masses. But behind the house an orchard of grapefruit and oranges had been cut from a false forest; from bois canot, out of which fishermen build their rafts; from tree-ferns whose branches make tracery of lace against the sky; from wild bananas called balisiers, that bear no fruit but only stiff flowers like the claws of lobsters, scarlet and crimson and yellow. Under their leaves the road ran in a pale translucent twilight, as though one stood under the sea.

Janet put a bucket beneath the bamboo stem that made a pipe from the gutter under the eaves; and when the rain throbbed on to the roof, gurgling off the shingles, it spilled itself into the bucket with a metallic resonance that drowned for a moment the eternal symphony of the two rivers. From each joint of the bamboo stem there had sprouted thin spiky leaves, bound by a spider's web.

"I found Miss Craddock on Neva Beach," Derek explained, "and insisted on her driving me home. Can we offer her lunch?"

"Oh nonsense," Teresa said. "Mrs. Morell, you mustn't dream of such a thing. This isn't a formal hour for calling, but I only came up to say how-do-you-do."

Janet took the full bucket from under the bamboo stem and replaced it with another. "Please stay," she said. "We live simply, but there's sufficient."

Her voice had enough of a Scotch inflection to be attractive, but there was no welcome in her eyes, and Teresa felt tongue-tied with shyness, regretting that she had come.

"I'd love to stay another time," she said, "but not today. The servants are expecting me at home, and I have to go into Grande Anse afterwards."

Janet's unspoken thought – it's to be hoped she changes first – was as obvious as Teresa's sudden determination not to do so. It was a pity, she thought afterwards, that Tommy was not there to appreciate the light and shade of expression, to sense the latent instinctive hostility between the two women, the cause of which lay in the future rather than in the present.

"I was just telling Mr. Morell," Teresa said, "that I'm afraid we've been trespassing shamefully on Neva. I love the ocean, and the high cliffs. On our side of the island the sea is tame."

"There are many that trespass, Miss Craddock, and steal too."

Derek said: "I've talked coconuts to Miss Craddock till my throat is dry as a husk. What'll you have to drink? Whisky? I'm afraid I've no soda. A rum punch? A pink gin?"

Teresa seldom drank in the daytime, but Janet's attitude made her require sustenance. "A pink gin," she said, "if you're having one anyway. But please don't mix it just for me."

"Oh, I'm with you. But Janet doesn't drink, poor girl." She looks it, Teresa thought. You couldn't imagine Janet uninhibited.

"Not even the wine of your own country, Mrs. Morell? It's the best of all, really."

"I'm afraid I cannot agree with you, Miss Craddock. My country has reason to be ashamed of its distilleries."

Teresa was angry with Derek for having forced this interview upon her. How could you think kindly of a person, appreciate her strength and uprightness, if she bludgeoned you with every word spoken, pierced you with the daggers of things unsaid? What had engendered this enmity, she wondered. A sleeveless dress worn in Grande Anse? A husband's too obvious interest? Or was there in truth something waiting beyond the horizon, something that only Janet could see or remember or imagine, some long ago happening that the circle of time was bringing round again?

Among the stones by the edge of the stream Teresa saw grey accumulations of dead leaves and sticks. Grass, and a few seedling

77

palms, had been flattened by water pouring over them. Now, the river ran quietly and softly, its waters spattered by raindrops. A heron stood motionless in mid-stream. "It didn't need to rain any more," Teresa said, "after yesterday. I can see that your river was in flood too. Ours roared like a printing press."

"It was terrible, Miss Craddock. My husband had gone up stream, and I was afraid. Water poured down like a moving wall, and what I had thought of as a little river became in one moment a foaming torrent, red-coloured, as though it carried blood to the sea."

Such intense speaking was embarrassing. Yet, for the first time, seeing it animated, Teresa realized how charming that grey-lined face might have been, and the trim figure wrapped in a grey overall. She was surely much older than Derek. And she guessed back twenty years to where a boy stood, frightened of life and resting on this girl-cousin's strength; and remembering her until the time came for him to need a wife. Since when she had managed his life for him, being clever with incubators, making vegetables grow, hoarding nuts, but inevitably crushing romance and fire out of a man who knew how the wind blew through cane-fields, and who looked for red flowers swinging like bells. Yet there was poetry, or something like it, in this queer Scotch woman who might be knowing their futures. "A foaming torrent," she had said, "red-coloured as though it carried blood to the sea." No artist could have made a better picture of St. Celian rivers in spate. But of what, Teresa wondered, had she been afraid?

"The worst flood in the world could never reach up here," she said.

"It was for my husband that I was afraid, Miss Craddock. I feared to see his body rolling, tossing, among those tumbling waters; his body, and not refuse of trees; his body, broken and inert."

"How horrible for you," Teresa murmured, taken aback, inadequate. "I'm so sorry."

The most futile of words, but she *was* sorry. This woman had been terrified for her husband, and he had come deliberately to Ça Ira, making the flood an excuse. In that moment she realized that she had forgotten to ask Derek what reason he had given for his absence; did not know if his wife knew where he had been. Which carelessness was almost a certificate of good character; showed at least how untrained she was in intrigue. Then she remembered that Derek had gone home wearing Tommy's clothes, his own wrapped into a damp bundle which at the last moment he had almost forgotten. So Janet must know. But she was thankful when Derek himself appeared, bringing rescue as well as cocktails.

"You mustn't forget to take your brother's clothes back," he said, almost as though he had read her thoughts. "I was extraordinarily grateful for them last night."

"But it's awful that your wife should have been here alone worrying about you, and you swilling tea at your ease, and stuffing stale cake."

"Perhaps Janet had cake too. She makes *good* cakes."

He shouldn't have looked at her in that teasing possessive way. No wife could like it. It was as though they two were sharing something illegal, something more than a joke about cake. "I'm afraid he's being rude about my cook, Mrs. Morell. Cakes are not her strong point. But I'll have to forgive him in return for this much needed cocktail."

"Drink to our success here," Derek said, "to the ultimate downfall of the forest." Then, turning to his wife, he explained: "I'm only teasing our poor neighbour. She turns pale and wilts at the thought of a tree being cut down. And stolen coconuts mean no more to her than blackberries or wild roses picked from high road hedges."

"It's no laughing matter," Janet said. "I deplore this incessant thieving. There's a lax standard in the island. Even the police give us no help."

"But *who* steals from you?" Teresa was beginning to find the subject irritating. "Why don't you hire a watchman and find out? It may be your own tenants, or strangers from down the coast. Frenchmen, even. I'll never believe that the whole population of Ville Rousse is organized to rob you. Not even in thieving will West Indians co-operate to that extent."

"They're all tarred with the same brush," Derek said. "Farouche, independent. I want them to plant bananas for me on the share system, but they've gone sour since I turned them off those gardens on the West End."

How difficult human nature is. Derek himself had gone sour when, eighteen years ago, he had been turned off his garden. But the gander's sauce never looked the same way to the goose. And in no case could you argue with a man, a man with whom you were a little in love, when you were drinking his gin in his wife's presence. Offensive arguments are apt to lead to intensive situations, to cope with which one should be free to draw a kiss from one's knapsack, or at least the right kind of a smile. "I'm sure things will sort themselves," she said. No one could go on forever crying: "Who's been digging up my nuts?" Soon there would be something else to cry about. Floods and landslides, blights and diseases. St. Celia had more tricks up her sleeve than a peasantry careless about the rights of property. "I'm truly sorry," she said, "that you've had so much trouble. It was on the tip of my tongue to say – don't do anything drastic, but after all there is nothing drastic one can do."

"One might close the beach," Janet said.

Teresa had been watching raindrops running off the leaves of banana trees. They hung for a while like glass balls on the ridge of the leaf, and then, as though pushed by playful companions, rolled joyously down the long green slopes. "How do you mean?" she said, "close the beach?"

"We own the foreshore and we suspect that nuts are exported to Guadeloupe. If no one was allowed to keep his boat on the beach it would be impossible to ship them."

"Yes, I see," Teresa said. If that happened then there would be no canoes and no rafts lying on all that long slope of sand. Hermit crabs would tumble alone among red mushrooms; and the little pink shells and the cowries would be unbroken by men's footsteps. "But, of course, you couldn't really do that," she said, "because there is no other beach for miles. How would the people get their fish?"

"That, Miss Craddock, would be their business, not ours."

Afterwards Teresa realized that she had been more puzzled than shocked. Here was a good woman; not a spinster, a woman of loose character, but a practising Christian woman. Obviously she couldn't be meaning what she said. Teresa wondered if this were a threat being tried out on her that she might pass it on. But from that moment she hardened against Janet, and her conscience was quietened. She said to herself that this woman, who was cruel, deserved to have her husband stray from her hearth. Which argument was illogical because life is not played by set rules, such and such an error deserving so much requital, but only by instincts and emotions that are fluid and irrational, spilling themselves in this place and that, without reason.

"I must go now," she said, "the servants will think I'm dead." And then, because situations should be outwardly tidy and if she meant to encourage Derek she must appear to encourage Janet also, she added: "Let's see each other now and then. After all we are rather isolated at this end of the island. Perhaps we are both lonely sometimes?"

Teresa was never lonely, never wanted people for the sake of having them. Implying that she needed Janet's company was an elaborate piece of politeness, and it gathered no moss.

"*I* am too busy to be lonely," Janet said, ending her sentence on a flat note that was deliberately meant to discourage.

Miss Craddock of Ça Ira had, perhaps, in some ways been spoilt. She was not accustomed to having her overtures rebuffed. Her eyes hardened, although her lips smiled more sweetly than before. The lives of many people, and of little fishes, were ultimately to be affected by this passage-at-arms.

She said: "Well, won't you both come over and lunch some day? If you're so busy, I imagine that Sunday would be most convenient. I shall be away this weekend. I have to go to Capesterre for a dinner party. But what about Sunday week? We lunch at twelve."

"I'm afraid we couldn't come as early as that," Janet said.

"You've forgotten church," Derek interposed. "If you'll ask us to tea we'd love to come."

Teresa had forgotten church, although she had heard that they favoured the Methodist brand. But she was glad that her projected guests had chosen the shorter meal. This meeting was meant as a gesture, and she preferred it to be no more elaborate than need be.

"That will be delightful, then. Sunday week. No, don't come out and get wet," she said to Derek, "I can find my way." The car, standing between high banks in the pale twilight of balisier leaves, was become a haven of refuge. The lace of the tree-ferns' branches covered a leaden sky. There was no bucket under the eaves now and water poured aimlessly through the bamboo pipe.

"This morning was a glimpse of Heaven," Derek whispered, standing bareheaded in the rain. "But I do wish that I'd kissed you."

"Be careful," she answered. "Remember there's an edge to the precipice." And because Janet's attitude had kindled provocative fires in her she added: "You might fall to unknown depths, and drag me with you."

IX

In the house next door there was a child practising scales. Church bells rang for vespers, and the town crier cried the name of the film to be shown that evening in the theatre. Teresa sat on the end of Tommy's bed, manicuring her finger nails. It was too dark for her to see clearly what she was doing, but electricity in Capesterre is turned on irrespective of the sun's setting, so that in winter there is a gap of half an hour in the town's life while streets grow cooler, and dust settles, and stars come out; a breathing space during which one must polish one's nails, or drink cocktails, or make love, because it is too dark to do anything else.

"I believe it's a ramp on the part of the gin importers," Tommy said. "I wonder what they're worth to them, those extra rounds when the sun has been turned off for tennis and the lights not yet turned on for bridge."

"It's a pity you're not a statistician," Teresa said. "You could work out (*a*) what the Government scores in customs revenue, and (*b*) what it loses in electricity charges. Talking of which, and by way of breaking it gently, Norah is in the family way."

"Good God, what a nuisance. Our domestic staff overdoes this breeding business. What'll we do?"

"Get in Rosalie for a month. I gather this baby isn't going to be featured as Fitzroy was. Norah's going to the Grande Anse hospital."

"And who is Papa?"

"The unknown soldier, as far as I'm concerned. A man of courage in any case."

"I bet it's Nicholas Nolette, Rosalie's younger brother."

"But, Tommy, he's half her age."

"*Ça n'empêche pas.*"

Teresa knew how true that was. Nothing prevented love, neither age nor temperament, nor colour. The spark struck in the oddest places. And sometimes it was blown out by a fortuitous wind and sometimes it burned fiercely, leaving behind it a black desolation. But you never knew that the fire had caught until it was too late to put it out.

"How's Georgette?" she asked. Georgette was Tommy's coloured mistress, slim and trim and elegant; chosen – Teresa pretended – for being her brother's physical antithesis.

"She's all right," Tommy answered. "Today's some fast day." Georgette was devout as well as seductive, which made her uncertain as a mistress, and also expensive. When money was needed for a cause she not only begged from Tommy but wrote to Teresa as well. Teresa generally sent the money, knowing it would be well spent, not on candles but on the undeserving poor.

The bells had stopped ringing now, and because she had been rubbing her buffer in time with them, Teresa let her hands rest idly in her lap, looking out of the window at the darkening sky.

"What's the matter, Teresa? One moment you look like a lovesick hen, and the next like the cat who's eaten the canary. Have you been up to mischief?"

"I haven't had the canary, Tommy. But I think I'm going to."

"Morell, I suppose. I'm afraid he'll prove indigestible."

"Tommy, sometimes I like him and sometimes I don't, and I hate *her*. But I do want to go to bed with him. I haven't felt that way for a long time." It was nice to have a brother you could talk to. They understood better than other men.

"Well, don't count on getting there. He's not that type, darling. Those sort of people don't come of the adulterous classes. They save up for alternate Saturdays at home."

Teresa shook her head, knowing better. Derek had been fashioned out of his time and class, or had been docked of his Saturdays. There was more to it than smoke in the way he had looked at her. Bed was waiting if she wanted it. And her mind swung back to the house at Neva where two rivers met; to the bucket under the bamboo stem. How shocked Janet would be by such talk, and Derek too, probably. The unadulterous classes never dotted their "I's". But even they got swept off their feet sometimes, or fell over precipices.

"What don't you like about him?" Tommy said.

"Oh, coconuts, gardens. It's an attitude, a frame of mind. Sometimes I almost think he'll say – damned niggers. And then he looks at me with those rather frightening eyes of his – they're queer eyes, Tommy, fanatical – and my backbone melts, and my throat goes dry, and I come over all girlish. I suppose it's what's called Nature's urge to reproduction."

"For God's sake, don't go as far as that, darling. Norah and Tilly do all the reproducing required in one household."

The unfair thing about Nature's urge was that it clouded and biassed your judgment. You couldn't see a man clear when you were in love. Teresa knew herself to be on the edge of a steep slope. Not a precipice, a slope, down which she would roll slowly, inevitably, like a drop of rain on a banana leaf, into blindness. She would be smothered as though in a snowdrift – (there was no metaphor you couldn't apply to love, making it fire one moment and snow the next) – and then everything that Derek said would be white and right. She would clothe him in virtues that fitted him no better than Tommy's trousers had done, and she would fail to notice any more his bony ankles and the damp black hairs on his legs. That was what love did to you. And being wise and experienced and knowing these things didn't save you from rolling. You fell as surely and as swiftly as an eighteen-year-old. Although, perhaps, sophistication brought you to your feet quicker, wiped your vision clean; and sometimes, all too soon, distorted it in the other direction, so that what had been pure white became almost absurdly a thing of bony ankles and black hairs.

"After all," she said, "it's not my fault that I'm not married."

Tommy followed her train of thought. Women needed a man sometimes. "It is, darling," he said. "You could have draped yourself in orange blossoms a dozen times."

"I could never have married anyone but Lewis, Tommy. Other men are good for one thing or another. But Lewis was good for everything. And so God took him away."

Tommy remembered those grey days after Lewis had been killed, when Teresa had nearly died of pneumonia, following on

85

shock. Above and beyond the Capesterre noises he could hear Paris ones, the quick snapping of taxi horns, the crying of "*Paris Soir*"; and see the red silk curtains and gilt chairs of the room in which he had found her. Afterwards, the doctors had said that she must live in a warm climate, and so he had brought her to the West Indies. Theirs had been a good life, a happy companionship. Some people thought Teresa heartless, her beauty superficial, but Tommy knew that it was not so. Lewis' death killed something in her, but the deeps were still there.

"I hope I'm wrong in my diagnosis," he said lightly, "and that you'll get what you want of him. Love's a disease, to be recovered from quickly." He knew that he was fortunate among humans in that he did not waste the substance of happiness in riotous loving. Georgette was a solace and an anchor. He had no need to go looking for trouble.

But Teresa was thinking that certain phases of life were made unjustly easy for the other sex, who were less subtle in their requirements. She passed in review the men of Georgette's world whom – if conventions were arranged differently – she might have bought as a man buys a woman; Georgette's brother, for instance, who drove a car for hire; or her cousin in the dry goods store. And shook her head hopelessly, because some women might settle their troubles that way, but not she. She had to bring love in; to complicate the issue; dream herself into a mental union before she could envisage a physical one.

She got up and stood by the window that was half curtained by creepers. Two or three streets away there was a breadfruit tree on whose leaves the sun's afterglow still rested, gilding the green foliage. Below, in the walled-in garden, a fountain played into a pool where goldfish sulked under lilies. Violets grew in cement-edged flower-beds shadowed by a red poinsettia that was now grey in the dusk. Through the slats of the jalousies masking the next-door window she could see that the house lights had been turned on, and knew that it was time to put cold cream on her face, and to have a shower before dressing. Town noises were louder at night, she thought; a child crying, scales playing, cocks crowing. For cocks in Capesterre crow at all hours of the twenty-four. Even at sunset.

X

The scent of gardenias rose out of the night to kill the petrol fumes from the hired car. Yellow squares of light, falling on to the green lawn from uncurtained windows, made the grass look almost blue. "It looks much as I feel," Tommy muttered, walking up the Government House steps arrayed – although not exclusively – in a white tie and his miniature medals. But Teresa, who wore evening clothes no more than twice a year and had that fancy dress feeling, was prepared to enjoy herself, regretting only that Derek couldn't see her; and sending silent thoughts to a faraway house at the other end of the island where two rivers chattered over stones and fireflies lit up the dark forest. The butler handed them the plan of the dinner table, showing them where they were to sit.

"Duds," Tommy groaned – he would have groaned whatever the turn of the wheel had brought him, not liking dinner parties – as he found himself placed between Gregg Corbin's wife who twittered, and a fellow councillor, who was also a coloured tradesman. "Remember not to discuss our grocery order," Teresa whispered. But she was pleased with her own fate, Geoffrey Hylton's sense of the frivolous matching her own.

They were announced to their host and hostess; grasped a few stiff fingers encased in white kid gloves. "Why won't you wear gloves, Teresa?" Dorothy Corbin said. "It's done at official parties." This was a ritual question, repeated twice yearly. Teresa explained: "It's my own brand of swank, my way of trying to be different." And added with a smile that was meant to be disarming: "Better *I* should say that than you." Last time she had pointed out that, as her hands were neither dirty nor cold nor ugly, she could see no need to cover them. Tommy had said once that Dorothy was bred of a convention out of a rule, but Teresa thought she was like a cross sparrow, always squeaking and scolding.

Few women attended the Council dinners. Some members did not bring their wives, and some had only mistresses. Being a mere sister put Teresa in the rare position of a red herring, neither flesh nor fowl. Maurice Collins, the Crown Treasurer, an immense fat-faced man, who had made a lifelong habit of keeping on the right side of the powers-that-be, apologized for his wife's absence with the well-used formula – "She has a touch of fever." Fever was a synonymous term for everything in St. Celia, from a hangover to an illicit weekend; and although everyone knew that Mrs. Collins was suffering from neither of these, but was going to have a baby, the decencies had to be thus observed. The extra men filed into the dining room alone, and the women took off their gloves, which subsequently slipped on to the floor and had to be recovered from among table-napkins and feet. It seemed inappropriate to Tommy that there was no grace said. Such grim proceedings, he thought, should have been opened by prayer as had been the Council meeting in the morning.

Long ago Geoffrey Hylton had moved that prayers should be abolished in Council, but he had been overruled.

"If communion with the Almighty will induce certain of the honourable members to speak the truth," he had said, "then I withdraw the motion." Geoffrey had been born and had lived all his life in St. Celia. A mischievous twisted smile was often on his grey lips, and always behind his eyes if you chose to look for it. Sometimes Teresa wondered what his anger was like, but she had never seen that; knew in her heart of hearts that he wore a mask against her, a piece of that defensive curtain hung out by coloured people to protect themselves from the impertinence of whites. "It isn't that we dislike you," a man had said to her once with whom she had been dancing, referring not to Teresa personally but to her race, "we distrust you." And Teresa had murmured: *"Et avec cause."*

One Capesterre dinner was very like another. Grapefruit; thin soup; fried fish on a lettuce leaf; chicken and ham, followed by ice cream or tinned fruit salad. Why couldn't they try Creole cooking for a change, Tommy grumbled. An old-fashioned pepper-pot, for instance, or at least crapauds. Tommy delighted in those fat-rich toads that barked on the hillsides on a damp evening. No one knew where they bred; their eggs were never found; but they kept on coming to their killing. From one end of the table the Administrator, hating the island and everyone in it, glowered at his guests as though he said to himself: "Scum!" That had been a line of Charles Hawtrey's once, in a play whose name Tommy had forgotten. "Scum," with a lot of sibilants in it. His wife – well-dressed and regal, although Teresa said that her pearls came from Woolworths and her teeth out of dead horses – was trying to be kind, but only succeeding in being frightening.

Not till the middle of the meal did Teresa hear the name that made her heart beat and her colour rise. "Do you see anything of the Morells?" someone asked.

"Teresa does," Tommy said. "She's dry-nursing them."

"And do they respond to treatment?"

"*He* does," she answered. If you deliberately stressed your interest in a person no one took it seriously. "But I'm out of my depth with her."

"Nearly naked in Grande Anse, what?"

"Oh, I'm making myself a douillette. I haven't broken it to you, Tommy, but they're coming to tea next Sunday." A douillette is an old West Indian costume, high in the neck and down to the wrists. An acre of stuff and a hundredweight of starch go to its skirt. "I'll wear it with a yashmak," Teresa said, "and economize in face powder."

"What I want to know," the Chief of Police said, "is why Morell can't look after his own property. He wrote to me complaining that the corporal in Ville Rousse was remiss in his duty. The man ought to stand himself a watchman."

"Let's institute coastguards," Tommy said. "Nice old men with blue reefer jackets and telescopes under their arms."

"Provided they put the telescopes to their blind eyes," Hylton insisted. But the Treasurer broke in: "I sympathize deeply with Morell. If you people would stop smuggling – "

"Smuggling has nothing to do with it," Hylton said. "Morell has got himself in wrong with the peasants. He has the Parham

Island manner. For years past they've been allowed to help themselves to the Neva coconuts, and because he's done nothing to conciliate them they'll go on helping themselves for years to come. If the man has any sense he'll let the thing slide. What's he losing per year, anyway? And who knows that nuts are exported?"

"He says his overseer knows."

"And I know the overseer. Harvey brings out of his head just what his questioner puts into it. Some things should be ignored, left dormant in the minds of Harveys. Morell has got nuts on the brain, like gnus have maggots."

Teresa tried not to listen. Hitherto she had always thought Geoffrey was right about things. Now she withdrew from the conversation, dreaming herself back on to Neva Beach where surf hissed on to white sand and brought tribute of pink-lined shells to the feet of the sea grape trees. She remembered a man's eyes teasing her, reading her inmost thoughts. "It isn't the island I'm going to love," he had said, "but you." What did coconuts matter, or peasants' gardens, when he had the power to make her a young girl again, a child with a woman's knowledge. But clamorous voices brought her back to the dinner table, back to the chicken and ham, and champagne, and argument of reality.

"Be a good influence," they were saying, as Tommy had said once. "Use your powers of persuasion, Miss Craddock."

"Your powers of seduction," Geoffrey whispered. "Let no stone be unturned, no sacrifice unburnt."

It was horrible and cheapening that they should be thrusting on her in fun a role that she was longing to play in earnest. "I have no powers," she said brusquely. "The Morells can manage their own business. It's not mine." But Hylton persisted: "It's every-one's business, Teresa. We must have peace in our time." Where-upon she saw the Administrator wince almost audibly at a coloured man calling a white woman by her Christian name, and rage at his ill-manners made her temporarily whiter than God had meant her to be. Colonel Grace, C.M.G., has an Anglo-Indian mentality, she thought; and remembered how in Calcutta they had called natives "wogs". She had walked home one night across the Maidan, and the young box-wallahs with her had thought it funny to push the wogs off the wooden rails on which they were sleeping; shrunken, skinny-legged wogs of the same shape and colour as the rails.

After walnuts and peppermints had been circulated, a wheezy gramophone was set in motion by the butler. Everybody stood up while the Administrator said: "Ladies and Gentlemen, The King." The crowd muttered in chorus, "The King," and stood to attention while the gramophone ground out the national anthem. The butler had been lazy in his winding, and the last "God save" sank to a peevish squeak.

Hardly had the party sat down before it was dragged to its feet again to drink to the Queen and the Royal Family. "How the welfare of those unfortunate people does interfere with our innocent prattle," Teresa said. And secretly drank the toast to a man against whom it seemed that everyone was prejudiced, a man who had longed for twenty years to own land and grow sugar, who had been disappointed and thwarted when he was young, and had a sour wife.

When the women had straggled from the room, Tommy and his neighbour settled themselves to discuss the port that the merchant himself had purveyed. Tommy asked what it cost, and was told. "Good God, it should be even cheaper," he said. And the merchant decided to splutter his amusement rather than to take offence.

"I could sell you something better," he said. And they fell into really good talk about wine and rum and such kindred spirits. Not till he was walking home through empty shuttered streets, across which starlight cast elongated shadows of stuccoed buildings, did Tommy realize that he had not only talked shop but had ordered a dozen bottles of old rum as well.

He sang as he walked, sang a song pertinent to the occasion.

"No matter how much we nozzle and souse
The sun never sets upon Government House

"Do you remember?" he asked Teresa. "The Adelphi, on our last night in London before we came out here for the first time."

"I remember," she said. They had thrown coloured balloons from the stage into the stalls, and Coward himself had been sitting in a box. "You've no regrets, have you, Tommy?"

"Wouldn't live anywhere else for the world," he said. And she knew that it was true. "I'm getting to be an old man, Teresa. Do you realize that I'd been at Eton for three halves before you were even born? I dandled you in my arms, woman, but you're catching up. Discrepancies in age shrink as one grows older." He didn't know the rest of the Government House song so he varied it with "Mad dogs and Englishmen". Teresa always complained that he never remembered a song until everyone else had forgotten it.

Sitting on the curb with their feet in the gutter, two old women talked under his bedroom window. "Clara is nasty-fingered," one said, "nasty-fingered. I do not know how Madam could have taken her into her house. She is nasty-fingered."

What was the matter with her fingers, Tommy wondered, that they should be nasty? "Hence, hag-seed," he cried into the night, quoting Prospero. But the fragment of talk troubled him, and before getting into bed he went to Teresa's room, holding out his hands to her and hoping that he wasn't nasty-fingered, although he knew they were short and fat like the rest of him. "Good night, Big Brother," she said. "You're sozzled and soused, but you've got lovely fingers. Nice, friendly fingers, that any man might be proud of."

XI

"Sir, everything is in order," Henry said. "But that girl Tilly, she say things behind my back that if she repeat to my face I will not answer for the consequences."

"What sort of things?"

"Things, Sir, that I do not express in the presence of Miss T'resa."

"They must have been hot things," Teresa said. "My presence has put up with a good deal in its time." She was leaning over the veranda rail looking out upon clouds that took on the caricatured shapes of animals. As the light faded, their tails and snouts elongated as though from the horizon they were trying to span the world.

"I bet she said nothing to matter," Tommy said. "I doubt the existence of the word Henry wouldn't repeat."

"He seems to have done no gardening while we've been away, so he's had time to quarrel. But he told me tonight: 'If God spare, come Wednesday, I prepare mould for the tomatoes.'"

"He put over a better one on me," Tommy said. "A strange bush has sprouted down by the runner beans, a thing with a yellow flower and brown seed pods. It seems you make a tea of it. 'You should try it, Sir,' says Henry. 'It is good for the wombs of women.' I said I hoped a cupful wouldn't change my sex."

It was getting dark now, and Teresa could see fireflies playing among the palm trees like falling stars, and a young moon slipping behind the horizon like a shy child at a party hiding among curtains. The clouds that had been animals were strung out over the sea in a thin streak, and there were more piling up on the mountain tops, beyond which no stars shone at all.

Next day the November rains broke more fiercely than Teresa ever remembered them. She could hear the rain sweeping down the valley, battering the treetops, minutes before it struck the house. There was a moment when, out of the storm, she looked upon a sea that was still blue. Then a grey shroud blotted it altogether from sight and there was nothing seen anywhere but a wall of water imprisoning them in a wet world that was all their own. Tommy had installed a new rain gauge, and spent a busy morning emptying it. Between breakfast and lunch it registered six and a half inches.

Henry loomed up out of the mud wearing a sack on his head as well as an umbrella. "Is everything all right in the valley?" Tommy called.

"Everything," Henry said, "is a total wreck."

They debated whether this should not be listed in the over-statement department, but they went to investigate. In three places a slice of the hillside had fallen into the valley, and the river, choked as many times, ran redly, turgidly, as though it carried blood to the sea. Janet had said that, and Teresa knew that the Neva rivers would also be running redly; but today Derek would be surely at home, so that there would be no fear of seeing his body rolling, broken, and inert, in tumbling waters. Last week he had come to Ça Ira by the Souffrière valley, but if he came that way now he would die, and the forest would bury him. And she thought how strange it was that Janet should so fear the forest, knowing it so little. What did she understand of vast trees, that with darkness became live predatory things, sending forth lianas and twisted roots that might deceive and trip a man, and, having caught him, broken-legged, hold him until it was their pleasure to grant him the boon of a green strangling death. Teresa knew the forest and loved it without fear. Was it true, what Janet implied, that it was like a dangerous woman? Had she affinity with it that she was not afraid?

"Henry hardly exaggerated," Tommy said. Together they looked down on to a total wreck of vegetables and fruit trees that, with the depressed appearance of yesterday's salad, lay in a tumbled mass among boulders or swirled with yellow foam in pools that were becoming lakes. "I'll be afraid for the village if this goes on." Only one foot's width of path was left where there had been three. Red wounds bled from the ground they stood on, and rain scoured these, carrying gouts of mud to the river, and heavy discoloured water. Torrents rushed through courses where they had not known that the land was creased, until it seemed as though the whole island was one vast waterfall, part of the grey skies out of which floods fell.

The village stood firm. No little grey houses were washed out to sea. But the bridge was broken, its steel girders twisted like silk, its stones tumbled and swept away. The road over the divide was blocked for two days by landslides – "The Government take a lashing," Henry said – and a watercourse, that no one had ever seen wet, rose suddenly and carried an old woman into the sea.

The veranda roof leaked until there was more leak than roof. When the rain was over and Ça Ira rose out of the water like the ark out of the flood, it was decided that something must be done. Tommy sent to the village for Français the carpenter, and together they fitted on new sheets of galvanized iron, and Français painted them. Tilly watched him at his work, making suggestions, irritating him to frenzy.

"What do you do now that your man is in the French country?" he asked. For Fitzroy's father had long ago crossed the channel, ostensibly to make money for Tilly, but had never sent any. Français was standing on a ladder with a paint-pot in one hand, and in the other a brush filled with green paint so thick, so luscious, that it gave him voluptuous pleasure to use it. He let a drop fall to make a round spot like a counter. Then he obliterated the counter with one glorious sweep of the brush.

"What do I do?" Tilly echoed, removing from her head a bucket of water, the fetching of which was the ostensible reason for her being out of the kitchen. "What do I do? I do the same as your wife does."

Teresa, overhearing, thought this remark capable of several interpretations, but the one that Français understood certainly touched him on the raw. He flicked his brush at Tilly, staining her frock and the handkerchief on her head.

Tilly was livid with anger. Like a mischievous puppy she had provoked the man, and now she growled and bit. Summoning

Tommy and Teresa as witnesses to the outrage, she demanded four shillings compensation for her damaged clothes. If the money was refused, she said, she would go to law.

Français ignored her. Secure in his elevated position he drew the brush backwards and forwards with long careful gestures, thinking how much more beautiful was his green work on the roof than had been God's on the lawn. The situation became very loud and very voluble. Even Isabel took it upon herself to express an opinion.

Next morning Français' wife said that she would pay for a new dress if Tilly would give her the old one. This offer seemed fair enough, but Tilly unhesitatingly refused it. Henry, who was present at the interview, was ready to explain.

"If her enemies get her dress," he said, "they might do her evil. Some people believe in these things." The word obeah was written clearly across the sky.

That day Tilly's genius suffered an eclipse. The omelette was a mess, the vegetables were burnt, the pastry fell with a dull thud into the cement drain where Tommy flung it, not in temper, but to avoid hurting the girl's feelings by leaving it on his plate. Eventually, for his stomach's sake, he gave her eighteen pence towards a new Madras; and next day, without rhyme or reason, Français handed over three shillings for a dress. Teresa never knew whether this was hush money on the part of Français' wife or a bribe against Tilly's obeah, but the incident was considered closed. "There aren't enough teacups in the pantry," she said, "to accommodate the storms we weather."

Meanwhile, Norah moved through the house like the majesty of God. Her scene with Teresa, the breaking down of her reserve, might never have been. Her duties were perfectly performed. She even managed not to look fat. To Tilly she never condescended so much as to box her ears. Tilly overflowed with the froth and bubble of life, but she tightened up when Norah was near. The two sisters spoke only on business – "There is fish-cakes for breakfast," or, "The master say to use a breadfruit." Once, on her way to Grande Anse, knowing she would be late, Teresa called to Tilly: "See that a lamp is lit before dark." And the girl protested: "Miss T'resa, I not understanding the sitting-room lamps."

"Well," Teresa said, "tell Norah to light one." Then she remembered, and ostentatiously suppressed annoyance.

"Of course, I forgot, you can't tell Norah." And she weighted her sarcasm heavily. "You must go down to the village," she said, "and bring back someone who can tell her."

Tilly had a sense of humour. She grinned as she answered: "That much I can tell her." All afternoon she had sat on a bench in the kitchen reading her Bible. "Because," she said plaintively, "it is all that I have to read." So Teresa offered her a volume of Boulestin instead, and told her to profit by it.

Henry said next day: "There is this to it, Sir. Tilly is a bad girl who go out to seek her man. But Norah wait for her man to come to her."

Teresa maintained that this was a distinction without a difference, the result being the same, but Tommy thought otherwise. "Norah's a modest wench; does the spider act. Will you come into my parlour? But Tilly, the feline, goes forth seeking that she may devour. There is a vast difference in technique," he said. And Teresa bowed to his superior knowledge.

XII

Derek said: "So much for your beautiful island, Miss Craddock. Now, we have seen what it can do. Immense portions of my property have disappeared into the sea."

"Ours fell into the river," she said. "The effect was the same. But a certain variety of mood is surely an attribute of beauty. Other islands can only boast the flat monotony of their own virtue." Janet gave a barely perceptible sniff, and Mr. Biggar the magistrate looked down his nose.

A recent shuffle of the official pack had brought a new magistrate to Grande Anse. Mr. Biggar was a veteran from the northern islands, his legal dinners so long since digested that he had ceased to derive benefit from them, but instead fumbled among precedents, and tied himself up in red tape. Whenever he opened his mouth there came forth toads of verbiage and phraseology. Harder to forgive was his persistent exposure, by wearing shorts, of knees that were dimpled.

"You cannot," Teresa said to Tommy, "expect me to be nice to knees like that."

"Knees are never nice," Tommy said, quoting their Aunt Louisa who, when she first saw Teresa in shorts, objected to her knees. "But," Teresa had said, "they're nice knees." And Aunt Louisa had countered with: "Knees are never nice."

"If your knees are not nice," Tommy said, "I don't see why you should object to Biggar's."

"I don't see why either, but I do."

They had to ask him to Ça Ira, so Teresa suggested getting him off with the Morells. The better the day, etc. Tommy had wondered whether it was wise to mix one's drinks, but now, seeing the sniff and the downward look, he decided that these drinks were blending. You never knew what would make a cocktail till you tried.

"Tell us your troubles," Teresa said to Derek, "and then we'll tell ours. You can begin because you're the party." She was strung up and nervous because seeing him again was very exciting although painful in public. She realized suddenly, and could share this with no one, that she had never before shaken hands with him.

"I went up on the cliffs at midday," he said, "and as far as the eye could reach the water was dirty and thick. Waves were breaking in orange spray, and opposite the mouth of each river there was a crescent of red mud that grew wider and wider. It seemed to me unfair" – and he smiled a disarming smile right into Teresa's heart – "that even the elements should steal from me."

"A plantation of young limes was altogether destroyed," Janet said, and her smile was not disarming at all but very grim, "and my vegetables were scoured out of the ground. Worse, the beating of the rain killed several young chickens. I couldn't get them into the house in time."

"I came home to find Janet shaking her fist at the forest," Derek said. "It was maddening to see those huge trees standing black and immoveable, while bananas crumpled and young oranges were uprooted."

Tommy was pleased to hear that Janet could do anything so human as to shake her fist. Teresa had been wrong about her legs. They weren't ugly at all, and she covered them with nice stockings, well pulled up. In fact, seeing that Biggar wore trousers and not shorts, the lower ends of the party were to his satisfaction. Socks hid Derek's bony ankles and Teresa could see no damp black hairs above them. The mists of illusion were closing in upon her, mists of love and desire woven so subtly into one another that none could tell where the seam was.

"Tilly's done her best with the cake," she said. "Your insinuation has rankled. I very nearly played the violin myself." No wonder Janet thought she was mad. What had violins to do with sponge cake? But Derek remembered.

"I hear you've got Jessaman as gardener," Tommy said. "We call him 'Partridge deceased'."

"If Partridge were not deceased I'd have wrung his neck long ago. Who was the bird, anyway?"

"A *rara avis* of a road surveyor who grew English vegetables instead of 'roots'. No problem arises," he explained to Mr. Biggar, "horticultural or otherwise, upon which Jessaman does not proffer the opinions of 'Partridge deceased'."

"We've got a gang of women clearing and planting, but Janet is sadly hampered by that dead hand."

Tommy said: "I met them in the road the other day. Jessaman was leading them home like a string of cows."

"Do you have trouble with your labour?" the magistrate asked. And Tommy and Teresa, with dread, saw coconuts breaking into the conversation as surely as fallen nuts sprouted among crab holes by the river's mouth.

Derek said: "There's plenty of it, and the people must need money, but they seem to be sulky. At present I'm only employing those who pasture cows on my land, or who have gardens. Then I can deduct my rents from their pay."

"I thought you had turned everyone off their gardens."

"Not everyone. Only those on the West End. I've got other plans for the land between Neva Beach and Ville Rousse."

Green cane-fields billowing like the sea. Wind blowing through feathery arrows. Red flowers swinging like bells. A foolish dream, Teresa thought, but how nice of him to have dreams when so many people go through life without them, sunk in a drab prose.

"What plans?" Tommy asked politely, but Derek managed not to give a direct answer. Teresa saw that he was sensitive about his fields, and was glad that she had told no one. She picked up her patchwork and turned to show it to Janet.

"What's the history of this piece?" Derek asked. And Teresa said: "That piece hasn't a history. It's Tommy's pyjamas. But the other basket," indicating it with a touch of her foot, "is my European collection. You can ask about most of them. They're eminently respectable."

The red and green plaid he was fingering meant Dresden, seven years ago. Teresa saw velvet armchairs set in a stiff circle, roses and cornflowers prisoned in gold frames, red chrysanthemums in a speckled vase with a black-bound grammar propped up against it so that crinkled shadows of petals fell on to the printed page. She remembered white wool wound about black shiny needles, and her own hands mechanically purling and plaining, and her lips mechanically repeating, reciting. Stitches and words went in rhythm together – one plain, one purl; *bis, durch, für, gegen*; and her thoughts had strayed like geese on a common while the curved shadows of red chrysanthemums lay on the book like her teacher's fingers, old shrivelled fingers with sharpened nails.

"Do you know German?" she said. "I hate it. To me it means prepositions clouding the atmosphere, buzzing in the brain like a murrain of flies. One sentence in my grammar has haunted me always. 'There are further five compounds that follow their substantives.' And I see them following – not humbly as poor compounds should follow their betters – but rudely, like dogs barking behind sheep, or prosecuting attorneys taking the accusative case."

Janet said: "You have a vivid imagination, Miss Craddock, but I admire your needlework. I'd like to make pretty things, but I have no time."

She was pathetic with her endless stressing of busyness. Teresa wanted to be sorry for her, but felt there was a rigid casing to the other woman's soul, rigid as the stays she wore on her body, that would never open to let in sympathy or intimacy. Why had she married Derek, Teresa wondered. To escape from that cold land to which she now longed to return? To escape into an existence that by very reason of its colour scheme must have seemed unexpectedly affluent, but of which scheme she took no advantage. Servants were cheap and she didn't employ them. Or had she married only for love, swept off her feet by the charm that was now so deeply affecting herself? Teresa felt that this woman would love strongly and hate to the same measure, a little grey rat to whom life and the people in it would always be all black or all white.

"Would you like to see my orchids?" she said. "Most of them are at the other end of the lawn. There's a new one flowering for the first time." But Janet answered: "I'd sooner stay here. Your view is so quiet and so wide. I'm tired of the forest and frightened of its closeness. And the beach at Neva is noisy."

At Ça Ira the sea was never noisy. Only rarely could they hear it whispering on the shingle or sighing as it withdrew itself from soft grey sand. Slate-coloured, tinted with mauve, peaceful to the point of oiliness, and empty of sail or smoke, it lay that night under the sunset with only a palm tree stencilled on it to break its flat placidity, its monotonous calm.

"I should like to see the orchid," Derek said. Was his eagerness too obvious? Was she oversensitive to what others would think?

"What about you, Mr. Biggar?" Some people felt as she did when they staked their fortune on a single number.

"Miss Craddock," he said, "this is the best chair I've found in the island, and the best view. Neither do I know an orchid from a sunflower."

"I'm mixing drinks," Tommy said. "Who likes what?"

It was almost too easy. Forbidden fruit fell into their mouths like ripe plums. They crossed the lawn slowly, fearful lest they walk too fast; and at last stood alone together under a pergola whose posts were the trunks of tree-ferns, and looked down at white blossoms that seemed to have gathered the dusk into their petals, and lost it. Each could have sworn that the darkness was less dark around those flowers.

So they kissed for the first time among lovely things. Exquisite terror came upon her, terror lost in delight, for there is nothing to equal the rapture of a first kiss. No later, stronger, tide of passion sweeping its victims into deeper water can give the same sense of elation, the same light-headedness. But before he touched her she cried out: "Tell me whether she loves you, Derek. How much would this hurt her if she knew?"

He drew her close to him and, because she was taller than a woman should be, their lips and eyes were on a level. He said: "Janet loves me as an elder sister or a maiden aunt. We haven't slept together for years." He lied about Janet's love, depreciating it, but whether purposely or not she never knew. He gave her the answer that she wanted, that he wanted to give.

"It had to happen, Teresa. Tell me that it was inevitable."

"Of course it was inevitable if we made it so. We are masters of our fate. But" – she laughed – "this is no time to talk philosophy. We must go."

They moved back into the world's vision again, for the measure of a kiss is longer than the time given to see an orchid. Where the lawn curved over into the valley there was a coping of old stones with ferns rooted in the cracks. They stood for a moment, watching the fading colours in the sky.

"Let me see you alone soon, Teresa. Meet me tomorrow by the blowholes." And she said she would try, longing already for his kisses to be repeated as a drunkard longs for his tipple. "If I'm not there," she said, "you'll know it's because I couldn't be." And she picked a handful of dead heads off a rosebush, sprinkling the petals on to the grass.

"You're not sorry I kissed you, Teresa? The precipice wasn't too breathlessly steep?"

"I ought to be sorry," she whispered, "but I'm not. I'm glad." And as they went back on to the veranda her heart echoed: "I'm glad."

XIII

Sometimes there were months when nothing happened. Then events piled up on top of each other with embarrassing swiftness. That night Norah had a grey face and was sneezing. "I have fever," she said, and Teresa could see that she was really ill.

"Go straight to bed," she ordered, "I'll put things away."

Next morning Rosalie the washerwoman was polishing tumblers in the pantry. "Norah arx me to tell you," she said, "that she not more worse this morning, but she have a leetle baby."

Such was her way of breaking it, and Teresa was properly amazed. "But it wasn't due for a month," she said. And Rosalie shrugged her shoulders.

"I sleep with her last night and at four o'clock she call me. I go down to tell Mr. Henry to fetch the midwife, but when we come back the baby is already born."

Teresa wanted to go and see it, but was told: "Norah is not open yet." Hours later they presented her with a black wizened creature looking incredibly old with the wisdom of all Africa in its eyes.

"Aren't you pleased with him?" she said to Norah, "now that you've got him."

"Yes, Miss T'resa, I pleased."

For an hour while Rosalie was away seeking help she had cried her pain to the dawn, and Tilly, her own sister, awake in the adjoining room, had given no help.

Tommy said: "I can't understand it. Tilly is normally a nice girl." It would seem that people are sometimes deflected like comets and behave so strangely that one must not judge them by what they do under a malign influence.

"Has anything been heard of Nicholas?" Tommy asked. But Nicholas was living in St. Patrick's Bay with his elder sister and her husband which – as Henry would say – was one long little distance. That night Tilly sat in the kitchen reading her Bible by the light of a smoking lamp, while the midwife prepared food for Norah. A cat sprawled in a kerosene box suckling her young, while another called through the darkness for a mate. Norah lay beside her baby in the little house under the pois-doux trees and cried out against Tilly: "She tell me that she, she, have her baby like Christian woman, but that I have mine like a dog."

"You had yours the very wisest bravest way," Teresa said, although she suspected that Norah had lied about her dates to avoid going to hospital. And she thought of Isabel, delivered of her first litter under the drawing-room sofa, while all afternoon Teresa had sat beside her, whispering loving words and suffering in sympathy more than the beast had suffered. Man's inhumanity – and woman's – was a hard thing to understand, and she felt bewildered by the contrasts that life offers, in the one hour love, and in the other hate.

She had met Derek as he had asked her to on the cliff above the blowholes. In the morning there was Norah's baby, and again in the evening. But in between there was love, sapid and strong-flavoured; a heady wine, intoxicating as the wind that blew across the open pasture. They sat beside a grey tree trunk that was bent over into the shape of an arch.

"When it was young," Teresa said, "it tried to grow straight, but the trade wind was too much for it, so it bowed itself to the ground again, defeated and now dead." Behind it there were bushes that had never struggled, but, yielding to the wind, had grown flat as roofs, covering rooms carpeted with old leaves. Here the breeze came to them as a soft caressing thing, no longer buffeting. Birds sang and lizards ran up the stems of trees. Fish swam in little pools and cattle grazed. Two people kissed and were amazed that such rapture could be theirs.

Some months have only torn memories in them, hanging like fragments of broken kites on to telephone wires. But others stand out clearly and distinctly, carrying with them beauty or horror, or an almost intolerable emotion, looming up on the plains of memory like black tarred posts streaking an empty landscape. Those months of winter, months when days were short, and the wind shifted to the north, bringing a sense of chill with it and a renewal of energy, were heavy with the excitement of stolen meetings, of stolen kisses; and the madness that illicit love is, love without future or purpose, a passionate fever bringing in its train light-headedness and delirious dreams. Teresa floated on air like spray blown from the blowhole, and drifted she knew not whither.

Norah got up from her bed and went about her work again. But for a full month she might not go out into the night air, and at dusk she shut herself into her room, seeing through the window fireflies imitating stars; hearing frogs call and the faraway noises of the river. When Tilly asked if she might take Fitzroy to Capesterre for Christmas, Teresa thought it better to let her go. And, as though by instinct, the instinct of the dog to which she had likened Norah, she left the child there with her mother and never saw him again. So had Teresa seen Isabel carry her children in her mouth to safety. She was never to forget Tilly as she saw her on the evening of her return, wearing a new red dress and a little straw hat that was almost a bonnet. That picture would be printed on her mind forever. Never had she looked prettier, more full of the joy of living, more radiant. And a fortnight later there was nothing left of her but a green coffin in the Capesterre cemetery, and the memory of a lovely laughing girl in a red dress.

XIV

On Christmas Eve Henry organized the village into singing carols below the veranda. There must have been fifty people, men and women indistinguishably massed together. From out of the darkness – darkness of night, darkness of negro faces – there flashed white teeth; the hem of a frock fluttered by the breeze; the whites of eyes rolling ecstatically. Behind them the light of the young moon etched the palm trees against the sky.

Henry opened with a speech. "Good night, Boss," he said. "We wish you happiness, prosperity, a rain of gold, Heaven after death. We cannot wish you more. God save the King." Then, waving a candle as baton, he signalled for the singing to begin. Teresa made a muzzle of her hand over Isabel's face, for the dog was not partial to carols nor, for the matter of that, to Henry.

"In my Father's house," chanted the women. "In my Father's house," echoed the men. "In my Father's house," sang everyone together until someone chimed in with the next phrase: "Jesus died for no sins of His own." It was strange sweet singing, one hymn drifting into another – "Twenty-fifth of December is Christmas night," and the familiar, "I heard the voice of Jesus say." But Teresa's thoughts had fled away from the present into the past. She forgot the palm trees, and the young moon that was making a gold streak on the sea, and went back to other Christmasses long ago, seeing herself a child again, chasing a fleeing dog through the snow, bareheaded and coatless; brushing her hair in the dark on a frosty night to see flame running through it like lightning. And at last, although she fought to keep it shut, her mind opened itself to the memory of that Christmas when Lewis and she had gone to a midnight Mass together in Paris and had prayed for a blessing on their love. And she found that she was able to probe the sore place; touching it was no longer an unbearable agony, because the anodyne of a new love was reducing pain to a mere ache. Five years ago, or even three, remembering that Mass would have brought on a shuddering fever. Together, they had prayed for happiness, and next day Lewis had been killed, mangled senselessly under the car of a drunken driver, and she had been left – unable to die. God owed her something, she thought, for those prayers. Ever since she had tried to catch up on Him, but had never succeeded. Sometimes she had won oblivion from other people or places, but never peace from God, who owed it to her.

The name of God brought her back from the past into the present. The music had almost lulled her into unconsciousness, and she woke to the singing of "God save the King," rendered in its entirety. Tommy dispensed rum and water and Christmas wishes. When everybody had gone away, and there was silence, she could hear the insects piping their eternal chant to the moon. A hermit crab dragged its huge shell across the veranda floor with a gentle scraping sound. A frog – large as her thumbnail – fell out of the roof.

"There's nothing so depressing as Christmas," Tommy said, settling himself to the postprandial slumber which follows inevitably upon turkey, "but thank God for no plum pudding, no snow, and no robins."

The rossignols – wrens and not nightingales – who were nesting in a box on the veranda, had done their best to supply the latter deficiency; and a bank of cloud resting on Morne Collat might, if put to it, pretend to be snow. But for the lack of plum pudding he had Teresa to thank. The Morells had a pudding, and Derek had asked them to share it, but Teresa couldn't have faced that. Not Christmas heartiness and good living from the oven of the woman whose husband was pressing her to the last infidelity, whose pressure she could no longer pretend to resist. Not Christmas heartiness with a new love on the anniversary of Lewis' death. There are some things that are not done, some vigils that must be kept.

"You're not a child, are you," Derek had said. "You've known love before?"

"I'm not a virgin, if that's what you mean."

"Well, then – "

It was true that Janet gave him nothing. She held – typical folly of a good woman – that because there was no longer a possibility of her bearing him a child there should no longer be intimacy between them. But Teresa knew, knew by instinct, that Janet still loved him possessively, would suffer from the unfaithfulness that she might sense without believing. "She loves me like a sister or a maiden aunt," he had said. How like a man to measure his wife's love by her bed-going.

But his wife did give him nothing. There was no element of sex in their life together and the strength of his desire nourished the longing that was in Teresa. Like Tilly she was under a malign influence, seeing her trouble as the result of too long starvation, telling herself that in future she must regulate her meals better. And she felt sore at the realization that her future must be inevitably a succession of snatched and unsatisfying meals. Freedom tasted sour and her inability to marry – farcical. But when it came to the ultimate surrender something drew her back. Virtue was it, or caution? And where do these overlap and become one? There is no taking away what has been given, no going back on the act of love; and perhaps some instinct warned her against becoming the pleasure of this man who had a sense of property, who might seek to own. But her vision was not clear all of the time. Nature's urge to reproduction worked strongly within her, and mostly she saw Derek all white and right as through a snowdrift. Although the things he said kindled fire.

There had been one brief flash of anger between them, on a day of grey seas, when storm birds flew low over the water. He spoke of his rage against another person, and she said: "I should be terrified if you were angry with me." Saying it lightly, but thrilling, even as she spoke, to the idea of an intimacy that could permit anger.

"Why do you say that?" he asked, suddenly unreasonably fierce. "Because you think I'm too uncivilized to control myself? A savage West Indian who doesn't know how to behave? Oh, half the time I know you're looking down on us. Not really thinking we're your equals." Quite unintentionally she had provoked the anger she had pretended to fear.

"You are talking utter nonsense," she said coldly, although a flame of passion was scorching her. "Of course I don't think you my equal. In brains and character you are infinitely my superior." Was this snow-blindness or an effort to placate? And who can tell where character finishes and obstinacy begins?

They buried their tiff under kisses, but Teresa knew then that the desired end was inevitable. She might drift vaguely as spray blown from the blowhole, but it was obvious that some day opportunity would come and that she would grasp it.

Tommy was asleep and Teresa stitched into her patchwork a piece of a scarf ruined on a trip to Guadeloupe. She remembered herself prostrate on the sloop's hatch, striving to retain dignity and her breakfast by the counting over and over of the three teeth in the captain's face, while waves broke over her sea-wracked body, and squalls swept down on them from beyond the Saintes. Now and again there had come a burst of glorious sunshine that, deceiving her with mild caresses, mocked at her gratitude, painted her skin scarlet and so blistered it that, on the return journey, she had been able to tear strips from herself and throw them as literal burnt offerings to the gods of a sea this time less turbulent. Now, five hundred feet below her, the Caribbean lay like a mirror, a mirror in which she sought to read the future, and could find nothing but a white-sailed ship twice pictured, once in fact and once in reflection.

Tommy was sleeping still when Rosalie ran on to the lawn. Tears ran down her cheeks and she cried: "My father's wife is gone clean crazy, and ten strong men cannot hold her down."

Rosalie's mother was dead, but her father's wife was, and always had been, somebody quite different. Bernard kept a rum shop in the village, a square house made out of a packing case, where you could also buy salt fish and tinned margarine and matches; but his dwelling-place was up on the hill above the village, and now it seemed as though half the population were gathered together there under the cashew-nut trees. Ten strong men – truly, Teresa thought afterwards, there cannot have been room indoors for so many – waited for another crisis, while from the mouth of the unconscious woman there came a dreadful moaning recitative, and her husband, his face ashen with the curious grey pallor that distinguishes a sick negro, prayed Tommy to telephone the doctor. But Tommy knew that the exchange was closed down for Christmas; would function, doubtfully only, for an hour in the evening. "Anyway," Teresa said, "Doctor Packer is in Capesterre for the holidays."

Fifteen miles away at Blanchard there was Doctor Crewe, eccentric and undependable, but there seemed nothing to be done but to fetch him. Tommy got out the car, and Teresa said she would come too for the "vep".

> *"Mâle cabrits qui dit,*
> *Vep poco fini,"*

she murmured, which song had a tiresome carnival tune to it that could not be got out of the head. Vep – short for vespers – has come to mean anything that one can get for nothing.

They crossed the narrowest part of the island, and at Woodstock turned south from Neva and Ville Rousse to follow the Atlantic coast. Here and there were curiously detached rocks sporting tufts of windblown foliage. The tide was so low that on Berricot beach the reef was bare, a dirty expanse of brown flecked by grey pools out of which little boys picked shellfish for bait.

The doctor was tall and skeleton-like, a Buddhist, a Welsh-man, and a believer in Social Credit. So many were the stories of his eccentricities that Teresa had suggested bringing out a calendar with an oddity of his for every day of the month. Long ago Tommy had suffered from boils, and the doctor's sole contribution to the problem had been: "They happen in St. Celia." Which phrase had become a singularly apposite catchword covering the fatalism of the island, the reluctance to better anything because – it happens in St. Celia.

"I don't know what a cenobite is," Teresa said as they lurched and bumped over the unmade road, "but Doctor Crewe makes me think of one."

Tommy said: "There's no bite about him. He doesn't eat enough to know how. I'll bet his Christmas dinner was a glass of water and a caraway seed, Let's keep him for supper tonight and force him to a good meal."

They found him alone in a gaunt room, on whose walls there were wood-ant runs, and from whose rafters cobwebs hung.

"I couldn't come over tonight," he said. "My car hasn't got lights."

111

The Craddocks had been shaken to the point of torture by the roughness of the road over which they had driven, and had suffered even more on the car's account, dreading its sudden disintegration; but Tommy remembered that frightening woman and the ten strong men. "If you come with us now," he said, "I'll bring you back myself this evening. Or tomorrow morning if you'll stay overnight."

"But there's no need," the doctor said. "No need at all. You can give an injection as well as I."

"I can *not*," Tommy shouted, and Teresa echoed him. But the doctor ignored them. "I'll give you two needles," he said, "you'll succeed with one or the other. I'm writing a most important article for the *Fig Tree* that must be finished tonight."

Obviously the man had hypnotic powers in addition to his faith in Social Credit. With no word of protest they followed him to the surgery; saw him break open a phial of heroin and discover that it had gone bad. "No matter," he said, "I'll give you morphia instead."

Too dazed to argue Teresa took over the box with the hypodermic and the two needles. "But supposing," Tommy said as they turned to go, "supposing the puncture goes septic?"

"Oh, they don't," the doctor said. "Not usually." Already he had taken his bitten pen from behind his ear, and his fingers twitched to be writing again.

"Look here," Tommy said when they had driven a short way without speaking, "you'll have to do this. It's a woman's part."

"Coward."

"Coward yourself. I bet you daren't." But Teresa was too old to be dared into doing things. She said: "You win, darling. Nothing would induce me to."

The trees came down very close to the road, hiding the sea. There was a chicken hawk sitting on a dead cedar. "I gave a horse an injection once," Tommy said, "seven years ago."

"Well, that qualifies you. You're God's gift to Ma Bernard."

"All right," he said, stopping the car, "then you can drive. I shall need a steady hand." He sat there looking very professional, practising the attitude of Luke Fildes' "Doctor". "I must grow a beard," he said; but Teresa suggested that he give the injection first.

Days are short in December. Already at five o'clock shafts of yellow light were streaking the sky behind Morne Collat. Pink clouds, and orange, floated over the sea. The strong men of the village were still standing by for emergencies, while the not-so-strong and the women waited in the little garden where cannas grew, and roses, Michaelmas daisies, and red poinsettias in broken pots. The patient, from whose lips there still came forth lugubrious noises, had buried her head in the bosom of her nephew. The room was crowded to suffocation, and the hurricane lamp threw grotesque shadows on to the roof.

The first needle was so rusty that it snapped in Tommy's hand. The other was rusty and blunt too, but somehow it stood up to its job, and the deed was done. The woman quietened, and one by one the strong men slipped away. "No, Miss T'resa," Henry said, having come to the Big House to ask for something to kill the pain of his sister's toothache, "It has not been a happy Christmas."

Next morning Ma Bernard was better, but still far from normal, and the rum shop remained closed. The anticlimax department suggested that she had been over-Christmassing. On the door of the shop there was a notice saying: "Cash sales from Ma Bernard. Credit from Bernard," with the unwelcome reminder, "please pay your debts." Ducks paddled in the soapy water of the estuary, and a litter of little pigs trotted along the seashore seeking what they might find.

Tommy was unbearably pleased with himself that Ma Bernard should have recovered. "If there's any little doctoring you want done," he said, "I shall be happy to oblige. There's nothing I don't know about Epsom Salts. I can cut corns. If any more of our servants give birth I shall put up a 'public midwife' notice."

"Steady," Teresa said, "who made a boss shot at a jigger and was laid up for a fortnight?"

"Jiggers aren't in my line. Besides, any good sister would take out her brother's jiggers for him."

Jiggers are fleas that burrow under the skin and cause an itching like chilblains. Clever people prize them out with a needle, and Tommy had always maintained that jigger hunting was one of the more amusing indoor pastimes; until the day he was careless about the iodine and his foot went septic.

XV

So one year died and another was born. Opportunity came to Derek and Teresa; came, or was made, or was blown to them on the spray of the blowhole. And as they waited, shyly and with pulses throbbing, the gates of Hell opened and the blast of its furnace drove them from their sin.

A felicitous allegory, for those who believe in Hell, or even in sin. Janet might have expressed herself that way. It may even be that she did. Janet had something of second sight, or a peculiar strength of intuition, and she may well have sensed the underlying motif of that night's tragedy, its repercussion on her own life. Others, who have outgrown Hell, might say that shock inhibited Teresa from that particular phase of fulfilment, or, even less scientifically, that desire for Derek was burnt from her soul by the sight of a flame that never touched her body. No matter how it is put the effect was the same. Derek and Teresa had meant to go to bed together and were prevented.

Tommy went to Capesterre, and Derek found a reason why he should go too. Not at the same time but later, two days later, by the launch that leaves Grande Anse at dawn. "I shall have to stay in town overnight," he said, "and the mere decencies of hospitality will compel you to ask me to dinner."

It is odd how a sense of guilt routs the sense that is called common. Teresa would unthinkingly have asked any other man in the island to stay the night at Ça Ira, but because she so desperately wanted this one she behaved as though the eyes of the whole world were watching, glaring as beasts' eyes glare, lit up in the dark by a car's lamps. "Come early," she said, "and we'll dine early. Then the servants will go away and we'll be alone." She hadn't the courage to make a room ready for him. And then it so happened that he did spend the night at Ça Ira, and the beasts' eyes saw nothing. Although – there being nothing to see – they might well have invented what was not there, such being the way of beasts.

He came to her before sunset, and together they watched for the emerald drop which she could never see – and he did easily. "You have to be brought up to it," she said. "Or else my eyes are duds."

"They're the loveliest eyes. Were you fishing for compliments?"

"I wasn't, but I'm glad I caught one. You know, Derek, people think – you've thought – that I'm superior and self-satisfied, but I'm not. I've built up that appearance as a buttress to my shyness. Down underneath I'm as greedy for compliments as though I'd never had one. I could swallow mouthfuls."

"Be careful, sweetheart, or I'll choke you with them. And then your pretty eyes will goggle and your lips will turn black – "

"Derek, you're revolting."

"Well, don't be greedy, then. You shall have your compliments doled out to you one by one after meals, and if you ask for more – "

"What'll happen if I ask for more?"

"You'll get them. I'd give you anything. And I've nothing to give but the fruits of my mouth, which are words."

The little silly things that one remembers. Things left far behind on the other side of a great gulf. That night the world was full of colour; of sunset sky and hibiscus bushes; of yellow patches on the hillside that were pale bamboos; of blue sea, and blue morning-glories dead after their half day's blossoming. So might she say that her love had died, save that it never came to its full flowering.

Derek asked: "You've no regrets, Teresa? You won't draw back? Change your mind?"

"I'm not that sort," she said. "Once I've decided to do a thing I'm not turned from my course." And Fate took up her challenge; let a pint of kerosene deflect her.

When it was dark and the moon not yet risen they went into the

115

sitting room. There was a sofa for each of them, a lamp and a pile of magazines. "Let's play we're married," she said, "and be rational until the great moment comes; and then we'll lose all sense and all reason, and be swept away by a delirious torrent of folly." So it had been long ago, with Lewis.

"Shall we get married?" Derek said. "Count the world well lost and run away?"

She had never thought that far; didn't answer at once. But in what should have been an immortal hour antipathy put out its first hesitating finger. It was true what she had said to Tommy, that there was no man she could have married except Lewis, and the good God had taken him away.

"Oh, I'll marry when I'm fifty," she said lightly. "Some beau of my childhood. The boy I snubbed at dancing class or spat at in the Park."

"You mean I'm not good enough to marry. That I'm not of your class."

"Oh, Derek, don't be foolish. Who's fishing now?" This assumption of inferiority was irritating. A woman wants to look up, not down, and now she had to grope for the right words. "You know," she said, "I don't think I altogether believe in easy divorce. I do in principle. I'd fight the Church's attitude to the point of martyrdom. But when it comes down to tin tacks you can't trade in an old wife like an old car."

"You put it very aptly, Teresa." And he went far away from her for a moment, seeking who knows what in the fifteen years of their married life. And she suffered a queer twinge of jealousy because there had been so many years through which Janet had loved him. "Janet has carried me well," he said, "I couldn't discard her now. And yet, things might be very wonderful." For a week – she thought – or a month. And hated herself for her self-knowledge.

All these were the fragments of things said, of things remembered; torn pieces hanging to the telephone posts like broken kites. They sat there as might married people, or a brother and sister, or strangers; apart from each other because there was only one sitting room and Norah was laying a table at the other end of it. Sometimes their eyes met, and their senses spoke more often

116

than their lips. With throbbing pulses they waited for their little hour to strike.

Then came the noise of the explosion, the screams of women. Tilly ran flaming into the room with fire flowing from her red dress.

XVI

Teresa had never known that the blackness of a negro's skin was so thin that flames passing over it would shrivel it away, would expose white flesh whiter than her own; flesh of a stark staring whiteness that, amid an accumulation of fear, was in itself frightening. When she came to, came out of the nightmare, found herself lying unhurt across the girl's rug-wrapped body and saw black shrivelled skin – curled up like the dead peelings you rub off yourself after sunburn – edging white horrible patches, this irrelevant surprise was on top of a mind that had been, for seconds, blank. It takes longer to write a thing than to do it, longer to do it than to think – what am I doing? The explosion, the first awful screaming, their mutual: "What's that?" must have been almost simultaneous. Teresa had time only to lay down a paper before she saw that flaming figure in the doorway, figure that she will see to the end of time, outlined against the darkness of the passage with the dress that was still red wreathed in orange flames blown upwards and backwards by the draught. But there was still, after that, the fraction of a second during which she lay, saying to herself: "This isn't true. You don't have to do anything. You're reading this in a book." Derek told her afterwards – and for her peace of mind's sake she prayed that she might go on believing it – that there was no appreciable interval before she, too, was on her knees beside Tilly's rolling, writhing body, crushing out flames with Persian carpets. But she knew that that fraction of a second was registered in time; knew that she had been afraid, afraid for herself, although she managed to crush fear as eventually they crushed the flames.

It was Derek who felled Tilly, and burnt his hand in so doing;

who forced what was no longer a human being but a screaming pillar of flame on to the rug in front of the bookcase. And Teresa helped him to roll her in it and brought up another, but from the moment that she had said to herself: "This isn't true," she had no recollection of her actions. For her the thing was not true – until she came to herself and saw the white patches on Tilly's legs, and a little red pattern of fire, that she pinched out with her fingers, creeping over the girl's hair like sparks burning soot at the back of a chimney. Then she was conscious of noise again; of the insects shrilling in the night outside; of Isabel, slunk under the table and barking savagely in fear; of Tilly's repetitive: "Miss T'resa, I gone," and of her own voice saying over and over: "No Tilly, you won't die," mouthing and enunciating the words in order to force them out of a jaw that was trembling to the point of uselessness; saying them over and over because she thought that if she said them often enough they would become true. And perhaps her faith did soak through into Tilly's, because her cry changed from: "Miss T'resa, I gone," to "Miss T'resa, de cauli- flowers is on de stove. De cauliflowers is still on de stove." That is why Teresa didn't believe that Tilly would die. She didn't think it possible that a dying person should remember cauliflowers, cauliflowers in a saucepan with water bubbling round them.

She and Derek had supposed the kitchen building to be burning. One of the other screaming women must have said it, that it should have registered in both their minds. It savoured of anticlimax to find the room as usual; a little darker, perhaps, because the lamp had been smoking and had blackened the chimney. But where a few moments before kerosene from a burst container had poured in flaming rivers over the cement floor, all was now tidy, ordered, quiet. Only a few bits of metal scattered, and on the stove cauliflowers bubbling, bubbling to their death.

They carried Tilly to her room, in the dress that wasn't red any more but black and shredded, while Teresa went to the tel- ephone, struggling still to control her quivering mouth. And knew despair when they told her – they, the near-white girl with red hair who sits in the little tin exchange near the jetty – that Doctor Crewe was in Capesterre; that Doctor Packer had gone to Colibri, and that the launch was late. It was an hour and a half late that night. Teresa never knew why. It never seemed worth while to find out. While she waited she pictured it creeping slowly through the dark sea under mountains, with a swinging hurricane lantern shining on to tired faces that, by reason of their blackness, were absorbed into the night, leaving only their smiles behind them and the whites of their eyes. And on the wooden jetty silent anxious people waiting under the stars.

No doctor could have saved Tilly. Too much of that thin shrivelled skin had been curled back off her body.

The flames had made a white girl of a black. That night there were two nurses in the village, the trained midwife and a girl from the Capesterre hospital, home on leave. The news spread quickly, quickly as flaming kerosene poured on to a cement floor, and they put oil and bandages on Tilly and covered her with blankets. Derek drove down into Grande Anse and brought back the dispenser who gave morphia; and afterwards, accepting a cigarette, found that his box had only three matches in it, whereupon Teresa gave him a new box and watched him, fascinated, while he fumbled interminably, trying to fit into it his own three. There was still a smell of smoke about the house. Rugs smouldered, and pieces of charred clothing blew along the passage. Isabel, not barking any more, crouched by Teresa, licking her blackened hands.

Derek went to Grande Anse, and when he came back Tilly's screaming ceased and she sank into unconsciousness. Together they waited for the doctor, their pulses throbbing no longer, and their hearts heavy with dread. This was to have been their love night, and the gates of Hell had opened. Was it Janet, Teresa wondered, who had called down the wrath of God upon the house; and had He flung His thunderbolt and missed, striking the innocent instead of the guilty? Well, Janet – and/or God – had succeeded in their purpose, for Derek and Teresa were prevented from their sin; and Teresa revolted from what she had meant to do, seeing love lying at her feet as a charred and blackened thing, a mere lust shorn of its tinsel. Yet the man was as he had been. She had no fault to find. He had shown greater courage than she and had burnt his hands. "Are you hurt?" he had said as they knelt one on each side of the girl's smoking body. And she had answered:

120

"Why, no," looking at her own hands with a sort of silly vacant surprise as though they ought to have been hurt, as though it wasn't fair.

His hands had been bandaged in Grande Anse while he waited for the dispenser, and at sight of them Teresa's eyes had filled with tears, but only as they might have filled for Tommy or for any other who had been hurt. "I've brought up my bag from Mrs. Bennett's," he said. "And I won't go into Capesterre tomorrow. I'll stay with you till your brother comes back. There'll be no beasts' eyes tonight, Teresa, staring at us through the darkness." And their thoughts met for a moment in ironic laughter, laughter that is God's silver lining to despair.

They waited an hour and a half for the doctor. Singly, then in groups of two and three, the people of the village gathered outside Tilly's room and stood in the starlit garden where the wind blew softly through the pois-doux trees, and the withered hibiscus flowers looked like dead coals tied on to their bushes. There was Français the carpenter, with whom she had quarrelled; Bernard the publican; and Jordan who had long ago been her lover. What were their feelings, Teresa wondered, as she watched their dark immobile faces on to which a flambeau threw queer shadows, making familiar features unaccustomed. How did Jordan feel who had held that white tortured body against his own? How Français, who had hated? How Norah her sister who for months had not spoken to her save in anger or on business?

Silently they waited till Doctor Packer came, driven in a lorry. And he took Tilly away, so that Teresa never saw her any more until she was in her coffin, although the people of the village went away with her, perched on the sides of the vehicle and clinging to the running boards. "They will get a free ride," Henry said. "And in the morning when the sun rise they will walk back."

Tilly's face hadn't been burnt at all, but she looked ugly and sallow in her coffin. Her hands were bandaged, and they had put cotton wool in her nostrils. Teresa had never seen a dead person before. She brought flowers to the hospital, a wreath of bougainvillea and cannas and marigolds that Henry had woven, and a bunch of tired pale roses. She would have liked at the last moment to put the roses into those bandaged hands, but she was afraid that it might be the wrong thing to do. This wasn't her party any more. Tilly was among her own people and their ways were not hers. Before the boards closed over her Norah knelt down and touched her sister with her hand. What message passed between these two, Teresa wondered. Was death stronger than hate? Would hate survive? She would never know now why they had quarrelled. The reason was buried with the roses and would never be resurrected. Then the coffin was nailed down, and they took it away by sea to Capesterre where the cathedral bells were tolling.

It is a very grand thing to have a second-class funeral. Many white people do no better. Everybody thanked and praised the Craddocks for what they had done for "Tilly deceased". Her mother wrote that "they were fully aware of the incident, that no more could have been achieved, and that the burial having passed off satisfactorily, they had somewhat consoled themselves." Some people said: "It makes it sadder that she was so pretty and so young." And others: "How terrible for the Craddocks to lose such a good cook." But Teresa had never believed that Tilly would die, because she had remembered the cauliflowers, cauliflowers bubbling on the stove to their death. Neither had she known that a negro's colour was only skin deep, so thin that a flame passing over it would shrivel it away.

XVII

Tommy and Teresa went up into the mountains and walked through the forest to St. Patrick's Bay. "Perhaps if I walk," she said, "I shall sleep without dreams."

Nicholas Nolette guided them over the old trace that Caribs may have made, or Spaniards, or French. He had hunted pig on it, showed them a trap he had dug himself – a deep round pit scoured out in its depths by snared beasts who had made a cave of their prison. Brushing a little depressed mud with the back of his hand, he said: "Here an agouti has rested."

Progress was slow in the forest. Rarely did sunshine throw chequered patterns on to the mud and the moss and the rotting leaves that lay at the base of tall trees. Trunks felled by hurricanes had to be crawled over or slipped under. Water had taken possession of the few miles where French pavé was, making a river where a road should have been, and piling one cobble on to another to build channels for itself, and miniature waterfalls. Where stones were not – and whoever made the track soon tired of metalling it – there were knee-deep sloughs where razor grass slashed at arms and ankles, and only logs and roots gave foothold. Nicholas, barefooted, carried a cutlass in his hand, a pack on his back, and a basket on his head; and as though insufficiently burdened caught a syrique for his supper, a yellow and black land crab tied with a vine-rope and swung from his little finger.

It was better to be walking; trampling underfoot memory of fire, and treading down into a grave of mud and leaves the flame of an alien love that had grown cold in her heart. Dead persons are buried, with coffins and roses and cathedral bells. Why not dead thoughts, dead longings, dead love? It seemed now that life had no reason or meaning to it; was aimless as spilt liquid spreading into inchoate patterns, and drying to no purpose. Nicholas carried fire in his pack. A case made of a calabash held pieces of hard wood which, with the blade of a chisel, he made to glow like live coals. In the bed of the river he found a brick-red stone from which he struck sparks with his cutlass. Nicholas didn't need matches for the lighting of his pipe, nor kerosene to make a stove burn. Teresa had sworn never to think of fire any more, never to mention it, never see it; although the sky flared at sunrise to remind her, and the wind blew through the nasturtiums in the garden, making them flicker on their stakes like flames on a hearth.

Beside and above the St. Patrick's River the track became mere notches in the cliff. Clinging to pendant roots she looked down on to a reach of sun-flecked water, which, save for one grotesquely exaggerated aspidistra, might have been part of some English trout stream. And as her fumbling feet tested a projecting stone and her fingers closed over a liana, she wondered irrelevantly – deliberately pushing her mind off her own imminent danger – why she must always estimate beauty by comparison, likening one plant to another and one river to other streams. Far away through the forest there came the soft coo-roo-roo of a ramier. "Pigeons bawling," Nicholas said.

Close to the sea this same river, no longer straight-waistcoated by cliffs, had been turbulent and undignified; had dug new channels through pasture land now soiled with sand and gravel; had piled barriers of dead trees against live ones and left up-ended roots indecently, absurdly, exposed. Nicholas said: "When the floods come last November I am in my garden and I see something. Stones rolling and trees rolling, and cattle carried to the sea."

The Old House at St. Patrick's looks down upon the Atlantic, whose breakers sweep out of the sunrise into the bay. Shutters, hanging from one hinge, creak in the wind. Floorboards are rotted and wooden walls embossed with the runs of ants. "Never while I am alive," said Joseph the overseer, wrinkled and shrunken, "have the family lived in the Old House. When I am a child Mr. Howker come for a day once a quarter, and then it is my mother's business to open the windows, but since he is dead no one comes. Miss Beth? I see Miss Beth thirty years ago when she is still creeping. Now, if I should pass her in the street I should not know her."

How strange, Teresa thought, to own acres and not know how many, to live twenty miles from a house that is yours and never to have seen it. Stranger, perhaps, to oversee an estate where nothing is done, nothing grown; where the river, unchallenged, has swept away the last of the sugar-canes; where strangling vines, unchecked, are crushing cocoa and coffee trees and withered limes; where wooden walls crumble and stone ones have fallen down. "Since the hurricane," Joseph said, "everything is mashed up. Here in St. Patrick's we live in darkness. God grant us a road that we may see light."

"Have you ever," Teresa asked, "been over this track?" And he answered: "Once, when I am a little boy, Mr. Howker send me to Capesterre to post a letter."

She sent her own mind back over the dark trail by which they had come. She remembered the dripping forest, the slippery watercourses, the sinister trees. She remembered sloughs and deep gullies, a cliff overhanging a sun-flecked stream. And thought of a little black boy, fifty years ago, running to Capesterre to post a letter.

All day they walked through the forest, and sleep came to Teresa in that Old House that was ready to fall at the touch of a finger. Listening to the beat of the sea on to grey sand she wondered who had lived and loved in this place, and whether those long-ago women – for there must have been women – had made a prison or a paradise of St. Patrick's, hemmed in between the mountains and the sea. But on the way home fever struck her, and the forest sought to hold her in its green choking embrace, sending forth roots to trip her and releasing rivers to sweep her through dark woods into unknown seas. Men saved her from these, carrying her in a hammock slung on a pole; and then she knew how a dead sailor would feel, bound up in canvas and thrown to the sea; and what it was to be a beast's carcase, or a fowl trussed for market. She likened herself to a sausage, to a chrysalis, to anything sheathed; similes running through her brain to the sound of rushing streams and tumbling waters; although always, overhead, there was the saving grace of a strip of treetops interlaced with sky. But because the sides of the hammock, acting as blinkers, made the trees trunkless and divorced them from all context, she could see nothing save a grey-green pattern out of which rain fell, seeping into her hair and filling her eyes as though with sorrow.

Miles away, hours ago – there were neither miles behind her nor hours, but fever elongated distance and made a farce of time – there had been a round black pool into which a cascade of foam fell from a great height, breaking the shadows under fern-hung cliffs, and muffling with its noise the thunder in the sky which came to them only as might the rolling of stones or the distant beating of a gong. Sitting on a rock among swirling waters they had argued as to whether this river ran to the Atlantic or the Caribbean, for not even Nicholas knew if they had crossed the divide. And Teresa – in whom fever was growing, and a deadly nausea, so that boulders shimmered like an asphalt pavement on a hot day – had suggested that there was only one way to settle the matter and that was to follow the river to its logical conclusion. This might take a week, clambering over rocks, dodging water-falls, tight-roping slippery trees; but the answer to the argument would be indubitably correct and established for all time. And now that she had given in, had yielded her trussed body to the carriers, rivers ran uphill and downhill through her mind, cover-ing all the map, all the island, all the world; a flood of waters, brown and white and tempestuous, flowing with rushing roaring sound. But at least she knew where the divide was because, from her prostration, she had seen the ridge outlined against the skyline as no pedestrian could have seen it, stumbling blindly – as he needs must – over the muddy track, watching only his own feet lest a stone twist them, or sloughs engulf.

After leaving the pool – how far away was it, how long ago? – that same track had risen to smite her, so that she found herself groping with hands among wet stones and trickling mud; listen-ing to the beating of her own heart pounding in her ears with a sound louder than had been the thunder above the fall. She had picked herself up again, plodding and stumbling from one mud hole to another because, from the forest, there is no escape save by one's own effort; until the miracle happened and light was where had been only darkness; a clearing among trees, voices, and the sound of an axe; noises improbable as a dream but recognized by the others; six men making a banana plantation, building a camp, having a hammock.

They cut a sapling – a young carapite – to be a carrying pole; and stripped another, a mahaut cochon, to make rope to bind the hammock to it. How unnaturally keen, she thought, must be a disordered mind that the names of these trees – the one so pretty and the other so ridiculous – should be for all time etched on her brain, lettered behind closed eyelids. Unnaturally acute also was her vision, so that she saw men stereoscopically against the forest; knew their faces better than loved ones; poignantly remembered black fingers gripping white peeled wands, and a black arm that, from behind a cutlass, felled one tree from among its fellows, tree whose refuse would rot to make a piece with the mattress of dead leaves on which she had lain, fingering each separate leaf. From some of these the flesh had altogether decayed leaving a tracery of veins only, things lovely as a coral fan and delicate as Chinese carvings. And upon some there lay snow-white patterns, painted by disease.

The carriers stumbled sometimes as they shifted her weight from one shoulder to the other, jerking her back each time into reality, and making her conscious of trees in which there was no bird, no touch of colour, not even a sunbeam to gild a leaf; but instead sinister growths – cactus-like – and the leaves of parasites weeping tears on to her bound and helpless person. They had passed a length of bark under her body, binding her with a girth to the pole; and upon this she rested, rested – she thought – as she might some day rest in her coffin, save that there she would no longer feel the shivering aching cold that was cramping her limbs and making her teeth chatter, till she longed to pluck from the passing foliage a twig to bite on, so that this other noise be not added to the incomprehensible arguing of the men and the booming of the rivers. Somewhere in her memory she knew that there was fire hidden, fire that would warm. Yet she would rather be cold than know fire again, that she had seen pouring in orange flames over a girl's red dress.

At last, when the pole was shifted and she was tilted upright on the slope of a steep hill, she saw below the treetops a streak of distant sea, and knew that soon – for time began to be a factor again, and "soon" a word that might some day mean something – they would come out of the grey-green twilight of the forest and she would be spilled from the hammock into a patch of sunlight for there would surely be sunlight at the edge of the sea. And she believed that if she saw sun again, the sun and the sea, she would no longer be afraid, neither of fire nor of love. But not for many days was the fever of her brain quietened, nor were the flames of her mind quenched by the remembered sound of water seeping through stones; of rivers falling over rocks into deep pools; but only by the ocean itself – oily and blue with a coating of sunshine on it – across which a white ship carried her to another island, and to freedom from dreams.

PART TWO

INTERLUDE

XVIII

The white clay road was so narrow that leaves of sugar-cane brushed against the sides of the car. A soft sea wind rattled the feathery arrows, swished through the untidy trash, brought with it the breath of mangrove swamps that are neither quite land nor quite sea. Between the canes there were dark tunnels speckled with shadows; and among the fields humped oxen, grey and biscuit-coloured and black, grazing on tracts of brown pasture dotted with thorny trees that carried burden of morning glories and small pink vines. Here and there the land was scarred by iron rails whereon the cut canes were drawn to the factory.

Parham Island is as unlike St. Celia as one island can be to another. Seen from the sea it has a prettiness of pale green cane-fields, of purple shadows lying on burnt hills. But when you come close to it and touch it you find that it is dry and dusty, and that the prettiness is only an illusion contrived by the sunlight and the clear air. There are no rivers in Parham, only pools, so covered with green leaves or with pink lotus blossoms that you cannot tell where water begins and earth ends. There are no forests, because for centuries the land has been tilled. No mountains, but only a few hills huddled into the south; and there the sea has found its way among them, filling interstices with the deep green waters of landlocked harbours. On the outskirts of the town bunches of sheep's wool hang on barbed fences between squalid unbeautiful houses; and torn shreds of kites have been caught up on telephone wires, fluttering like shattered memories strung on to the cable of the past.

Teresa's disappointment in this place was tinged with a bitter humour. "If this," she thought, "is what Derek loves, how can he have loved me, to whom this is alien?" Alien, and yet through intimacy with his own thoughts strangely familiar; as though, knowing a writer's fiction, one afterwards read his biography, finding there the raw material from which he had drawn his creations. Here were cane-fields billowing like the sea; and others patched, as he had told her, with date palms and scrubby cotton. At sight of a stone chimney she wondered – was this his home? And realized that the landscape, as well as the life of the island, was dominated now by the twin steel chimneys of the sugar factory from whose shining sides the sun struck fire; and from which the wind carried a stench that came of dead fish, of minute creatures called "millions" that were drawn up out of the water into the machinery to perish thus nauseatingly in the making of sweetness. Stone sugar mills were crumpled into disuse now, and a few chimneys only were still standing as landmarks of dead centuries.

The white clay road ended in the strip of pale sea that cut off Surinam from the mainland. Those whom Horace Canning wished to receive were ferried across to him by a pontoon bridge. Surinam Island was long and narrow, and very low; and there Teresa found beauty as she saw it, beauty of an untouched jungle, flaunting the subtle and macabre loveliness of logwood and balsam, and manchineel; of cinnamon and tamarind trees; of grotesque cacti thrusting skywards stalks that were like those of giant asparagus, and which died of their flowering. Upon the sea ringing the island God had painted every blue that He ever thought of; the blue of a peacock's breast, of a turquoise; the blue of harebells and of ice. In shallow waters above the reef, fish stood on their heads, letting their tails wave on the surface like coral fans; while to white-sanded beaches there drifted the refuse of the Atlantic; electric light bulbs, and the disgorged fat of whales coalesced into rectangular blocks; mauve and green balls made of glass that were once floats of nets spread to catch submarines.

"Bubbles that symbolize our ephemeral memories," Tommy said. "How little comes to the surface any more from that long ago bitterness."

From even before the War, Teresa remembered the Cannings' old house in Yorkshire; remembered a ruined church in whose smothering ivy she had lain hidden, hoping to see a ghost; prize bulls that she had longed to make mad, but which were never anything but somnolent under their loads of fat and their coloured labels; footmen with powdered hair, wearing plush breeches in the evening.

"No powder now," the General laughed, "nor even footmen. Parlour-maids, and I'm better valeted."

At Surinam slow stately negresses moved through the rooms, more impressive than men in red plush, more impressive even than Norah. Tilly had never been impressive, not even in her coffin; only pretty, and very naughty, and a good cook. And now – nothing.

Surinam had been lived in for two hundred and fifty years. Slave labour had built the house, and the stone sugar mill, and stone cisterns to hold the rainwater caught by the stone catchment. Now there was a steel windmill to bring the water from the cisterns into the house; electric light shone out of an evening, and a car stood in a wooden garage. But sometimes in the jungle you came across reminders of the old days; a pile of vine-covered rubble that had been a dwelling; a tamarind tree marking a boundary; a frangipani planted on the burying place of a slave.

This was the first time the Craddocks had been to Surinam. They never wanted to leave Ça Ira, and the General was in England all summer. He didn't know the long hot days when the cane-fields shimmered like the sea and the sky was streaked with mackerel clouds piling up for a storm. He spent his summers doing the things a gentleman does; following the mayfly by little southern rivers; walking the Scotch moors in August; meeting the first touch of autumn with the partridges among the stacked corn; and his winters in doing the things a gentleman should do – helping the poor and oppressed of another race who had no claim on him, no right to his help save that they needed it.

Tommy and Teresa had remembered him, thought of him, as a die-hard Imperialist; a Tory of the string-'em-to-lamp-posts, shoot-'em-down-like-dogs variety. He was their father's contemporary, and their father, unlike their mother, had been all these things. But here in the mansion that slaves had built he took up the burden of black men who had been free for a hundred years. "I'll be glad of your point of view," he said to Tommy, who was a Legislative Councillor. But between St. Celia and Parham Island there was no view in common; no point of contact. Every mental outlook was different, and even the faces of the people.

XIX

Sanders, Andrew, Luther, and John, mouthpieces of a landless peasantry, sat on the stoep built two hundred years ago by slaves. Andrew was a carpenter, but "Times are so bad," he said, "that for seven years I have not plied my trade."

Luther had ten children, and earned only five shillings a week. "I hear that in other countries animals are housed better than we. My house is breaking down, and the rain comes through."

John's aquiline nose and thin mobile lips showed traces of East Indian blood. "No planter," he said, "will sell us land for they fear to lose our labour. We must pay twenty shillings a year in rent for one acre, and are given no lease. So it may happen that, although we have dug and prepared the ground, if we offend the owner or the overseer we are evicted before we can reap our crop. Yet the estates own thousands of acres that they have let go out of cultivation."

Sanders was old and wrinkled and could remember many things. "The factory," he said, "gives a shilling a ton less to the peasants than to the estate owners. And our cane is as good. A field that is fat yields more tons than a field that is lean, but one ton of cane is as good as another. And we must pay to the planters another shilling per ton for weighing and carting, for what they call administration. And they let cane be our only crop because only so can the factory be kept full. Once we had a Peasants' Association, and we were going to administer our own cane, but they" – (the planters, the factory manager, the merchants) – "they mash up the Association." And with the word "mash" he brought down one fist on to another with such force that you could almost see the grinding of the poor between millstones.

Now, for the first time, the voice of the peasant was heard in the land; heard, but listened to no more than the crying of a ground dove which is the saddest sound ever uttered, although very continuous. "And the overseer tell us," Andrew said, "that if we do not vote for the estate manager we shall be turned from our fields." Whereupon Laertes the donkey walked up the stairs on to the stoep, and, standing in line with the men, brayed for his afternoon tea. So that it was amid laughter and the dispensing of stale crusts that Horace Canning, an old man seeking peace who had taken up the sword in a cause that seemed to him just, tried to convince them – tried perhaps to convince even himself – that the ballot was secret.

"If the donkey have no bread," Luther said, "he can eat grass. But if they turn us from our land then we have only our labourer's wage and we must go hungry."

Some people in St. Celia wanted the old estates to grow cane again; wanted a sugar factory; wanted, so it would seem, to be wage slaves. Yet those without land of their own were able to make their gardens and grow their food on Crown land, and the Crown turned a blind eye. In St. Celia there was no need for a man to be hungry, and when his roof leaked he cut a new one from the Crown's forest. But humanity is never satisfied; must always be asking for more; not realizing that, seen through the glasses of envy, it may be only a widow's mite that is shining like gold. "In St. Patrick's," the overseer had said, "we live in darkness. God send us a road that we may see light." Yet here there was surely a greater darkness, though the estates prospered, and cane-fields billowed like the sea. "Things couldn't be like this in our island," Teresa said. And remembered for an instant the little gardens on Neva cliffs and Janet's tight-lipped mouth saying: "We might close the beach." But it seemed to her that not even Janet could do that kind of thing in St. Celia. The mental outlook was different, and the tempers of the people.

When the men had gone away the sea was not blue any more, but silver grey. There was golden lining to the clouds behind which the moon had risen, and scarlet streaks threaded through those among which the sun had set. Sanders, Andrew, Luther, and John went home to the huts that were once slave quarters, although the great houses on the hilltops had fallen away. "The house fell to pieces," so Derek had spoken of his own mansion. "The peasants took away stones as they wanted them." But his cane-fields were there still "speckled with date palms and made scrubby by patches of cotton. Some damned land settlement scheme," he had said. Some long-ago Government scheme to assist the Sanders of this world, and the Andrews and the Luthers and the Johns. So, as always, there were two sides to the picture; and Teresa's mind, made foggy by the snows of illusion, hadn't known which side was positive and which negative.

But on Surinam, where manchineel trees and cacti spread their sinister beauty, and waves whispered among the bleached roots of mangroves, there was peace and a great quietness; peace broken only by the aching sound that is a dove's cry; by the deer that moved slowly towards the water troughs below the cisterns; by the ghosts of black men of long ago, who built the house and the catchment and the sugar mill, and who were never, technically, free.

XX

There was no fire on Surinam. Teresa recovered from her fever and forgot her dreams. Often Derek was with her in spirit, bathing off quiet beaches; walking the long rides cut through the scrub; pottering in a boat among outlying reefs and cays. She rehearsed letters to him that she would never write; told him things that she would never say. Pushing far from her the fact that she didn't like his cane-fields and his burnt brown hills, she shared with him the sea's colours; showed him in imagination deer tracks in the white clay; a shark moving through clear water under a yellow cliff. On Surinam there were neither cane-fields nor hills, only a flatness of strange trees, in the impenetrable depths of which – impenetrable to man by reason of their thorns, their toothed leaves, their poisons – deer lay hidden, and wild sheep, and unknown birds. Here there was no forest of giant trees, sinister as a woman, carrying green choking death hidden among lianas and parasites; but only manchineel trees, innocent to the eye as apples in an orchard, and deadly in bark and fruit and leaf; and cactus plants, throwing up giant asparagus and dying of the effort, ready to tear and rend and destroy. But one didn't venture among these to touch them, as one ventured under tall trees that allowed no undergrowth to clutter their roots, but only red mushrooms, spotting the floor of the forest; and decayed leaves from which all flesh had vanished, making a tracery of veins delicate as Chinese carvings.

Teresa thought of Derek, but without passion; loved him with her mind and not with her body; didn't realize yet that her body had set up a graven image for her mind to worship. Tilly's death, or the manner and the moment of it, had cut off something, some power in her, as surely as a burnt-out fuse cuts off electric light; and she felt that love, blasted in such a fashion, could never sprout again, nor bear fruit, for there were only ashes left where had been flowers. To give herself utterly to Derek, as she had planned to do, was now impossible. No reason implemented her instinct; she didn't believe in the gates of Hell; but a gulf had opened at her feet, a gulf that would be unbridgeable unless he saw it, felt it, too. In which case friendship might span it, or perhaps a deeper love.

"I don't understand myself, Tommy," she said. "It's as though half of me had died."

"It doesn't matter, old girl. Don't think about it." But she had to think; bringing her mind continually to a problem which it refused, like a horse refuses a fence; and her will power was not strong enough to compel the horse over. Yet she knew that if once she could leap the fence, or span the gulf, she might be altogether normal again.

"You don't really sympathize, Tommy, do you? I mean you wouldn't feel the same way?"

"No, darling, I don't think I should. What happened wasn't your fault or Morell's. It had nothing to do with your need of each other."

"I feel pretty foul, you know. It's bad to meet a man half way, and then draw back."

Tommy agreed. It was foul, but often done. "He'll understand," he said to Teresa, not really thinking that Derek would. And then he added: "But without any question of morals, my dear, and cutting out the 'honour rooted in dishonour' business, I don't think Morell is your man. I can see that he is attractive to women" – he didn't tell the things he'd been hearing, because heard things should never be repeated to another's hurt – "but your relationship wouldn't be a happy one. It's not in your character to be furtive."

"It was happy, Tommy. The furtiveness didn't matter. I was alive again. Now, I'm haunted by a promise that I can't keep." She was no more stable than spray blown from a blowhole, and of all things hated inconstancy.

Days after, among the ruins of old dockyards where the spirit of the past was so strong that even personal memories surged like

139

a rising tide, it came to her that she was of those women for whom there is one man all their lives and one only. Nature's urge to reproduction had made a fool of her, letting her dream that she could love twice. Forsworn to Lewis, was it now his memory that was making her forsworn to another? There were no visible links between her long-ago lover; Tilly, who had died under her fingers like a snuffed-out candle; and this old sacred place where it so happened that she spent an hour dreaming in sunshine. But there, possessed by this spirit, she knew herself to be once more very close to Lewis; and it seemed to her, then, that no reasoning and no argument, no sense of honour or obligation, could drive her back into the arms of the man from whom flames had sundered her.

XXI

"Nelson," Teresa quoted from her guidebook, "was troubled by many things in the West Indies. He suffered from frequent illnesses, recurring headaches, and the impetuosity of youth. He quarrelled with his admiral and with the Governor of the island to whom he tried to teach their business. He was woefully pinched by mosquitoes, and eventually, of course, he married. But" – and she added this on her own account, watching men filling in potholes whose luscious ooze gave her an itch to play mud pies – "he never tried to get to his naval dockyards by motorcar."

Tommy said: "These roads are the worst that civilization can offer. Better a desert track or a watercourse than good macadam gone wrong."

"But at least," the General observed, "something is being done. Only last month the Governor himself got bogged, and the whole population of the village – all four of it – was called out to haul the car on to *terra firma* again."

As a result of this *lèse majesté* on the road's part, men were removing boulders so mysteriously protruding from a once level surface, and were building a causeway over a swamp where small grey crabs slithered into bubbling holes; where manchineel trees were made more sinister by the grey parasites trimming their branches; where white cranes stood gracefully contemplating their own slimy reflections.

"We'll have to walk," the General said, "but it's not far." Tommy and Teresa were accustomed to walking, because in St. Celia one has to. But in Parham Island they have these terrible roads.

All along the coast there were ruins of stone houses, quarters of long-ago sailors and soldiers once attached to the district. Negro huts, some made of mud and trash and some of wood, stood in the lee of old walls upon which trees had rooted. A rim of soft white sand edged the sea, and in the shallow water there floated silvery fishes so pale, so much the colour of their element, that only by their shadows could you detect them. On every hilltop, hard to distinguish from the natural rock, were ruined fortifications; here and there gun emplacements; sometimes the blank staring eyes of windows that had no rooms behind them, but only space.

Clarence Harbour is an inlet so landlocked that never a wave beats on its shore, nor does a breath of wind find means to ruffle its blue opaque water. Wrapped in a silence, a stillness, that is almost mystical, lie wharves and storerooms, boat-houses, barracks. A notice forbids the admittance of all strangers, foreigners, and women. But not even the latter are suspect now, when wooden walls are rotting and stone ones tilting a little under the stranglehold of lianas. No ships sail any more through the narrow entrance once guarded by an iron chain. Only pale fish and basking lizards, ground doves and gross red sea-slugs compete with the shades of those long-dead sailors who fought with the French for possession of the West Indies, and won.

"So much these islands mattered to us once," the General said. "And now so little."

Nelson's house had been sparsely refurnished with three beds, half a dozen tables, as many plates, and a couple of chairs. There were prints and pictures of the period; a wooden box lined with tin, reputed to have been his bath; an earthenware jar three feet high, in which it was suggested that he caught rats. In the garden a sandbox tree was now – as probably then – most viciously inhabited by bees. And, lonely on the porch, there stood a painted bust of the great man himself.

"Whatever he may have looked like in life," Teresa said, "that thing is indubitably libellous." It stood there, uglier even than the two bleached figureheads – "Male and female created they them," muttered Tommy – that faced the still water and the green hills beyond it, with vacant eyes and goitred throats and disintegrating anatomies.

It was not in this house that she recaptured the spirit of the past, but among dead stones under trees; beside capstans that sun had blistered and rain rusted; on strong sea-walls upon which oysters grew, and feathery annelids.

"Today's great thought," she cried, poking at these with a stick. "Nelson and William the Fourth played with them just as I do."

Annelids were born to be teased, an irresistible temptation. Worms that live in tubes, they put out feelers like brilliant plumes and at a mere touch withdraw them again; spit mud to show contempt of conduct unbecoming to ladies or admirals; then slowly, cautiously, with infinite beauty, unfold again.

"There was a beach in Australia," Teresa said, "facing the South Pole and the Southern Ocean from under immense cliffs; and there I found starfish of such exquisite colours that I laid them out in patterns like Persian carpets, patterns that shifted slowly, and were each morning dissolved.

"You've seen a lot of the world," the General said. And she answered: "I'm glad of it. When the nations of the earth are so ugly it's good to have lovely places to remember."

Ugly things had happened in the old dockyards; murders, floggings, the cruel discipline of the old-time Navy; for wherever man is, or has been, he has brought ugliness. But these had left no impression on Clarence Harbour. One read of them and forgot. Here, there was no reek of blood, no sense of fear. Frame houses and grey shingled roofs had mellowed and grown old without dwelling on their sinister memories. Here, there were only the sweet peace of a summer's afternoon, a hot, still silence, and the beauty of empty hills.

XXII

There was grass growing on the old stone jetty, and black-rimmed oyster shells fringing its sides. Below it starfish slept on grey mud, and coloured sea-slugs with skins wrinkled into obscene folds. Top-heavy pelicans stood sentry over a rusted iron cable and a wire fish-trap. Where sodden paths bifurcated there was a patch of growing cotton – white woolly tufts bursting out of shrivelled pods – and a few shabby wind-torn coconuts.

At right angles to the jetty a high stone wall fronted the sea, broken by an imposing gateway that had no gates but only posts, with moss outlining the crumbling blocks of their masonry. Hens perched on a ladder under a sandbox tree; and from a wire rope, stretched between two ragged palms, there hung patched garments swollen by the wind. Ducks paddled in the sluggish stream oozing from the courtyard of what, three hundred years ago, had been the treasury building of the island's capital.

"For this wetness I apologize," said Mrs. Darvel, the ex-postmistress. "Last year I drain the yard at my expense. Ten shillings and sixpence I pay for the draining of it. But when I write to the Colonial Office to get my money back they say that I had no authority to drain it. So this year the water lies in the yard."

The old house was dark and massive, with carved ceilings and heavy beams. Creepers wreathed the veranda posts. Sandflies bit viciously at strangers' ankles. The front room was labelled "Post Office and Telephone Exchange", but now the Post Office was closed, and only one coloured girl sat in front of a box and table pulling out and pushing in plugs. One window looked to the village street, to wooden two-storeyed quaintly varied houses smothered in bougainvillea and Barbados pride; and the other to the sea – a flax-blue bay deepening on the horizon to purple, stained, where the coral reef peered through, with brown freckles whereon fishing birds stood motionless.

Mrs. Darvel, rocking in her chair, wrinkled a coffee-coloured brow over the local press. She knew that politics had suddenly obtruded themselves into Parham Island. Not politics implying the vague activities of a faraway government miserly about drains, but politics with a personal meaning; the giving of votes to, and the using of them by, a peasant people. "I have not registered as a voter," she said with the quiet dignity of an aristocrat who has kept her fingers unsullied. "*I* was never one to push myself forward. I have not wished to see myself in front of another."

"That is truth you speak," answered Prudence, the washer-woman, sitting humbly on a hard chair, a Madras handkerchief wrapped round her tight plaits, and her hands hidden under a white apron. But the planters do bad things to the people, and the boys tell us that we must vote to obtain justice. I myself have had my land taken from me, and now have nowhere to plant cane or to grow provisions."

Mrs. Darvel's foot tapped the floor rhythmically to the rocking of her chair. The telephone girl studied her own face in a pocket mirror. Prudence looked down at the ants scurrying over the rough boards, but with the eyes of her mind she was seeing only a sweet potato patch; the green stalks of okra; ripe corn. "All summer," she said, "my dead sister's child work in the cotton fields, and when October come I send her to school. 'Where is that child?' say Mr. Pond, the manager. 'She must come back to the picking.' But I say to him: 'No, for it is the law that a child of eleven years shall go to school.' 'Let her come to the fields,' say Mr. Pond, 'or I will give you notice to quit your land.' And a week later the ranger call with a printed paper telling me I must leave in June. The law is that I should have a year's notice, but Mr. Pond, he give the notice that pleases him."

A door opened with a great agitation of flies, and Mrs. Darvel's daughter put down a tray on to her mother's newspapers. "Hard times," she murmured, "these are hard times. For if one man grows hard so does another. George Lucas, by Exton, tell me that the doctor would not come to his child until George pay him five shillings. And because he had no money at all the doctor drove on in his car, passing the very house-door where the sick child lay."

"Often I hear that same thing," broke in the telephone girl, who had access to more gossip than anyone else, and frequently embroidered it. "Without they first see their money the doctors will not visit the sick. But they are Government servants just as were you and am I, Missis Darvel, and are paid to help poor people."

But the old lady in the rocking chair was loyal to her caste. A Government doctor; a postmistress; both served the Empire and should be as Caesar's wife.

"Poor people must help themselves and each other," she replied tartly to the upstart chit in charge of a machine that, sometimes efficient and sometimes not, savoured always of magic. But the chit, already engrossed in other and distant conversations, did not realize that she had been snubbed. And Prudence the washerwoman, appreciating the crosscurrents of loyalties, discounted Mrs. Darvel's remark. She would never herself hear anything said against a family for which she had washed.

Stirring her heavy cup, Teresa looked out thoughtfully over the sea. The purple shadow of a cloud covered the brown patches of the coral reef. A pelican dived, falling from the air into the water with none of the grace implied in the word dive. Far away she could hear the noise of a motorboat, itself hidden behind an island.

"Mr. Pond he go fishing," Prudence said, adding inconsequently, "Pelican live by fish alone, but we, Miss Craddock, we must rent land to grow bread. Sea food is not enough." For a moment Teresa's mind dwelt on the oysters under the mangrove roots; on the pile of empty conch shells that she had seen lying in the yard with pale pink interiors – delicate as rare porcelain – broken and exposed. But the chuffing of the motorboat, insistently monotonous as the shrilling of crickets, swung her thoughts back on to politics.

"The ranger," Prudence was muttering, "say that we must vote for Mr. Pond because he is a benefactor. But I ask you, what is a benefactor? Is it a man who signs a receipt for rent? That is all Mr. Pond has done for any of us."

"Ah, this voting," sighed Mrs. Darvel, and her chair creaked wearily as she picked up the paper again. "I do not understand all this voting. I never was one to push myself forward."

"But the planters," Prudence began again patiently, while Mrs. Darvel's daughter collected the cups and went back into the kitchen, "the planters – "

She had told her story a dozen times, why not thirteen? And as she spoke a flicker of sunshine pierced the tangled vines wreathing the veranda. The heavy beams, the oppressive ceiling, the dark dusty corners of the Post Office, were lost in shadows. But that one sunbeam, filtered through flowers, fell like a smile from Heaven upon the peasant people to whom a vote had been given.

"It isn't like that in our island," Teresa said passionately, "it isn't like that at all." And thought for a moment of Derek's coconuts, seeing the pile of empty husks by the river's mouth. "Morell comes from Parham Island," Tommy had said long ago, "and has brought his ideas with him." Now she began to understand what he had meant. But Derek wasn't like this. These were not his ideas. Derek was kind and charming, and his eyes melted your heart. Her body had set up an image for her mind to worship, and she had not yet discovered that her idol had feet of clay.

PART THREE

COCONUTS AND A CATTLE

XXIII

The bar of the Cintra Hotel in Capesterre is a grey room lined with shelves, on which stand bottles of every known variety of liqueur. But no one ever opens the bottles to see if they contain what they pretend.

"I wonder what would happen if anyone insisted," Teresa said. And remembered the old story out of *The Virginian* about the traveller in Texas who asked for *vol-au-vent*; whereupon the proprietor, running a pistol into his ear, observed: "You'll take hash."

"Olive wouldn't run a pistol at you," Tommy said, "but she'd very rightly serve you whisky if you asked for any of that fancy stuff." Olive was a grand person, stoutly beautiful, as a barmaid should be, and, with the business of the island at her tongue's end. Under the bottles there were showcases full of dusty chocolate boxes featuring lovely damsels displaying silk legs and garters.

Tommy and Teresa came off the boat in the middle of the morning, and waited at the Cintra for Gregg Corbin and Geoffrey Hylton. From the other half of the room they could hear the click of billiard balls and the voices of the players. Above and below the swing doors into the street there were hot rectangles of light, slices of sky and pavement whose glare intensified the cool quietness of the bar.

"Well," Hylton said, "you've heard the news? His Grace is leaving us. The Colonel, C.M.G., retires to England to preen His Honourable tail in Whitehall."

"We may get worse," Corbin said. "You never know. When Gammage was here I prayed God to take him away. But the Almighty's sense of humour was too subtle. He granted my

151

prayer, and sent us first Denton and then Grace." His sentences drooped at the end, fading out into little sighs as though they were never quite worth finishing; a thin unhappy man with a tired moustache, who was supposed to have had a disappointment in his life that no one knew the truth about.

"I don't care who we get," Tommy said. "Since I've been to Parham Island I know we've nothing to complain of here."

"Oh, there," and Hylton shrugged his shoulders, "they're still practising slavery. But the minions of the Colonial Office are not to blame."

Teresa saw in her mind's eye Sanders, Andrew, Luther and John, putting their faces against a background of logwoods and cinnamon trees, deer grazing in long rides leading to a purple sea with a red cloud over it. And she remembered Laertes the donkey braying for bread, and peacocks screaming, whose breasts were the colour of the sky. "Surely," she said, "the Home Government is ultimately responsible. They hold the colonies in trust. All you little Legislative Councillors, who run around looking important, have only the powers of prefects. There's always the headmaster in his study. And it seems to me that if an ignorant little boy in the third form is being bullied, it is fundamentally the headmaster who is to blame."

"I'm glad that at least we look important," Tommy said.

"Some of you do."

"Well, don't say which. I shouldn't like my colleagues to feel slighted." Olive carried their drinks on a tin tray that had black and white dogs painted on it. She wore a bright red dress and gold earrings, and the Madras that bound her head was mostly blue.

"Comparisons are odious," Corbin said, "even between islands. But something will have to be done about labour conditions in Parham. Only – granted that you're right, Miss Craddock – the headmaster of a democracy can do nothing drastic. He has to keep faith with the inevitability of gradualness."

"Then my analogy falls flat, because headmasters of schools have to act quickly. Otherwise the bullied boy dies, or runs away, or grows up warped. Parham Island peasants don't die noticeably enough to cause a scandal; they can't run away; and nobody cares if they're warped."

"Sometimes the little bullied boy grows up and becomes a bully on his own account. That has happened before in the history of the Underdog."

Geoffrey was on the side of the Underdog, but had one of those balanced minds that are the despair of the enthusiast. "That's the equivalent of being warped," Teresa said, "and exactly proves my point. It's of prime importance to the Home Government to see that the boy is not bullied. Rebellions and revolutions – oh, all right, then – serious discontent, are expensive."

"Teresa is talking too much," Tommy said. "Can't you stop her mouth with something?"

"We'd love to," Geoffrey responded, smiling gallantly with his own, "but I'm afraid that in this respectable establishment it must be done with a cigarette. She has a drink already. Or shall I be, as well as look, important, and buy her a box of chocolates?"

Teresa made a face. She wasn't the kind of girl that men gave chocolates to, although Derek had sent her one of these boxes at Christmas time, and she had eaten some for sentiment's sake. Now she knew that when she went back she would find the rest of them penetrated by white worms; and cockroaches would have nibbled the cardboard picture.

How often we think of a name only to hear it mentioned. Or is it the power of our thinking that draws it to another's lips? "I believe we have Miss Craddock to thank for good work done," Corbin said. "I was in the Grande Anse Section the other day and heard that Morell had settled down into a live-and-let-live policy. Nuts don't rattle at all any more. You *were* the good influence, weren't you?"

She had half wanted to hear that name, half hated it; took a long pull through a straw before answering. "Tell me how they are," she said. "I don't think I've had any influence at all, but inevitably, after what happened – well, I can't help being interested." It didn't matter at all that she was blushing. She didn't even have to pretend that she had choked.

"Of course," one of them said. "I'd forgotten. He was with you that night." So the beasts' eyes had not even been glaring in the darkness, let alone seeing anything. They had forgotten that Derek and she had been together for any purpose whatever.

"Yes," she said, "and thank God he was. I'll never hear a whisper against him after his kindness to me that night." Would she have spoken so strongly if she were still fearing the beasts' eyes? Why should she be easily praising Derek with her lips, and yet feeling in her heart this leaden depression? Even before seeing him she knew that fire had melted some of the snows of illusion.

"I've nothing to whisper against him," Corbin said, "except that he won't take advice. Did you know he was putting a hundred acres of Neva into sugar?"

"Good Heavens, no," Tommy said, "what for?"

Here were Derek's dreams lying in mud for oxen – or men – to trample. Once they had danced like sunbeams piercing a dusty room where only she had entered. "Did you know that, Teresa?" Tommy asked.

"He told me he was going to. It's not a thing I can understand." Green cane-fields billowing like the sea were all right from a distance, but since she had last seen Derek she had been close to them and touched them; had seen a people groaning under their burden.

"Some people seem to ask of life what they've always had," Tommy said, "and others react the opposite way. Here are Teresa and I, brought up on a pavement, and we've never once thought of planting one at Ça Ira."

"There's one there already if we chose to dig it up," Teresa said. "But, Tommy, what a sublime picture of us – brought up on a pavement. It makes me think of the canvas huts men have when they're tearing streets to pieces. I can see nurses cooking our Cowangate on braziers. But I definitely remember being taken to the seaside once."

"That was done out of a charity fund for mental defectives," Tommy said. "You were better afterwards."

He and she were playing the old game of sidetracking when the conversation was becoming bothering to one or the other, but their friends could hardly be expected to know that, and went on chewing their bone.

"Tommy and Teresa being perfectly foolish doesn't tell me why Morell wants to grow sugar at Neva," Geoffrey said.

"Because he was brought up on sugar and he's used to sugar,

and he likes sugar. To look at, I mean, not to eat. And he can do what he likes with his own land."

"He can do what he likes, till he brings a factory on us. And grow what he likes if it sweetens his attitude towards the poor of his parish. Aren't people borrowing his nuts at all any more?" Everyone else's nuts were "borrowed". It would be interesting if Morell had found a formula.

"If they are he's turning a blind eye," Corbin said. "But I hear that he and Mrs. Morell are very thick with old Biggar. What do you make of that veteran?"

"Biggar?" Tommy said, shrugging his shoulders. "The people in our village call him – *philosophe*. Henry tells me that means – busybody." Teresa had worked out that this piece of etymology was derived, via the French colonists of the eighteenth century, from contempt of the encyclopaedists. "Mr. Biggar's all right," she said, "when he has trousers on."

"Meaning exactly?"

"I don't like his knees."

"What's the matter with them?"

"They've got dimples."

"Good Heavens," Geoffrey said, "I hope mine haven't."

"No," Teresa said, "they haven't. I made sure of that before I made friends with you." His skin was the colour of dark oak, and when he was stripped for swimming his body reminded her of Benga's, the African dancer. There were no dimples in Derek's knees either, but his ankles were bony, and there were damp black hairs on his legs. And she thought, looking at Geoffrey, how ugly white bodies were on a tropical background, and how out of place. But she sheered off the contemplation of bodies because it brought her to the edge of a great gulf, a gulf of her own unreason that she could not bridge.

Tommy said: "I saw Biggar click with Mrs. Morell the day we had them all to tea together. I suppose she isn't fussy about dimples, or has never had them exposed to her."

"She'd look the other way if she didn't like them. Those sort of people really have blind eyes when it suits them."

Teresa laughed. "She's not blind to *my* knees." And Corbin said: "What a trouble she'll be if we ever put women on juries."

"Haven't you got that fixed yet?" Tommy said. "I don't believe you people even think when I'm away."

"We're against it," Hylton said. "I don't consider that in St. Celia we have women of suitable mentality to sit on juries."

Teresa gaped at him. She could have named offhand a dozen women, including his own *maîtresse-en-titre*, who ran admirably their or their husbands' business; cultivated estates; brought up innumerable children. There was nothing the matter with their mentality. "I find your point of view oriental," she said, lighting a cigarette from the one she had just finished and fitting it into her holder. Derek had said once: "Are you smoking because you want to, or because you think you look seductive behind that holder?" And Teresa *had* thought she looked seductive, had wanted to; and now was bitterly sorry that she had succeeded in her ambition. Here she smoked solely because she wanted to, these men being proof against her holder.

"But, Miss Craddock," Corbin protested, "think what awkward situations might arise. Supposing I were ill, and Dorothy called to sit on a jury. What would happen?"

"Why, you'd get better," she said. "Or, on the other hand, you'd get worse." But the vision of Dorothy measuring crime with her little yardstick of etiquette almost swung her to the other opinion.

"Gregg wouldn't get worse," Tommy said. "The thought of his wife sweating in a jury box would cure him of anything."

"*I* have sat on a jury," Teresa said. "It was the most infernal nuisance, and I hope I'll never have to do it again. But if the jury system is to continue it's a civic duty that everyone, male and female, should be ready to perform. It's got nothing to do with what sex you are, or who's ill."

"I asked old Judge Settle the other day what he thought," Geoffrey said.

"And what did he?"

"He said it didn't matter. That people forgot it was the old man on the bench who had the last word."

To Teresa this conversation was like an old-fashioned cameo, having the sad fragrance of another world. She hadn't known that men anywhere, men one knew, could still be debating as to whether women were, or were not, fit to sit on juries. She could remember faintly, and Tommy extremely well, their mother's suffragist activities, and knew that they wore her to her deathbed, with the War following so soon after. And she marvelled that in one generation women should die to put match to a candle, and in the next hardly trouble to use its light. Did not need to use it, for the matter had been fought out long ago in the headmaster's study, and soon the inevitability of gradualness would bring illumination to the whole school. Women – as women – don't die for their rights any more. Only left-wingers nowadays, or Chinese.

Teresa was pondering these things, letting the men's conversation drift over her head, when Maurice Collins blew into the bar; the very apotheosis of a right-winger, pompous and prosperous, exuding heartiness from every sweating pore. That he "blew" in was a cliché Teresa found essentially justified, for his coming had the effect on the rest of them of an east wind, an east wind when the temperature is below zero. You could have heard them stiffen. Strangers, meeting Collins for the first time, thought him a prince of good fellows, but later they discovered that he was like beer. When the froth was blown off there was a bitter taste underneath.

"Well, well, well," he said. "What's everyone having? Black velvet, Miss Craddock? That's the stuff after a sea voyage."

Teresa shuddered audibly. Eighteen hours' journey on a placid sea, of which six had been spent at anchor, was no more her notion of a sea voyage than was black velvet her idea of a drink on a hot morning in Capesterre. "Thank you," she said, "I haven't finished my gin squash yet."

"And how's Parham?" Collins went on, ordering a whisky for himself, as nobody else seemed to want anything. "I'll be going up there myself next month on Federal business."

Tommy said that Parham was very well, thank you.

"Have a good trip? Those C.W.I. boats are pretty classy, what?"

"We've no complaints." The east wind had made icicles of four pleasant people, and they couldn't help it.

"They charge outrageously for deck chairs," Teresa put in, feeling that someone had got to keep the ball rolling, even though it were a ball made of snow.

"Oh, I agree," Collins said. "Fraudulent. I never hire a deck chair on a C.W.I. boat."

"Don't you?" Geoffrey said, and the hatred between the two men was so strong that it tainted the air, taking the ice off the frozen feeling. "I thought that was how you made something out of a trip, charging up a deck chair to your expenses account."

The silence echoed out into the street, making the hooting of a taxi like a blasphemous intrusion into a sacred moment. The very beggars were quiet. Then Tommy's chortle broke the tension, and Collins himself mimicked it.

"Ha, ha, ha. Very good, Hylton. If I thought you meant it, I'd rook you double duty on your next consignment."

"I never mean anything," Hylton said. "It's so much safer."

"All the same," Corbin expostulated afterwards, "you shouldn't have said it. We've enemies enough on the official side of the Council."

"The man is getting altogether too important. He needs deflating."

"Well, you don't have to be the one to stick in the pins." Corbin was a white West Indian, a creole, born in the island. "Collins," he said, "is one of those Englishmen whose slogan is 'the Empire for the English'. That hypothesis must be disproved, but by the steamroller of our own integrity, Hylton, not by pinpricks."

"Good Heavens," Tommy cried, "what a wonderful expression. The steamroller of our own integrity. Where'd you find it, Corbin, where did you find it?"

"It's my own," Gregg said modestly into his glass. "My very own."

"Well, it won't be any longer," Tommy said. "I'm going to make it mine. In future, 'the steamroller of my integrity' will be blazoned across my notepaper; will be embroidered by Teresa on my underpants. When I die you'll find it written on my heart like Calais on Mary what's-her-name's. I'll – "

"You'll come home, Tommy," Teresa said sternly. "You're getting overexcited and above yourself. What's more, it's lunch time."

The billiard balls had stopped rolling now and the players were standing by the bar. For this brief hour the grey room was alive and vital. Even the lovely ladies on the calendar advertisements and on the chocolate boxes in the showcases had become part of the human picture, making what they could of their colours before those fierce slices of light, that were above and below the doors, paled them into the uniform greyness of the walls. Outside in the street, light was waiting; and heat, that leapt into the room to take possession of it whenever a door swung open.

"I'll see you tomorrow, Craddock," Corbin said. "There is an unofficial meeting at my house."

Teresa wondered with motherly feeling whether the prefects got through any more business at their private sessions than at those she was permitted to attend. And gravely doubted it. Outside on the hot pavement there was a cripple sitting in a square box on wheels, and she dropped a threepenny bit into his hand, thanking God that she was not as he was. Beyond and above the houses of the town she could see three mountain peaks outlined fiercely against the paler sky. Tomorrow she would have left streets behind her and would be home again at Ça Ira, where the threads of life, some of them so badly broken, would have to be picked up and mended again. And some would never mend.

XXIV

One broken thread was the friendship between Norah and Rosalie. During Teresa's absence they had quarrelled *à outrance*, and it did not seem possible that peace could be made. Rosalie had claimed a length of material from among Tilly's effects, saying that the dead girl had been working it for her, and Norah maintained that this was not so. She had called Rosalie a thief, and had driven her from the house with a stick.

"Two shillings I pay to the doctor, Miss T'resa, for him to see my bruises."

"The transaction should have been reversed," Tommy said. "Doctors have all the luck." But Henry told them that Rosalie was going to law; was suing Norah for the doctor's bill and for defamation of character. "They say hard words to one another," he said, "but my daughter will stand as witness that Rosalie lifted a stick first."

This ridiculous and everlasting going to law, symptom of slave mentality; a legacy, like gout, bequeathed by our ancestors' errors. A hundred years of freedom have not eradicated the characteristics of irresponsibility from a people, who, for generations, were allowed to make no decision, to have no independence of thought or action, so that now they seek always for help outside of themselves. "The Government must do this, the Big House will give that." And above everything they go to law, wasting magisterial time and their own money.

Norah's baby had grown, but was still wizened. The creases in his face hadn't been ironed out. One couldn't imagine Norah being a cow-like mother.

"No, Miss T'resa, I feed him arrowroot."

"Gracious," Tommy said, prodding the infant with the ignorant courage occasionally displayed by bachelors, "he looks quite pleased to see me."

"Why, yes," Norah answered simply, "it is a brave child."

Teresa asked what the baby was called. "I call him Albert," Norah said, "but he not christened yet. Next fortnight he will be christened."

That was something that Teresa had never been able to understand. It happened among rich and poor, black and white. You had a tenet of faith that unbaptized children went straight to Hell, and yet believing mothers ran these inconceivable risks. Albert was already three months old, and little babies died so easily. Does this prove, she wondered, that after all reason is stronger than faith, or faith in a good God stronger than in a cruel one? She tried to persuade Norah that cow's milk would be better for Albert than arrowroot, but she did not succeed.

"He must have always the milk of the same cow," she said, "and of that I cannot be sure."

There were more superstitions about milk in the island even than about Hell. For instance, it had to be watered, else the cow would run dry. A superstition as surely invented by the milk vendors as at the beginning of things it had suited the Church to invent Hell.

But – Teresa sighed – was this to be inevitably her future, tendering unwanted advice to mothers who would never heed her because she was not herself a mother? And she remembered how once, for a moment, she had imagined herself having Derek's child; which fancy had lasted no longer than the time it takes to draw breath, a dream child dying of its conception.

Below her the sea was fiercely blue, darkening to the horizon. Superimposed against it there was a yellow-leaved croton bush, filled with sunlight; and a yard or two beyond, leaving a square of sea like a window, a spathodea with scarlet cup-like blossoms over which hung a cloud of hummingbirds, black creatures, their plumage shot through with red or green. Sometimes this same scene was painted in pastel shades and sometimes in tones of grey, but that morning the colours were laid on crudely, each one clear and rich and distinct. And her heart was saddened a little by the beauty that surrounded her; for loveliness, unblessed by love, can be sadder than rain that may cheer by contrast. She took out her patchwork, and sat in a long chair under the saman trees. Creepers, wreathed about the branches, fell in long streamers, swinging in the wind, and there was a bee orchid, early flowering, trailing from a rugged bole. She fitted in a pale blue piece of material that had come, a long time ago, from the Pyrenees.

"I shall be glad when you've finished that magnum opus," Tommy said, "it makes you go all broody."

She said: "I've nothing to brood on but my past," but said it more cheerfully than the words sounded. "Do you remember," she went on, "the day we went out of France into Andorra?" No customs authorities, no passport formalities; the frontier a little mountain stream and beyond it two stone buildings, cowsheds rather than houses, on one of which was written in all simplicity the word – Andorra. Droves of half-wild horses grazed on the treeless hillsides, trampling the Alpine flowers and munching with equine indifference white mountain buttercups and purple gentians. To make a village, stones had been piled one on another without mortar, and roofs were flat. "The whole impression of that day is blue," she said. "Blue skies and blue views; columbines on the edge of the precipice; and irises growing wild in hayfields for pigs to lie on."

"I remember only the precipice," Tommy said. "You forget that I was driving." *La Route des Pyrénées* had been a narrow shelf without a parapet, chiselled out of sheer rock.

Here the sky was blue also, and there were morning glories on the wall and plumbago in the flower-beds. "I don't know what's happened to Andorra," Teresa said, "nor even which side it's on in the war. But if I wanted to smuggle myself from France to Spain, or back again, I should do it by that road."

"Perhaps by now they've got machine guns in the cow-houses," Tommy began, and then they saw Derek Morell crossing the lawn towards them. "Don't leave me," she whispered in sudden panic. But he said: "Don't be a coward, Teresa. All this is your doing."

She *was* a coward. She had told this man that she loved him and now couldn't honour her own cheque. A mist of shame dimmed her eyesight, and the waspish brown and yellow heads of the bee orchid seemed to swim into each other to make one huge menacing blossom. Isabel barked, and was wagging her tail so that with each wag she struck her own flanks, and did this so quickly that she made a fan of the tail, which one saw moving as a solid piece.

"I'm glad you came," Teresa said nervously. "You'll stay to lunch?" Perhaps if she saw him often, and a great deal, the charm would work again, the spring be wound up.

"I've only come for a minute," he said. "I heard in Grande Anse that you were back. I felt I must know if you were well again."

Tommy did leave them, melted into the middle distance, disappearing behind mango trees. He hoped that Teresa would find the solution to her own happiness, and be done with it. "What do they see in that man," he wondered, aware that many women had been foolish about Derek, but not knowing whether Teresa knew this, or cared. "I'm saved a good deal," he thought rather wistfully, "by being fat and obvious instead of the tall dark man of mystery that girls meet when gypsies tell fortunes." And reflected further that Georgette loved him very nearly for himself alone; that his sex life was simple, and living with Teresa better than being married. How much happier he was than those two on the lawn who were playing a dramatic farce and thinking it tragedy. Their trouble had been self-induced, was never inevitable. Quite soon, perhaps, they would look back at themselves and laugh.

"It's a long time," Derek was saying. "I've been hungry to see you." And the sight of him was making her heart beat to a faint echo of her former feeling so that she knew she was really glad to see him and not afraid any more. She thought he would ask nothing that she could not give.

"You wouldn't be complete in my mind," he said laughing, "without Isabel and the patchwork. Isabel and I have been lonely. Now, tell me quickly about Parham Island. I'm still homesick, you know. St. Celia remains too big for me, too grandiose."

What could she tell him? Would he care for the troubles of Sanders and Company, or Prudence the washerwoman? She liked him less for liking his island, but that was not a thing you could say. "We got mixed up in politics," she said. "It's terrible how the poor live and are treated there."

"I hear Canning is doing a great deal of harm," he said. "Disturbing labour conditions is a dangerous experiment, although I wouldn't put it past your friend Hylton in this island." Horace Canning turned over stones to reveal the scurrying suffering creatures underneath, but Geoffrey never disturbed anyone; frequently oiled the troubled waters of others. Derek's petulant jealousy was flavoured with colour prejudice, a thing that happens to some people on both sides of the line, and Teresa changed the subject.

"I met people who sent you messages," she said. "Especially a pink and white blonde called Dossie. She detested me on sight."

"Oh, her." And Derek's stress of the pronoun implied both an apology and a sense of embarrassment.

"A past of yours?" Teresa laughed. "I suspected as much."

"She was never important," he muttered, but Teresa interrupted: "Don't be silly, my dear. I never supposed myself to be a unique experience. You haven't the manner of calf love."

"But you are unique," he protested. "There's never been anyone like you since Time began."

"Surely, to a connoisseur, every experience is unique; as to an epicure. Every woman, every dish, has its own special qualities."

"But qualities differ in degree," he said. "Dossie was low in the scale. A cornflower shape, with not enough strawberry jam."

"Don't depreciate her, Derek," Teresa said rather sadly. "We all slip very easily into being a past. Some day you'll refer to me as – oh, *her.* If you don't say worse things."

She cut short his "never". "Tell me your news," she said. "How's Mrs. Morell, and – everything?"

"Janet is well, but not – everything. Coconuts still fade mysteriously into thin air."

"Oh, dear, I heard in Capesterre that all that was all over."

"By no means; but you told me to hold my hand and I obey my mistress' orders. That is to say, my very nearly mistress."

She ignored the implication in his voice, bolting like a scared horse. "It's a pity that the leading men in these villages can't or won't deal with thieving," she said. "They should stop it from a sense of civic pride."

"They probably share in the thieving. I don't put anyone past it." But she told him that was nonsense.

"There are boys everywhere nowadays," she said, "for whom there seems to be no future, who have nothing to do but to pilfer and smuggle. After all, smuggling's a sporting game." She saw them in her own village, wearing French caps and smoking French tobacco, sometimes drinking French brandy; wriggling their bottoms and calling it dancing, while one strummed on a guitar and another rubbed two tin lids together, or made horn noises through a bamboo stem.

"It's a game that makes me very angry," Derek said.

"Have you spoken to the priest in Ville Rousse?" Teresa asked, "he might help you." But Derek hardly knew him. "We send him milk," he said, "because it seems to be an estate tradition. But, after all, he's French and a Catholic. Not much in Janet's line."

Janet was ridiculous and a menace, with her little hidebound prejudices. "I'll go and see Father Dolet tomorrow," Teresa said. "He's a very dear old man."

"Can't I come with you?" Derek asked. And she thought they were on a safe and friendly basis, and that it would be nice to walk on the cliffs again. But almost at once she knew that she had made a mistake; had seemed to promise more than she meant.

"I'll meet you by the beach," he said, "and afterwards we can talk properly. But, Teresa, won't you – I mean, haven't you an orchid to show me?"

The first time they had ever kissed she had made excuse to show him an orchid. That had been in half darkness, with white blossoms gathering the dusk into their petals, and the afterglow of the sunset colouring their faces, their whole lives. She didn't want to be kissed now, in broad daylight. Perhaps didn't want to be kissed at all. What had been soft and happy and subdued then would now be vivid, with a hard forced brightness. She said: "We've no lovelier orchid than the one in front of you, although its a wild and common thing. And – the world is awake."

He made no effort to persuade her. Tomorrow would be another day, and, under the dark trees, where rooms were whose windows looked to the blowhole, he would love her again; and perhaps within sight of the water would rebuild what fire had destroyed. But she, catching his thought, wondered if it were not rank folly that had prompted her consent to meet him, but later consoled herself with the thought that there would be no need to be hidden and alone. The high road would chaperone them, and the priest, so that whatever happened would be her own fault. She held the wheel in her hands.

XXV

Nicholas Nolette made a garden on the bank of the St. Patrick's River. He cut down immense trees; burned branches and undergrowth; left the trunks to rot where they fell. Then he planted dasheen slips and banana suckers; put in cassava roots and a little corn. A year later, when he had reaped from this garden, he left it derelict and passed on to another patch, stubbornly believing that his provisions would grow only on virgin soil. Razor grass and tree-ferns and wild eggplant sprang up where the garden had been; and when heavy rain came, and there were no longer roots to hold the earth in place, the cliff cracked and a slice of it slid into the valley, choking the stream with red dirt and leaving a raw wound on the hillside, whose blood ran with the river and stained even the sea.

Walking to his new garden Nicholas found his path blocked by the landslide. As he cutlassed another, never thinking that this had happened by his own fault, his eye caught the gleam of unaccustomed metal, and, wondering, he filled his basket with pieces of clay out of which stars were shining. That night his sister's husband, who had been to Demerara, and had known men working in the fields, told him that he had found diamonds. Behind closed windows they plotted what should be done, while outside moonlight shimmered on little broken waves, and long tongues of surf licked the canoes drawn up on the beach.

Next morning Nicholas went north to consult with Mr. Craddock, but Abraham, his brother-in-law, boasted: "I have travelled in far countries and I know Town ways." He crossed the mountains by the Lake road, which is so high above sea level that clouds hang on little stunted trees and swirl about a traveller's head like wisps of hair; and came by the Palmiste valley into Capesterre, where the first tradesman that he questioned would give him no more than a shilling for a few pieces of his clay; but from another he got five pounds for a saucepanful, whereupon he regretted his first bargain and returned hot foot to the St. Patrick's River. But already – because in Capesterre nothing can be hidden, and no story remain unembroidered, acquiring in the process fungoid growths – news had spread like a rushing flame that wealth was to be had on the Windward Coast for the picking up. Men, lusting for diamonds, plunged through the forest and over the divide; ravaging Nicholas' old garden, scrabbling at the cliff, making with their trampling a slough of the river trail; and returning with their utensils – their biscuit barrels and their kerosene tins – full of clay for which they got precisely nothing, it having, in their absence, been discovered that these gleaming morsels were not diamonds at all but iron pyrites of no value. And the man who had paid five pounds for a saucepanful was the mock of his fellows. Where the flame of rumour was first kindled there was it quenched. But, in far away valleys, and by lonely beaches where the dousing of the story had not reached, little flickering fires of speculation crackled and spluttered, and for many weeks people came into white men's houses, hoping to sell stones for the price of bread.

Nicholas walked all day from dawn until late afternoon, following the red coast road that passes sometimes through the lonely silence of the forest and sometimes vouchsafes blue three-cornered glimpses of ocean and the crashing of waves beating against iron cliffs. As he walked he dreamt of what he would buy with the money that Mr. Craddock would surely give him. A gramophone and a safety razor; blue silk pillows for his house and grand clothes for his person. After which he would hire a motorcar and would have himself driven round town. He, the rich man, would be driven by a paid chauffeur whom he could order as he pleased. And when his dream came to that point he slashed with his cutlass at the unoffending branches of shrubs, and spat into the road fibres of sugar-cane upon which ants made a black smother for the sweetness that he had not sucked.

Nicholas crossed the island at its narrowest part, and, passing through Grande Anse, mounted the Ça Ira valley and came on to the veranda of the Big House. He lifted the goat's skin that covered his basket and revealed lumps of clay wherein stars shone with a pride that he might have displayed had he created them, and not picked them from among stones and rubble and the upended roots of trees. Tommy, always the optimist, was very much intrigued.

"I have a friend in England," he said, "who is director of one of the biggest diamond firms in the world. Not," he insisted, "that I believe there's anything in it." But he said this so that Nicholas might not be unduly set up, although his own enthusiasm made him already visualize fortunes for all concerned. It amused Teresa to think of those lumps of clay from the St. Patrick's River being poured with contumely on to the table of a dingy London office and afterwards carried – they that had been "headed" under a goat's skin – in Roger's Rolls Royce to be shown to Mildred, playing the invalid in her heated loggia; and she, having laughed at the clay, telling some footman to throw it into the river; river that bore no resemblance to the St. Patrick's save that both carried water to the sea. That evening, long before news of the Capesterre diamond debacle had been drummed along the coast, Tommy got out a cigarette tin, filled it with the clay and posted it with a covering letter. Weeks later, when the "rush" had been altogether forgotten, he received from Roger Hallenstein the discouraging report that might have been expected.

"I told you so," Teresa said, and this made Tommy very angry. "Not to say that," he explained, "is the hardest lesson life teaches us. I hope by the time you're my age you'll have learnt it."

"Aunt Louisa never learnt it," Teresa said. "She even used to say it when she hadn't." But this was a long time after, when she had a bad taste in her mouth, and lovely days made the burden of her mind heavier.

Meanwhile Nicholas asked for an advance on his diamonds, and Tommy refused it. Not even his optimism extended that far, although while his right hand remained adamant his left slipped over two shillings as a gift. Norah purloined these to pay for Albert's christening; so that Nicholas, boasting in the kitchen of the brave things he would do with his money, of the gramophone and the blue silk cushions that he would buy, of the motorcar that he would hire, was in fact penniless for his trouble and footsore into the bargain. Norah didn't believe in diamonds any more than Teresa did, nor in blue silk cushions either.

Next morning Teresa woke early, wondering if it would rain, and half hoping that it might, for her assignation troubled her a little, and she hated herself for this new inability to know her own mind. But the clear Carême weather held promise of further loveliness, and already she could see little scrubby bushes on the lower hills touched with pink and yellow to imitate autumn. On the seashore huge leaves of almond trees were brilliantly scarlet, and even in the forest the uniformity of green varied more than was usual. She said: "It must be spring that is making a weather-cock of me." And considered how, when you first lived in the tropics, there seemed to be no change of season to indicate the year's passing. You found beauty monotonous, missing the sudden flush of green on to winter's greyness; the brilliance of decay that ushers in winter again. But soon you realized that not even here did Nature ever stand still. Trees lost their leaves, although never all together. Flowers bloomed in their seasons. You watched for pois-doux as once for hawthorn; for red lilies as for tulips; for petrea instead of lilac. But it was disconcerting that only in this dry season of spring could you find autumn colourings.

Crossing the lawn to water her orchids, orchids that she had not shown Derek, she saw that the sun – rising behind mountains and still invisible – was casting a yellow sheen on to the sea and on to a bank of cloud massed on the horizon. The slope beyond the garden fell so steeply that she could almost have thrown a stone into the river, river whose murmur made part of the morning noises, blending with the singing of the rossignol; with the shrilling of the green crak-crak grasshoppers; with the loud voice of Henry driving a young cow to pasture before coming to his work. On the far side of the valley banana leaves were touched with shining gold, and there was a flash of silver from the cutlass of a man working in the field.

This was no morning on which to feel depressed, although nervousness made the hours drag on braked wheels and duties seem leaden tasks. "I've had too long a holiday," she thought, but knew that in fact housekeeping lacked savour without Tilly. A cook had been burnt, but the world had to go on; and she remembered how, on that fatal night, within five minutes of the tragedy, within five minutes of seeing that screaming writhing mass of rug-covered flames upon which she and Derek had pressed their own bodies, Norah had come to her and had said: "What for dinner, Miss T'resa, that I may be getting it ready." She had told Norah then that never, so long as they both should live, was she to mention food to her again; although next day and the day after she was served four meals as usual, and ate them. But now, when she had to order food, sickness came upon her, and tears rose.

Susannah, the new cook, was in any case rather a pain. "You should have found out beforehand," Tommy said, "that she was a Protestant. All good housekeepers pry into the religious convictions of their servants. It's well-known that Protestants don't cook as well as Catholics."

Teresa didn't know where Tommy got his statistics, but there was no doubt that Susannah came to her work with an Anglican outlook; with an inability, for instance, to put butter in the right place, and a tendency to puddings. But Protestant or not she had her share of superstitions, refusing to sleep in Tilly's room lest it be haunted. "No, Miss, for many weeks I not resting there. Tilly will seek to return to her room, for the dead are very cold."

They had found lodgings for her in the village, and she was not satisfied with these. "At Sylvie's," she said, "there is no basin, no utensil, no happy feeling." Before going to meet Derek Teresa gave her a basin and a utensil – euphemism for *pot-de-chambre* – but the happy feeling, she told her, she must provide for herself.

XXVI

The town of Ville Rousse stands on a steep hillside facing the sea. Old grey stones make doorsteps and foundations for wooden houses faded to the same shade of grey. A massive flight of stairs – stairs planned on a grandiose scale for some vast city rather than for a huddle of houses clinging to a windswept cliff – leads to a grey church with a red roof whose inside walls are whitewashed, and whose blue-painted doors have been fret-worked with Sacred Hearts. Trifles of painted glassware decorate the altar, and paper roses mix with tight bunches of marigolds and cockscombs. Statues, once brightly painted, are shabby now and the faces of the saints are tired. But on every feast day and throughout the month of May a light shines in the tower from dusk until nine o'clock, telling whoever may sail that lonely sea that the lamp of Christ is still burning in the church at Ville Rousse. And sometimes, on nights that are not calendar feasts, another beacon shines out to guide smugglers from the French country on to Neva Beach.

"I take it that rousse means russet," Teresa said, "but it isn't the right word. I don't know what could be the *mot juste* to describe this particular red. It's fiercer than brick, and none of the obvious shades fit at all."

"I was in Devonshire once," Derek said. "The cliffs there gave me the same impression."

"But in paler tints. Coming from here I always feel that England looks washed out, like an old frock whose colours have run."

As they walked through the town to the priest's house they saw with distaste albinos, having pale skins and negroid features, skins of a dead leprous pallor, unnatural and horrible. "It happens that way sometimes," Teresa said. "There's a colony of them here; or perhaps just one family. Over in the Saintes, those French islands, there are really white people, descendants of Breton fishermen. That's on Terre d'en Haut. On Terre d'en Bas the people are black, and they say it's only recently that they've started to mix." Only now, in this speedboat age, was race prejudice weakening between peoples who for three centuries had faced each other across a narrow strip of sea and been hardly on calling terms. And whether it was that her eyes were unaccustomed, or whether inbreeding had been carried beyond what was reasonable, it had seemed to Teresa that these "poor whites", their pale flesh peeping through rags, had the bleached unnatural look of things grown in the dark or kept in cellars; so that the black faces of the sloop's crew had shone like good deeds in a naughty world, refreshing to see.

At the top of the Ville Rousse stairs a child with red hair stood malevolently staring, and then fled. The presbytery was gaunt and bare, sheltering only a few hard chairs; books grey with mildew; a portrait of the Pope stained with damp and nibbled by cockroaches. The old man, whose halo of white hair surrounded a tonsure that was one huge freckle, always seemed pleased to see Teresa. He could talk French to her, real French as opposed to patois. And she lent him books of which the bishop might doubtless disapprove, but which brought him a taste of an old life twenty years behind him, twenty years in which he had not seen France. And because she was not of his flock he found her a pretty picture in her sleeveless shorts.

"Can you help me, Father?" Derek said. "Who are the people who rob me and why do they do it? I have tried to be just."

"They do wrong to rob you," the old man said. "I have made a sermon to tell them so. But long ago these people, or their fathers, planted the palm trees. They think they have a right to reap a third of the crop."

"But can't they understand that now I have bought the estate? It has nothing to do with me who planted the trees, nor what arrangements were made by my predecessor. The whole crop is mine."

The priest hesitated before speaking again. Teresa could hear the crying of the sea, muffled and far away. There was a cat chasing a beetle under a chair and a moth beat its wings in a dark corner. At last he said: "Mr. Morell, I come of a poor family. In the Vendée my parents held only an orchard, a few fields. But is it not so that when one buys or inherits a property one acquires at the same time certain responsibilities, the duty of administering the land for the greatest good of the greatest number? For instance, Doctor Crewe has told us that the fat of the coconut is necessary to health."

Derek muttered: "That faddist. So I've got him to blame." But aloud he said: "I won't commit myself by agreeing with your notions, Father. Miss Craddock is a more receptive audience. But this is not a question of a few nuts taken for food. Many are being exported."

"There are bad men, alas, in every community. It is not just to blame our whole village for the sins of a few."

"Who are the few, Father? You must surely know."

He never noticed how the priest recoiled, sensing the suggestion that he should break the sacred confidence of the confessional.

"Why not pay watchmen, Mr. Morell," he said coldly. "So might the thieving be prevented."

"To pay watchmen costs money," Derek answered. "There's little enough profit to be made nowadays. However" – and he got up and peered round the room as though the information he wanted were lurking in a corner, "if you can't help me" – Teresa saw his lips hover over the word "won't" – "you can't."

"Everyone is trying to help you," she said irritably. "We all know that the people are exasperating to strangers, but you must realize that, rightly or wrongly, the average St. Celian looks on a fallen coconut as a 'mango on the ground', something to pick up and eat. And the system has worked. Where other islands are threatened with unrest, here no one is hungry enough to make trouble."

"You're all leagued against me," Derek said. But said it with a smile as though he realized that he'd been behaving like a nutmeg grater, harsh and rasping. "I must bow inevitably to beauty, and" – with a look at the priest – "to wisdom."

"Miss Craddock has wisdom as well as beauty," said the old man. And he took some green fruits off a shelf, handing one to each of them. "The first Julie mangoes," he said. "You will please to take one to Mrs. Morell, with my compliments. And I thank you again, Mr. Morell, for letting Harvey send me the milk. I am a sick man and can take little else."

They said goodbye to him and went away, coming out into sunshine again from out of that grey room. The police station had neat flower-beds in front of it, and the lance-corporal's horse was cropping grass on a small patch of lawn. "No, Sir, Mr. Morell, I not knowing who stealing from you, but when you catch the thief I ready to arrest him. What you should employ, Sir, is a great detective."

The fame of Hercule Poirot and Lord Peter Wimsey has penetrated even to Ville Rousse. Books come to stranger ends than their makers dream of. Torn by cockroaches, pierced by yellow worms, their titles obliterated from the covers, they lie at last in earth's remote corners and are read by black policemen, even though a page here and there be missing.

Mr. Buffon, the storekeeper, saluted them as they went by. His was a little rickety store where canvas shoes and soap and onions rubbed shoulders with patent medicines, rolls of coloured cottons and Madras handkerchiefs. Over the door there was a signboard with the notice – "Gent.'s In and Outfitters".

"When we first came," Derek said, "Janet quarrelled with Mr. Buffon. We get our meat from him. One week it was high, next week just nasty; and Janet wrote a sharp note saying that if in future it were no better we should have to deal in Grande Anse."

"I should never have had the courage," Teresa said.

"Neither will Janet again. Mr. Buffon replied in three pages of almost illegible calligraphy that in twenty-four years of butchery he had never had a complaint. And Madam could buy meat where she chose."

"Whatever did Madam do?"

"Went to make peace, and was told that the offending pig had been purchased in Woodstock and had walked to its killing, been prodded rather, along the coast road. At sight of the Loubet hill it had grown tired, had sat down, declined to go further. 'I'd as soon be killed here as anywhere,' it said. And was killed, all weary with its walk."

How nice Derek was in this mood, telling his story with that touch of exaggeration, that appreciation of the pig's point of view. He struck a false note when stressing his sense of property; and Teresa reflected how oddly ownership of land affected different people, giving to some pomposity or hardness; and bringing dignity to others, and self-respect.

They had left the car by the Ville Rousse cemetery where croton leaves and cannas, and in the summer flamboyant trees, carried on the red effect of the cliffs. The graves were piles of earth banked up by conch shells, and at the gate there was a white cross, accidentally perfect in its simplicity, for they would have ornamented it if they could. When Derek came on to his own land he pointed to a cow standing among lime trees. "That's not mine," he said. "Someone is helping himself to free grazing."

Teresa said: "It's loose, strayed from somewhere up river." Cattle owners found it cheaper to use a vine or bark rope than a chain, but these did not last forever, and so beasts escaped. Often she wished that the ropes broke more easily than they did, for in this unfenced country men tied their cows to stakes; and sometimes were careless and cruel, or floods came to cut them off from their cattle, and these were left shackled and helpless. Then you might hear a lowing and a moaning of thirsty creatures in the forest, and stakes stood in a circle of bare earth, trampled like the mud surrounding a sugar mill whose machinery is turned hour after hour by a harnessed bull, walking always in the same place.

"Let's go along the cliffs," Derek said. "Let's make sure that the blowhole is still blowing, and see if the bent tree has fallen."

"It won't have fallen," she said. "Long ago it bowed itself before the wind, but its heart is strong." The wheel was in her hands, literally as well as figuratively, but the trouble was that her mind resembled one, turning first this way and then that. The sun had been hot in the village, and the wind did not reach the high road. It would be pleasant and perfectly natural to go up on to that sweep of open country where they had kissed long ago and been happy. To fear a scene at all was cowardly, but if a scene must be faced, why not get it over? Derek had done nothing to deserve being treated like dentist's appointment, put off till the last moment, dreaded. And, after all, if she were kissed, it wouldn't hurt like having a tooth stopped.

So they came down on to the beach and saw that there were three boats drawn up under the sea-grape trees and a half dozen rafts. White terns made a shrill screaming over an isolated rock that had grass on it, and little sandpipers ran before them, barely escaping from under their feet. Isabel scrabbled for crabs, crabs that – unearthed – pinched her nose till she tossed them high in mid-air, leaving them to find their own way to the sea while she dug feverishly, crazily, for others. The boats were native built, trunks of gommiers hollowed out high up in the mountains and then carried down to the shore with singing. Square rigged, their sails were made of flour sacks opened up and sewn together. It took twelve sacks to make a sail. The rafts were the stems of bois canot, bound together, with rowlocks added. Beside the boats the sand had been newly trampled, and there was a pile of husks under an almond tree.

To reach the foot of the cliff they must wade across the mouth of the river, an undependable river whose estuary was constantly shifting. On a muddy bank under palm trees, where the ground was riddled with crab-holes, women were washing clothes, and the stain of the soap drifted down to them, thickening the already opaque water.

Teresa led the way, and when she came through the trees and out on to the point she went right down to the edge of the sea. There were two seas in that place, one inside the bay, and one the open Atlantic. "Look," she said, "there's a pool here with fishes in it. Only seventh waves ever reach it, so that seaweeds have been able to grow."

He stood beside her watching yellow and black striped fishes browsing on green weeds. And because she knew he wanted to say other things she went on talking about fish that interested neither of them. "At Surinam," she said, "I caught one in my hands while I was bathing. I saw a lump of seaweed drifting towards me, put my hands under it for no particular reason, and drew up a fish that I hadn't even known was there. Not one of this kind. It was flat and golden brown, and it lay in my palm for quite half a minute before it flopped back into the water."

Derek didn't want to hear about fish. They two were alone together, and by her fault were silhouetted against the sky for all the world to see; although, indeed, there was no one but his own sleek cattle to see them, immense creatures, half zebu, who stood there motionless, ruminating upon two intruding people and staring at them with soft brown eyes through a multitude of flies.

"Don't look at the fishes," Derek said. "Look at me." And he turned her face towards his, watching the light and shade on it, the change of expression. "What's the matter, Teresa? Are you afraid of me? You've changed somehow."

She said: "Yes, Derek, I've changed."

"Does that mean that you don't love me any more?" She turned away from him irritably, kicking with her foot at a tuft of grass, and thereby squashing a caterpillar. "Do *we* die that way," she wondered, looking at its dead body, "through the casual carelessness of some Being so large as to be inconceivable?"

Aloud she said: "I don't know. That's the awful part about it, Derek, I don't know."

"My dear child," he said, and now it was his turn to be irritable, "that is ridiculous. If there is doubt in your mind then you don't love me. It isn't a thing about which there can be shades of opinion." He was already bitter in his pain, wanting to hurt.

She said: "Listen, Derek, I know I'm ridiculous. It's always absurd not to know one's own mind. You've interested me more than anyone has for years. I want your friendship. I'm happy with you. But the other side of love is dead, or in a coma. Be patient with me and it may resurrect. But I do loathe myself for feeling this way. It's so shaming to break a promise."

A shower of spray rose out of the blowhole, and its rainbow colours floated westward on the wind. So her words floated, chilling his heart. "I don't understand," he said, and she answered miserably: "Neither do I. That night, the night Tilly died, I was in a state of complete exaltation, my whole self dedicated to love. In some curious way shock paralysed all that side of me, and I hate myself because I can't do what once I wanted to."

And in that moment he hated her. He didn't want to walk on

cliffs chaperoned by a dog; to hear a woman prattling about the island's beauty or see her weaving past scenery into her patch-work. It wasn't for these things that he endured Janet's sourness, suppressed his own anger with thieving peasants, wasted his time. He wanted, nakedly but furtively, to go to bed with her. Wanted her body, and not her friendship. Tommy had been wrong on that evening in Capesterre when he had said: "Those sort of people don't come of the adulterous classes." At that time Teresa, thrilling to a new music, had been wanting this man as now he wanted her. But it would seem – and she smiled wryly at herself – that neither did *she* come of the adulterous classes. Even then she had admitted that women always complicated an issue, had to dream themselves into a mental union before they could envisage a physical one. Well, God knew, she had complicated this issue, or He had. But at least she had controlled her wanting with scruples and patience; whereas now Derek had no patience, but tore roughly at the tender, almost intangible, membranes that had grown over and closed her desire.

The ocean was smashing itself to pieces at their feet when these two smashed up their intimacy; but the ocean was not to blame, for this would have happened as inevitably if they had spoken together at dusk among orchids. Their relationship had never been established on rocks but rather on the sands of solitude and illusion, and would have had no importance at all in the scheme of things save for its consequences, its backwash on to innocent people. And Teresa blamed herself bitterly for the beginning of it; but, as regards the ending, she felt sourly that whereas she understood Derek's reactions he made no effort to find sympathy for hers. From the moment he had first seen her on the Capesterre jetty that was half crumpled into the sea he had desired her, had sensed the response in her; had seen her white body as a kiln in which fires were banked down, requiring only his touch to burst into flame. And now, having apparently changed her mind and denied the promise which she had given not only with her lips but by her whole attitude, she was pretend-ing that an actual flame had burnt passion altogether, leaving only charred fragments that she was pleased to call "friendship". He had no patience with such complexities. Inhibitions, that now popular word, were excuses for not doing what you didn't want or were afraid to do. There was an ugly look in his eyes that Janet knew, and his overseer, but which was strange to Teresa who had seen those eyes lustful or appealing, but never unkind.

"This is pretty bloody for me," he said. "I've loved you honestly and told you so. You met me more than half way – "

She flushed scarlet at this gaucherie, holding her head high for very shame. There was a touch in her manner of – who is this clerk turned planter that he should throw my former condescension in my teeth.

"I might have forced love on you," he was saying. "Even that night when you'd promised yourself to me there was no reason why you shouldn't have come. But I respected your distress and I've been badly paid for my self-denial."

He hurt her out of all proportion to his words. A man does that when he is noisy on his gears. Not what he said bewildered her so much as the withdrawal of all sympathy and understanding, the harping on one thing. "I've told you that I'm sorry," she said quietly. "If you want to hold me to my promise you can take me now. But, by God, you'll give me a receipt in writing so that all my life I can be reminded that my debt was discharged."

"Don't be melodramatic, Teresa. What you offer is false currency. I don't want a slab of cold fish on a marble table." He was digging a hole in the turf with the point of his shoe, and she remembered noticing the green stain on the white canvas. "I was a fool to believe in you," he said, "and a conceited fool to suppose that I meant more to you than a flirtation, something to keep your hand in."

"And what more," she wondered, "was I to you than a woman to sleep with, cheaper than a prostitute yet of more value, an exhibition medal for your male complacency." The snows of illusion were all melted now and he stood there, bereft. Her body had built up an image for her mind to worship, and not only were his feet shown to be of clay – bony ankles with damp black hairs above them – but his whole self.

"It's horrible that we should quarrel," she said. "Let's respect the decencies and leave hard things unsaid. I am genuinely, humbly, apologetic for my change of feeling, but some things are beyond control."

Then he lost his temper and said: "How right you are. I'm tempted now to grab what you just offered." And he seized her and held her close as though to rob her body of breath. "Come to me with love, Teresa" – but he made an order of it, not a plea – "break down this absurd barrier of your mind and let me teach you passion again. I'm not unpractised. I can wake fires to warm you."

But she tore herself from him, shuddering. The barrier of her mind was not absurd but a very real gulf, ever-widening. His touch had become horrible, grating on every nerve. She could have plunged into the sea to be clean of him had not Isabel, sensing her distress, barked savagely at Derek, tearing the hem of his trousers, so that Teresa – who had been savage herself for a moment – had to pull the dog off and laugh hysterically at the anticlimax.

"Oh, Derek," she said, "she's defending my honour. Do laugh with me. It's the only way we can be friends again. Nothing matters except laughter." God's silver lining to despair – she had called it once. But she must revise her values. Now, silver was of little worth and laughter a more precious metal, to be prized above rubies.

But Derek was too angry to laugh, his pride too damaged. He strode away over the grass, passing by the bent tree that had not fallen, and by windblown bushes that made rooms under their branches, leaving her still laughing, at Isabel and at him. Which laughter turned easily into tears, so that with one arm round the dog she lay there sobbing on the turf and hoping against hope that Derek, not the Derek of fact, but of her imagination, would return. But when she lifted her head there was nothing but the ocean in front of her, and tumbling dangerous waves which might well smash to pieces a body thrown to them by mischance. And above the waves there was the blowhole, spewing spray for the winds to scatter, spray that was like the useless empty words a man had not understood.

XXVII

Derek wasted no time in crying. There was a snake sunning itself in the grass and, although it was harmless, he killed it with satisfaction; for no proper man, he had often said, could see a snake and fail to destroy it. So already a serpent and a caterpillar had died for their quarrel. On his way up to Neva Ford he met Harvey the overseer.

"I saw a stray cattle on the West End," he said. "You had better impound it."

Harvey said: "I think it is Robert Nolette's cattle. That same that keeping his boat on the beach."

"Well, in future he won't keep his cattle in my lime-fields. And if conditions don't change he won't keep his boat on the beach either."

Harvey looked thoughtfully after his master. The boss was in a passion, and how could a man tell whether the cause was the loss of coconuts or of Miss Craddock. The affairs of their so-called superiors, bewilderingly innocuous as these appear to be, are not hidden from the peasant people; but there is no censure in their attitude, only a mild astonishment that white people should talk so much and do so little.

Harvey found the stray cattle and impounded it. That is why, two days later, Tommy was handed a note from Robert Nolette. "Dear Sire," he read, "I am now asking you to be kind enow to help me in this mater, even there is a pig I will sell to back you. Neva estate has pound my cow and I don't have are penny to take it, so I am asking you kindly to lend me four shillings until I sell the pig. I will back you the money. I am yours, Robert Nolette."

"What's Morell been up to now?" Tommy said, throwing the

paper over to Teresa. He knew that they had quarrelled; guessed rather than knew the details, for she had told him nothing. He was sorry for his sister and had sympathy to spare for the man, but he couldn't perpetually avoid mentioning him, behaving with a *figure de circonstance* as though there were a death in the house.

Teresa read through the letter and remembered the stray beast in the lime-field. Was this trouble of Robert's due directly to her? Had Derek vented his disappointment on a cow? How curiously, she thought, are people's lives linked, that her own sexual inhibitions should affect the son of an old witch woman who had died with her name on her lips. Her tears of two days ago had been long since dried. She, too, was angry now, but coldly angry, and her sense of shame had shifted its direction. She regretted, not having broken her promise, but ever having given it. How easily is an idol shattered. How frail had been her love that it should have died at a blow. Yet a dull ache in her heart, a sadness for what had happened, warned her that it might rise again.

"What's Morell been up to?" Tommy had asked. And she answered: "Obviously 'pounding cows. I should have thought that there was grass and to spare on Neva, but he's within his rights."

"What shall I do? Lend Robert the money?"

"I don't care what you do, except buy the pig."

"Robert is a good man," Henry said. "You will see your money. But there is little pasturage near Ville Rousse save on Mr. Morell's land." Henry had been noisily drunk the night before, making excuse that all the men who had ever slept with his daughters had been in the village together and had paid rum for him. Henry had only two daughters, but he had had a great many drinks. Now, he was stern and a little pontifical, suffering a recovery.

"It will be nice for Derek to get the money," Teresa said over the teacups. "The four shillings will be paid to him. And a shilling a day extra for every day that he isn't paid. 'Pounding cows is a profitable business."

"Behold the female of the species," Tommy thought, "deadly already." And took a mouthful of cake which he straightway spat out again. "Christ," he said, "what has the woman put into it?"

Teresa took a careful nibble and echoed Tommy's sentiments.

"She did tell me," she said, "that the baking powder had run away with her, but I never supposed it had run as far as that. Oh, Tommy" – and the sorrow of all womanhood was in her eyes – "don't tell me that the end has come, and that I must make cake myself."

"Never, darling," he cried gallantly. "I will die first, as I almost certainly should after. You know, Teresa, what that woman Susannah needs is a pride of elders at her heels."

"A what?"

"A pride, darling. You have them of lions, why not of elders? The etymological sequence is sound. Elders *are* proud. I feel that Susannah requires stimulation. As she is she gives me the creeps."

"The creeps are better than a tummy-ache. But, Tommy, don't qualify as an elder."

"Good God, no. Fancy chasing that girl to the bathroom."

"I suppose we'll get used to her in time," she said doubtfully, "but I'm beginning to dream of good food like I did at school."

She had dreamt not of food, but of spray blown from the blow-hole, spray that had crystallized into hard words. Tommy talked on for the sake of talking, and his words were not as hailstones, but soft and comforting in their irrelevance to her trouble.

"Do you remember," he said, "that pub in Saulieu where they treated us like geese bred to provide *fois gras*, stuffing us till our eyes bulged? There was a *pâté* of duck; mushrooms in flaky pastry; a cake smothered in whipped cream and strawberries."

"There was a lot else. And I remember that the owner of one self-respecting Anglo-Saxon tummy reeled into the courtyard vowed to a perpetual diet of roast mutton and mineral water."

"Which vow I have not kept. But I could do with just one of those dishes now," he said wistfully. "Just one."

Teresa said: "It would be fun to be on French roads again." The tropics had turned sour on her in the last two days. Derek had given her life the flavour of stale cheese, and she was glad to take the taste out of her mouth by reconstructing an existence in which he had no part. Lewis had died in Paris, and the city was anathema, but there was still France. There were still the Landes, where cork trees lined the roads like soldiers holding back a crowd; Auvergne, where she had trampled daffodils and wild narcissi to swim in a river under cherry trees. There was still Provence with its Sleeping Beauty atmosphere, its olives and cypresses, waiting for a magic kiss to bring to life the lords and ladies, the minstrels and the knights who once thronged the narrow streets of Beaucaire and Tarascon.

"There was a hotel at Tain," Tommy said, "where they did *a crême de volaille* – "

"You greedy hog," she laughed. "I was lost in 'Memoirs of my Dead Life'. Now, you've broken the spell. Yesterday I found Susannah cleaning the veranda floor with a piece of fish skin. It gave a good polish, but after all fish is fish, so I told her to use a scrubbing brush. Today she has revenged herself by having a sore finger. She says the brush scratched it." Susannah was the type of servant who always got the better of you.

"Tilly used to scrub floors with sour oranges," Tommy sighed. "And carried up black sand from the coast to scour pots and pans with."

"Tilly was a nereid, darling. She even ate seaweed."

"Norah does that, made into jelly, and she's no nymph."

It was good to be with Tommy, forgetting that silly scene on the cliff, getting back to normal again after her attack of love fever. A lassitude remained, but from the beginning she had had no illusions about heartaches, knowing that they must follow upon indulgence as inevitably as liver attacks. But this time – morally speaking – she had indulged herself so little, her pain on that score being no more deserved than would be indigestion after one taste of Susannah's cake. In future, she decided, she would cling only to Isabel, who asked nothing and gave all. A lizard on the veranda rail was going through the process of sloughing its skin. A white wrapping, like clouded cellophane, seemed to be holding it motionless, and by the look in its eyes it suffered. Some must suffer from a change of mind, she thought, and some from a change of skin; and in no time at all both agonies would be forgotten, ephemeral as red dragonflies lighting on honeysuckle flowers. Soon the lizard would dart up a tree again, and she would have added another memory to her dead life.

"A woman to see you," Norah announced. "She not telling me her name."

Long ago Tommy and Teresa had formulated a code of behaviour. "We have leisure and a little money," they said, "and these force upon us a certain responsibility." So when people called they saw them, and this was no light burden. They were importuned at all hours; had to give patient consideration to trivial problems. Tommy was lawyer, moneylender, doctor; telephoned to hospitals and police stations; dispensed as required quinine and iodine and Epsom Salts. "Please, Sir, a grub sickens my stomach. I beg you a draught to cure him." "Miss T'resa, my wife will be confined and my children make their first communion. I beg you a little something for their clothes." Much of the borrowed money was repaid; sometimes it had to be worked off, necessitating a figurative digging of ditches to be filled up again. Sometimes there were bad debts and sometimes free gifts. Often the people brought them presents; an egg or a cucumber, or the heart of a palm.

The woman was a stranger, wanting to start an infant school in the village. A certificated teacher, she had had to give up working in Capesterre in order to be near her mother who was bedridden. Her papers referred to her as Mrs. Pollit. "Where is your husband?" Teresa asked, "is he working?"

"He and I not agreeing," she said. "He give me nothing."

Teresa was enthusiastic about the idea. Some of the children who lived up the valley had to walk five miles to school in Grande Anse. Often she passed them on the road bunched like a flock of sheep and carrying their lunches in tins that had been purloined from the Ça Ira rubbish bin. It was surprising the things that one recognized in the neighbourhood; discarded clothing, broken crockery, magazine advertisements prized for interior decoration.

"Mr. Bernard at the rum shop have promised a piece of land to put the school," Mrs. Pollit told her. And Teresa volunteered that if the matter could be arranged she would contribute building materials. "I'll speak to Mr. Craddock and the magistrate," she said, "and we'll see what can be done." But nothing ever was done. It happens like that in St. Celia.

The woman went away down the hill, and as Teresa watched her diminishing figure zig-zagging over the rough road between stunted sandbox trees and logwood, she noticed with pleasure how the evenings had lengthened. Here, where the twenty-four hours were almost impartially divided between light and darkness, an extra sixty minutes of twilight – in winter they lit the lamps at five-thirty, and in summer an hour later – were regarded as treasure trove and prized as the loveliest part of the whole day. That night Teresa went down into the valley and came to the banks of the river that was running clearly now, and unstained. Rocks, which for a long time no flood had covered, were bleached grey; and she could see mullet swimming and immature crayfish, and those dark green snails that the people use to make soup. "They cause milk to flow in the breasts of women," Henry said once, being full of such wisdom. At that hour night had already fallen among the cocoa trees. The sea might still hold the dying sun on its bosom, but here there were only shadows and black branches and ghosts walking. No one but Teresa would go near this place after dark, for Ma Nolette's spirit had been seen there, sitting by the path side and making the cows run dry.

Beyond the cocoa trees there was watercress growing in a gravelly side stream, and she groped for it under huge dasheen leaves whose purple stalks rose straight out of the water. The river itself, running swiftly in these reaches, had made of itself a series of pools that were like individual hip baths; and when Tommy and Teresa bathed in them, each under their own waterfall, they thought of the Great God Nquong in his bath in the salt pans; and of the other two gods in their baths, dwindling to the edge of the picture. And she was glad that it would soon be the mango season, when they brought down basketfuls and ate them there in their baths, tossing for the upper pool and the right to float refuse down the other's fall. Mr. Golightly's mare, she remembered irrelevantly as she climbed the hill again with the watercress in her hands, ate mango stones. At the right time of year the roads were littered with them, and she picked them up and scrunched them as she walked.

XXVIII

Robert Nolette paid in Tommy's four shillings, and got his cow out of 'pound. He had been away in his boat for three days, and the cattle had broken its rope and strayed almost on to the beach. If he sold his pig well he would buy a chain as well as repay Mr. Craddock, but meanwhile he twisted a new rope and led his cow back to her pasturage. Robert had a garden on Crown land, and there was a patch of good grass beside it; but this was a long way up the valley, and he had meant to ask Mr. Morell if he might tether his cow on Neva, paying a shilling a month in rent. He had put off doing so, and now it was too late, so that in his heart there was a sense of grievance against Derek, who might have given him warning instead of penalizing him for what was not his fault. Now, he was too proud to ask for pasturage, even though he paid for it.

His way led through a lime-field that Derek had not yet cleaned. The trees were old and withered, hung with grey beards and trimmed by ferns and minute orchids. Teresa's orchids, holding the dusk in their petals, were gorgeous and flamboyant; but here there were humble members of the family, poor relations, so to speak, picked out in buff and red and green, too inconspicuous to be coveted, and yet none the less interesting. Fruit was yellowing on the lime trees because no one had troubled to pick it while it was green. Robert thought that perhaps Mr. Morell did not consider the trees worth saving, and would plant the field in bananas or grapefruit. Bananas were a paying crop nowadays, although sometimes the buyers were not fair to the peasants; and sometimes it seemed that there was a glut in Canada, and then the Association would be instructed to reject as many bunches as possible, so that a mere scratch on one fruit, such as a lizard might make, would be enough to disqualify a whole eight-hand bunch. And there was Panama disease that rotted the trees and turned their leaves yellow, spreading no one knew how; on men's feet, they said, or on their tools. These things were talked about of an evening, at Buffon's store.

An old canal ran through this lime-field, a stone aqueduct that had not been used for many years, and was damaged in places. The forest sees to it that if man does not care for his toys they are soon broken; and if someone was building a new house, or repairing an old one, he borrowed a stone or two upon which to rest his timbers. The canal was long, for the Neva River was sluggish in its lower reaches, and at one time swift-flowing water had been needed to turn wheels. Now, the roots of the mango trees made stagnant harbours in which mosquitoes bred; and flowers, smothering the treetops, cast their dead blossoms to rot on the surface of water too lazy to carry them to the sea.

Robert heard perdrix calling, and said to himself: "Now is not the season, but when the time comes I will take a bird to Mr. Craddock to thank him for lending me the four shillings." But his heart was heavy when he remembered that he must sell his pig. Lent was a bad time for killing, and people would know that he was forced to sell, and would not offer him a good price. Even so, for it was a fat pig, he would receive more then four shillings, and Mr. Craddock would send to Capesterre for a chain. His was a strong cow, and nervous too, so that if she were disturbed she plunged and strained at her rope, weakening it. Sometimes Miss Craddock walked in these valleys, and her dog barked at the cattle, frightening them.

Robert Nolette paid his money and got his cow back. And if he grumbled a little, not only to himself, but among his friends at the rum shop, he harboured no thought of revenge. Things were hard for a poor man, and one must be patient. In the hereafter all men would be rich and of the same colour. But on the day after he recovered his cow, there was a young bull missing from Derek's own herd. It vanished as though a hand had been stretched forth from Heaven to catch it up into Elysian fields; or as though an octopus had put out tentacles and drawn it down into unknown depths. A cattle had been, and was not.

Harvey saw that there was a boat missing, and over the sand where it had lain palm branches had been drawn, as though to conceal footsteps, or to cover a beast's tracks. He looked hopelessly at the beach, finding it unreadable as a letter over which ink has been spilt. Inland, under the coconut palms, he found fresh dung, which proved nothing. For twenty-four hours he waited, hoping against hope that the beast had strayed. That evening Nicholas Nolette brought in Robert's boat with a catch of dolphin, and blew shells to summon the people. The fish were sliced with a cutlass on an upturned raft, and their blood ran down into the sand, while the silver of their scales shone in the sunset. If, on the way to cooking their fish, women picked up a nut to use with it, no one, least of all Harvey, could blame them. But the loss of a cattle was a serious matter, and he knew that next morning it must be reported. He had been slow about doing so, for he feared that Derek would make trouble.

And trouble was made. "This is the end," Derek said. "I have no more patience. I shall close the beach." So had Janet spoken to Teresa once, and she had not believed it.

Harvey said: "How do you mean, Sir, close the beach?"

"I own the foreshore. From now on nobody may keep a boat or a raft on my land."

Harvey had not envisaged anything as drastic as this. Ever since he could remember, and his father before him, boats had lain on the Neva Beach. It was the people's right. "But Mr. Morell," he said, "there is no other beach. How shall the men bring in their fish?"

"That is not my business," Derek answered. "By closing the beach I shall at least insure that my property is not removed by boat."

"But without fish, Sir, the people cannot live."

"You exaggerate, Harvey. Fish can be caught off the rocks. What's the name of that river on the other side of Ville Rousse? There's room for a boat there."

"There is room, Sir, but when there is even a little storm rafts are mashed up. It is no place to keep a boat."

But Derek wouldn't be softened. "You must manage as best you can," he said. "I mean to insist on my rights and protect my property. You can give a fortnight's warning. I'll write out a notice and you must put it up in Buffon's store and wherever else you think fit. In future no man is to beach his boat on the sand, and no woman is to wash clothes in the river. If they do they will be summoned for trespass."

"But, Mr. Morell" – it was not easy to go on with those hard cold eyes compelling his acquiescence – "there is no place else for them to wash clothes. The Coriac River is dry, dry, dry; and from the Bourette the people of Ville Rousse get their water to drink. If washing is done in the river it will pollute it."

"I have given my orders, Harvey," Derek said. "If you don't care to carry them out, I shall doubtless find someone who will."

Harvey didn't believe this edict would stop thieving; thought rather that it would encourage it, for the inhabitants of Ville Rousse were a proud people, and Mr. Morell was punishing the innocent with the guilty. Many of the former, Harvey thought, would now be numbered among the latter. He couldn't see the pain that was lying behind the hardness in Derek's eyes. Had he seen it he would not have understood that a man's thwarted desire for a woman should be making him stubborn and cruel.

It was only half consciously that Derek tried to hurt Teresa by this hurting of others; by doing something she would dislike in the hope of assuaging his own hurt. Time gives a bird's-eye view of events, and Teresa was able in the end to see how a burst of ill-temper made him start this ball rolling, and having once started it, lose control of it; with his own stubbornness, and Janet, keeping on kicking it further and further down the hill. And from this same bird's-eye view events in their sequence could be seen as neat links in a chain, binding one person to another so that their lives were crossed like the sticks of a charm. Because a cook was burnt, a distant village was deprived of fish. Because a woman's passion died in the flames a man whose mother she had be-friended was unjustly persecuted. Robert Nolette knew nothing of the stolen cattle, but because he had a grievance, and because his boat had been missing, suspicion lodged in Derek's mind and obstinately remained there.

XXIX

After giving his order that the beach should be closed, Derek went home to tell Janet what he had done. He found her picking beans in the garden, liking the hot smell of earth rising out of the ground, and the feeling that all about her there were useful things growing. The beans were twined on stakes, whose little sharp branches had been insufficiently cut, so that she had to move warily lest she tear her hands and dress. A kingfisher skimmed down river with a noise like a child's rattle. Every morning at dawn he alighted on the same branch of a dead tree, a tree so covered in parasites that it appeared to be more alive than its fellows. Teresa had told them that this was a very rare kind of kingfisher. You hardly ever found its nest, and only one museum in the world had its eggs.

Derek carried Janet's basket back into the house. His hurt had made him feel warmly towards her, and he turned to her like a child coming to its mother to be kissed and made better. Only he couldn't tell her where the sore place was, thinking that she would not understand. And indeed he was right. Janet had guessed more than he knew, but she could not understand. She could only endure.

In the grass below the veranda, and even – unasked – among the vegetables, red amaryllis flowered in a profusion that Janet found disconcerting. These grew wild at Neva, spreading continuously, but Janet was suspicious of all beauty, and these exotic blossoms had a way of flaunting theirs that was almost indecent. There were some women like that.

"I'm glad," she said, when Derek told her what had happened. "It was about time." She saw this as a blow aimed at Teresa, and

192

triumphed in consequence. Janet was a good woman according to her lights, but her lights were fogged; her virtue being of that unaccommodating variety which demands an eye for an eye, or even an eye for a tooth. Coconuts had been stolen, and a cattle; it was only just that retribution should follow. And a loose woman, who had flaunted her naked beauty in that place, would understand that her influence was waning. Janet knew that Derek would have taken action sooner but for Teresa.

Lima beans take a long time to shell. When she had finished them she took knives and forks from the kitchen table, and with scraps of newspaper wiped off the grease before putting them in the sink. A lizard sat on a window ledge, puffing out its yellow throat. A chicken hawk circled over the bois blanc tree in front of the house. Janet was full of thought, for she knew that Derek's decision was important and might have serious consequences; and although she welcomed it her mind was troubled. She did not really believe that she had second sight, but sometimes her instinctive fear of some person or action was so strong that it was almost as though the future rumbled a warning. So had it been when she had first seen Teresa, and, hating her for no reason, or for a reason hidden in the future, had sensed that she was as menacing to her as were the dark trees of the forest. Now, in the moment of her apparent triumph, she hated Teresa again; and the kitchen was filled with her presence as sometimes it was when Derek had been at Ça Ira and come home with her scent hanging about him, clouding him as though in a foetid miasma. With a shudder she turned to her newspaper, studying each piece of it before running it up the knife blade between her fingers. It was an old paper; its news, in the light of after knowledge, stale and unprofitable as yesterday's pudding. But she lingered over each fragment for the sake of the picture that it made; or because of the dread that it shut out.

Derek had taken a cutlass and had gone into the orange field. A tête-chien snake was curled round a ripe fruit, waiting motionless for pecking birds that it might crush them with its body. Derek, crushed in spirit, hoped that physical effort might bring peace to a man's soul. But the smell of the blossom, mixed with that of the lemon grass above the orchard, was so overpowering that it disturbed and sickened him. He found that he could settle to nothing; that his arm, like his mind, swung aimlessly to and fro. Three months ago Teresa had told him that she loved him, which knowledge had been exquisite as a jewel. Now, she had snatched herself from him, and his diamond was only iron pyrites, of no more value than the metal found by the St. Patrick's River about which the whole island was talking. Men had come even to him, hoping to sell stones for bread; and he likened himself to the Capesterre tradesman who had paid five pounds for a saucepanful and had been the mock of his fellows. Because he couldn't understand Teresa he had ceased to believe in her; thought she had played with him wantonly and then tired of her sport. But not believing did not prevent him from desiring. His body ached with its longing, and it was only for a moment that his orders to Harvey had soothed his mind. "Perhaps if you are patient," she had said, "my love will revive again." But Derek was wiser than she, knowing that love never flowers twice in the same place, and that it was of no use to be patient, because there was no hope for desire to feed on. He threw down his cutlass and went out of the orange field. Crossing the river by the ford he took his unhappiness to the forest, the forest that long ago Janet had likened to Teresa.

XXX

On the day that Norah's baby was christened Mr. Biggar, the magistrate, came to tea. The diamond debacle had already broken on Capesterre, and Tommy told about those that Nicholas had brought him. "I thought there was a fifty-fifty chance," he said, "so I sent a sample of the clay to an expert in England."

"Make it seventy-five-twenty-five," Teresa muttered. "You believed in those diamonds." But the magistrate was not listening. His ears were pricked and his paw lifted, like a pointing dog's. "How did you send the sample?" he asked Tommy.

"By post, of course, in a cigarette tin."

Mr. Biggar unpricked his ears and put his paw down. "Mr. Craddock," he said, "forgive me for saying so, but that was an improper thing to do. The clay was from Crown land. Do you tell me seriously that you exported a portion of His Majesty's property by the ordinary mail? Surely His Honour should have been consulted first."

Teresa hooted with laughter, but Tommy was very angry. "Damn it all," he said, "it went by His Majesty's mails." The official attitude, breaking like a rash over this dug-out, made his blood boil to fever point.

Teresa, scenting danger, hastily changed the subject. Mr. Biggar was more than a magistrate, he was almost the King's representative. She told him about Mrs. Pollit, and put forth an appeal for the infants' school.

"It's very charming and generous of you, Miss Craddock," he said, "but I hardly think that the Government will be prepared to subsidize a private scheme."

"But surely, Mr. Biggar, the Government is like God. God

helps those who help themselves. If Bernard the publican gives the land, and we sinners provide the building, I should have thought money might be found to supplement the woman's salary. The children's parents will contribute something."

"Unlike God," said Mr. Biggar with a flash of wit, "the Government is hard up."

She knew how true that was. There was never enough money for roads, nor for medical services, nor for education. Only – she thought rather bitterly – for the salaries and pensions of white officials; which opinion she refrained from making audible to the specimen sitting beside her.

"If you like," Mr. Biggar said, "I will make a memorandum of the proposition and forward it to His Honour."

"Oh, don't bother," she answered. "My brother will be seeing the Ad. next week." Definitely, knees or no knees, she did not like Mr. Biggar. But Derek liked him, and Janet. He always went to Neva when there was a court at Ville Rousse. It is a queer thing about social contacts, how seldom you like your friends' friends. Which aphorism did not apply in this case because Janet was never her friend, nor, for the matter of that, Derek either, who had wished only to be her lover.

The school idea came to nothing, although the sequel was funny. The Government would give no assistance, and the Craddocks couldn't take sole responsibility. It was like that in St. Celia. People got excited about something, and ran round importantly in small circles. Then nothing happened, and the dust settled again.

The sequel came three weeks later, but the telling of it belongs here; a fragment of a torn kite hanging on to the wires of memory, a portion of God's silver lining gleaming through dark clouds. Mrs. Pollit sank into oblivion, but her husband played his tiny part in the subsequent scheme of things. One day Tommy and Teresa wandered into a valley that was new to them, for St. Celia is so crumpled and compressed that one can never know all its creases, and sitting by a stream to eat chocolate, were joined by a stranger who volunteered somewhat surlily that this was his land. "And how far does the trace go?" they asked, to which he replied not very helpfully: "You can go as far as you can get."

Isabel had chased a sow that day and scattered her litter. There was always a risk in a strange valley that you might stumble on a mountain-dew still, or some other thing that was better not seen. So, for these two reasons, they were very forthcoming to this person on whose property they had inadvertently trespassed, and Tommy pulled an Eno's bottle of rum out of his pocket and offered him a drink.

"I am that same Pollit," the man said, "whose wife asked to make a school in the village."

They agreed afterwards that they had behaved with perfect foolishness, but they wanted to placate Pollit. Tommy did not even know that the woman had said: "He and I not agreeing." So they blethered words at him, dribbling them – so Teresa described it later – out of fawning mouths. "We were so sorry." "We did all we could." "We think the Government's policy is wrong." All that sort of thing, while the man listened without expression, smoking a cigarette that he had accepted from Teresa's case.

When they had stopped talking, having nothing more to say and being run down like unwound gramophones, Pollit remarked gravely: "My wife not a good woman. She keeping the corporal," which, being interpreted, meant that she was the corporal's mistress.

It was one of those moments. With immense presence of mind Teresa decided that this was Isabel's cue. She had been holding the dog by the collar, Isabel having a strong colour prejudice and disapproving of this impromptu party, but now she loosed her to create a diversion; because there is, after all, no recognized answer to a man's statement that his wife is keeping the corporal, although Teresa wondered afterwards whether his eyes had not twinkled at their embarrassment. Later, he sent down a present of cush-cush, that root that turns out mauve mashed potatoes; and was their very good ally in the trouble that came upon them. But "she keeping the corporal" became part of the family vocabulary. "It sounds so expensive," Teresa said, remembering at the same time that neat patch of lawn with the corporal's horse on it, and the detective stories lying – worm-eaten – on shelves.

When Mr. Biggar had gone, Teresa asked Norah, who was

collecting empty glasses, how Albert was. She hadn't seen him for two days. Norah said: "He not back yet."

"Not back? Where from?"

"Today he christened."

She was furious with herself for having forgotten. "But Norah," she cried, "I'm so sorry. Why ever didn't you tell me? You could easily have gone."

"No, Miss, I not go."

"It was dreadful of me. You should have said something. We could easily have got tea for ourselves."

"No, Miss T'resa, I not going. The mother never go to the christening except it be so far to the church that she must feed her child. Ma Bernard take Albert. She standing for him. It not fitting that I should go."

Here was an altogether new notion. Teresa would have hated to have her child wrested from her and handed over to the church in her absence. But she had noticed that Norah never looked well nowadays, was coughing a great deal.

"Yes, Miss," the girl said, "I getting fever."

"Have you seen the doctor?"

"He give me injects. They not cure me. Soon I ask you to let me go to Capesterre for nine days. There I shall drink a tea and shut myself into my own room. So will my fever be cured."

Was Albert to endure incarceration also, Teresa wondered. And sighed at the prospect of coping with Susannah alone.

Meanwhile, Rosalie's case came on against Norah. Tommy and Teresa had reasoned with, implored, even threatened both girls in their efforts to get the matter settled out of court. But it seemed they would have lost face by so doing. Invoking the law was a national pastime, and the farce had to be played out to a finish, with the whole village as audience. It didn't matter any more whether the piece of material had been Rosalie's; whether Tilly had drawn the threads and begun to embroider it. As an exhibit it had been lost sight of. But Rosalie had paid two shillings to the doctor that he might see her bruises; and not only blows but rude words had passed between them, and things had been said that Henry could not pronounce in Teresa's presence.

In the magistrate's court her presence was less respected. It appeared that Rosalie had screamed at Norah: "You have a man for the price of fish." And Norah had retorted: "You, you have a man for dasheen."

"And what," said Mr. Biggar, laboriously taking down the evidence, "is dasheen?" while the crowd outside giggled and nudged each other, there being no room inside the court for more than the magistrate and his clerk, the contending parties, one witness and a policeman.

"Here is a very Darling come to judgment," Tommy whispered; but Teresa wondered how a man could dispense justice among a people and not even know that dasheen was their most common food, a starchy root of the arum lily family that grows wherever men make gardens, which is everywhere. But the *philosophe*, meaning busybody, showed wisdom in assessing the case at its face value and dismissing it; making Rosalie pay three shillings costs and Norah the doctor's bill of a florin. This was a virtual triumph for Norah, inasmuch as her expenses were less, but a great waste of everyone's time.

"There'll be Français' case next, against Bernard the publican," Tommy said. And Teresa groaned. The carpenter had come to Ça Ira one morning looking like an Arab with his head bound in a bath towel, and carrying pieces of glass and a broken bottle with which he said Bernard had mashed him, having waylaid him in his garden. "And for the reason," Français said, "that I complain that he have my wife."

It transpired that as publican and dispenser of credit Mr. Bernard took many wives. And Teresa remembered Tilly, with a bucket on her head, teasing Français like a puppy, and saying: "I do as your wife does," which had so angered the cuckolded husband that he had spattered paint on to Tilly's dress. "But Français was always a difficult man," Henry said. "He go once to build me a house and he leave it in the middle, saying he cannot see what I want with so large a house." And he drew breath to add: "You will please, Sir, to give me a remedy."

"A remedy for what?" Tommy asked.

"For nothing, Sir. Just a remedy." And left it at that.

XXXI

Before Français' case came on there was Robert Nolette's, wherein the *philosophe*, whose legal dinners had been so long since digested, showed less wisdom, lighting with Derek's help a fuse that flickered and spluttered for many weeks, making a noise that echoed from one valley to another, and the reek of which was wafted to other islands. Derek had posted a notice outside Buffon's store, and Harvey had gone among the people telling them, that henceforth no one might keep a boat or a raft on Neva Beach, nor wash clothes in the river. But rain blurred the notice, which anyway few people could read; and nobody quite believed what Harvey told them, nor thought that it applied to them. For twenty years Robert had beached his boat on Neva and his father before him. It was not reasonable that anyone should prevent him. He had stolen nothing, harmed no one. His boat stayed where it had always been.

When the fortnight was finished, Derek himself watched by the bay side. He was alone with the sand and the sea and his own bitter thoughts; but he saw on a raft a basketful of sprats, such as are caught from the shore with a cast-net, and thought to himself that if he took these the owner would come to claim the basket and thus be identified. Boats were licensed, but not rafts. His first impulse was to spill the fish into the sand, but on second thoughts he decided that he had a right to them and that they would eat well. He put them in the car among the white cedar blossoms that had drifted into it, as once, long ago, they had drifted into Teresa's.

It so happened that on that day only the Nolettes were using their boat. The sea was high and they caught no more than would feed themselves, and had trouble in landing. For though Neva was the only safe beach on all that rocky coast, even there the surf ran high, and a man took his life in his hands when he went out on a rough day. They were two tired men who pulled the boat to a safe resting-place under an almond tree. Derek recognized Robert. Once he had given him a razor blade, that same blade with which he had cut the swollen limb of his sister Rosalie, and had brought her relief from her pain. Nicholas he knew only by hearsay as the reputed father of Norah's baby and the finder of diamonds. He told Robert that he would summons him for trespass; and he took the numbered licence plate off the boat and put it in his pocket.

All day Robert and Nicholas had fought with the hard sea and had conquered. The ocean had numbed their faculties, beaten the breath out of them, left them unfit to battle with a hard man. Robert was bewildered to the point of hardly understanding what Derek meant; but Nicholas was younger and more acute; had heard more talk, had seen the notice. "My brother paid sixteen shillings for his licence," he cried angrily. "You have no right to take it."

Derek said: "You have no right to bring a boat on to this beach. I gave you warning."

"But always I have kept my boat here," Robert said. "Where else should I keep it?" He looked out at the grey sea lashed with white; at the storm clouds massed in the south-east; and knew that it was no weather to take a boat elsewhere, and for sailing it without a licence plate he might be arrested. There was an anchorage three hundred yards out, inside a reef; but tonight surf was crashing over the coral, making a thin sinister line of foam. A boat left there now would be mashed up by morning.

Robert had cut his boat in the forest, high up on a ridge of Morne Collat. With laughter and with singing, he and his friends had carried it to the seashore. Every year he paid a shilling to the Government for each foot of its length. He loved his boat and would never let it be mashed. "Tomorrow I will remove the vessel," he said with dignity, "but tonight it is not possible." Even tomorrow it would not be easy to sail round the northern capes into the Caribbean, but he would try.

"You are only aggravating your offence," Derek said crossly. But he knew well enough that to force the men to sea now might be driving them to their deaths. "Whose rafts are these?" he said. "It will help you to tell me."

They had never heard of King's Evidence, but they wouldn't turn it. "We not knowing," they lied stubbornly. And Derek, irritated, aware that he was in the wrong, said: "So much the worse for you." And turned to go back through the coconut palms to the place where he had left his car.

He never knew how nearly Nicholas struck him and took back the plate from him by force. Robert sensed his brother's feelings, and put out a restraining hand; but although he prevented an assault he could not stop the younger man's tongue, and Nicholas called out: "You have done an ill thing, Mr. Morell, and will suffer for it." Derek paid no attention, but told the magistrate next day that he had been threatened, and that, although he had no proof, he was sure that these were the men who had stolen his cattle.

Robert and Nicholas went with heavy hearts to warn other owners of boats and rafts, passing on their way through that part of Neva which Derek had cleared to plant cane. Already there were green fields billowing where gardens had been, and scrubby flowering shrubs, and white orchids. Now, the people must go far up the valleys to grow provisions, and the compensation money had been long since spent. But the clearing of the land had given work in the village. There had been a little cash circulating, and no grumbling. Mr. Morell had a right to grow what he pleased. Now, however, the Nolettes brought ill news, which spread and was at last acted on. One man anchored his boat at sea, and lost it; one raft capsized, and its owner came ashore with broken fingers; but no one claimed the basket with fish in it that Derek had taken.

At the mouth of the Bourette River there was room for a few craft, but only a few, and landing was so dangerous that men dragged their boats into the shelter of bushes – low windswept bushes that had flowers on them like pale oleanders – and there left them; not fishing any more, although it was their means of livelihood and they had paid money for their licences. Some made new cast-nets; but it seemed that not even on foot might they use Neva Beach; for to throw a net a man must stand waist high in water with his loins naked; and Mrs. Morell had been affronted by this indecency, and in court Derek cited it as a grievance. Long ago he and Teresa together had watched a naked man fishing, but then he had said nothing. The man had been an essential part of the picture, in tune with the scene's beauty, and no offence. So boys were driven to throwing lines into the sea from rocks, baiting their hooks with crabs that tiny fishes nibbled away before an edible one could be brought even to the point of temptation. Women collected whelks and another flat kind of shellfish; and when Mark Ludovic hooked a cong so large that he could not kill it, but was on the other hand nearly killed himself by the lashing of the creature's eel-like body, only landing it at all by screaming for help, then there was a feast day in the village; for the lack of fresh fish was felt sorely, and there was much ill-temper and discontent; some of it directed against the thieves who had stolen Morell's cattle; and some of it against Derek himself, who had provoked thieving; and some against his wife, who was an unsmiling woman, paying only three farthings for eggs when the known price was a penny. So that the village of Ville Rousse was like a seething cauldron whose contents are out of harmony with each other, making the resultant stew indigestible and a little dangerous.

On the evening of the day after Derek had spoken to Robert and Nicholas there was no craft of any kind on Neva Beach, and no women washed clothes in the river. On all that long expanse of sand there was no sign of life save for the purple and red crabs scuttling under the almond trees, and the black frigate birds hovering over the stormy water. For a long time Tommy and Teresa had not bathed there, nor taken guavas from the garden of the ruined house. Cowries and fan shells and pink-lined clams lay unbroken for hissing foam to play with, and the ripening almonds fell to crabs and ants. Derek had got what he wanted, and his beach was empty. But like all such victories it was sour tasting; bitter as aloes growing on the cliff-side; salt as the sea foam that melted at his feet.

XXXII

Robert and Nicholas Nolette sailed their boat round the coast to
Ça Ira village. It was a long and dangerous journey in such
weather, although the wind was with them through the channel.
The north end of St. Celia is a sheer-cut cliff without break in it;
a blank wall of rock like the sightless face of some gorgoned
monster, at the foot of which lie sharp pointed pinnacles that
might be its fallen teeth. When they had rounded Cape Benedict,
and come into the peace of the Caribbean, they found there was
no wind at all. Out of a dozen valleys mist rose like steam, and a
woolly cap lay on the head of Morne Collat and woolly wreaths
about its middle. For the last few miles they had to lower sail and
row. Robert beached his boat on the shingle, throwing out ballast
stones and scattering little pigs rooting for filth as many months
since he had scattered them when his mother lay dying and
Rosalie had been suffering from a sore finger. He remembered
that night as he walked through the village to the old house with
the stone doorstep where Rosalie now lived with a man who had
chosen her to be his "keeper". Fire blazed from under the coal
pots, and in the smooth lower reaches of the river water ran clear.
Only tonight there was no moon, and the darkness of the sky
reflected the darkness of his own heart.

Robert would have come to Tommy in his trouble, but the
others dissuaded him. Rosalie was disgruntled because she thought
that Teresa had sided with Norah against her; and Nicholas felt
foolish over his diamonds and a little uncomfortable about
Albert. That is why Tommy, who could have been so helpful,
who would have had a lawyer to defend the men, who might have
squashed the whole business at its inception, knew nothing about

it until it was over. People came to him continually about things that did not matter; involved him in trivial arguments, consulted him in petty quarrels that had not even the saving grace of being funny. Now, on a vital matter, they had not liked to disturb the master; thought, perhaps, that in a quarrel between black men and a white he would not be on their side.

Robert and Nicholas were summoned for trespass and were fined three pounds each; a sum so fantastic that the people gasped like breathless fish, for surely no one in the world had so much money, or at least no one in the island. The fuse that the white men had lit flickered and spluttered, and the seething cauldron of discontent bubbled over. Strange things were muttered, and at last said out loud. That the magistrate, for instance, was unaccustomed to his work, and that Mr. Morell had influenced him. This no one could dispute, because when it was asserted in court that Nicholas had said: "You will suffer for it," Mr. Biggar had turned to the complainant and had said: "Do you take this seriously?" And on Derek having answered: "I do," the magistrate fined Nicholas the same sum as his brother; although the boat had been licensed in Robert's name, and so the trespass was his. But the licence plate was returned, which should never have been taken.

Now, Robert had no choice but to go to Ça Ira, although he was ashamed to ask for more money, having so recently borrowed four shillings and not repaid it. And on the same day other boat-owners came; and people of importance from the Ville Rousse side of the island; Mr. Buffon the storekeeper, and Pollit, whose wife kept the corporal. Some came by road and some over the mountains by the Souffrière valley, from which the wind blew the smell of sulphur as though to symbolize the stink that was already spreading over the whole island. They came to Tommy as their member of Council, swarming about him like gnats, and suggesting first this thing and then that; until at last he drafted a form of petition to himself, requesting that he ask the Government to investigate the matter of the Neva Beach foreshore rights; and he told the people that if they felt strongly about this business as many as possible must sign it. Meanwhile he would consult Mr. Golightly and see Mr. Biggar. For it did not seem to him just, either in equity or in law, that a man should be able to close a harbour to a village that had used it for generations; to reserve a mile-long strip of sand to himself and his crabs, thereby depriving of their means of subsistence persons who had already paid money for their boat licences. Teresa agreed with him that such things were not just in equity, but feared that the law was more subtle than justice. You never knew where it would nip you; nor where it would be on your side.

Tommy lent Robert and Nicholas part of their fine, and arranged with Mr. Biggar that the payment of the rest might be postponed. The magistrate was already a trifle scared by what he had done; was hiccupping mentally, as after an undigested dinner; realizing that Morell had made outrageous use of him. Even in Capesterre there was comment about those preposterous fines. Meanwhile, the people of Ville Rousse sent over for more paper on which to put their signatures, for the number of these was very great. And the petition was ultimately presented with over three hundred names on it, some illiterately scrawled, and some with a blotted cross against them – "Eleanora Samuel, her mark". So many, in fact, were the Josephs and the Benjamins and the Samuels that one might have suspected a Jewish community had one not known the nomenclature to be religious. Most people in St. Celia have two names, the second a haphazard one for everyday use, a nickname; the reason being that the devil, who knows only their baptismal names, will be prevented from recognizing and catching them. But on Sundays, when the devil does not function, they use their own names again. And their surnames are called titles.

First among the signatures was the parish priest's. And before long Doctor Crewe's had been added to the list, he having volunteered his name as health officer to the district, knowing that the people were already undernourished, and would suffer from the loss of fish and coconuts. He asked Tommy to bring over the petition, and came out of the hospital to meet him, lanky and wild-eyed; signed it; and stayed for a long time talking theosophy till he pulled himself together suddenly and said: "Excuse me, but I'm in the middle of an operation." And vanished to take up his knife or his scalpel again where he had dropped it, leaving Tommy wondering whether the signature of a madman might not weaken his cause.

"What am I to do?" he asked Mr. Golightly the lawyer, whose office, shaded by breadfruit trees, looked out upon the blue waters of King Charles' Bay. "This man Morell has been my friend." He couldn't add: "And my sister's lover," although he wondered whether Golightly hadn't suspected that. One's business is always known in St. Celia by some subtle underground method of communication. And he remembered that Mr. Golightly had been on the launch when Derek and Teresa had first met, they two seemingly alone together in a little circle of their own intimacy, with a strange stillness lying on land and sea, and a flying fish whispering. That was only a few months ago, yet how much had happened. Some years spun round emptily, without landmarks; and these were the best, on the principle of – happy is the country that has no history. Now, there was this new trouble spluttering and crackling all round them, a trouble that might make history.

"You have no choice," Mr. Golightly said. "Your duty to your constituents compels you, irrespective of private feelings, to lay this petition before the Council. You have no choice at all."

Tommy had known that all the time. There had never been real doubt in his mind as to what he should do.

XXXIII

Teresa was very unhappy about this thing, although she knew also that Tommy had no choice. She was sitting in the garden on the morning that Robert came, thinking of the Ville Rousse people as she stitched a piece of a torn Madras into her patchwork. Only a year ago they had attended Father Dolet's blessing of the boats on St. Peter's day. A little chapel had been made at Neva of sticks and palm branches lined with coloured bedspreads and gaudy handkerchiefs. After Mass – the people kneeling on the flat waste ground beyond the almond trees, while dogs quarrelled and raced foolishly among their upturned feet – a procession had sung its way on to the beach where a half dozen boats were drawn up with sails spread; at every masthead a bunch of flowers, flowers decorating thwarts and rowlocks. The priest had sprinkled holy water, blessing and commending each boat to St. Peter; after which they had sailed gaily from under the shadow of the coconut palms; gallivanted out to sea, and, having found the passage in the reef, quickly returned again; for this was no working day, and the boats were but frisking on the ocean as colts might kick up their heels in a field. All afternoon and all evening the beat of drums had sounded on the seashore; while the wind that blew through the empty chapel, tearing its bedspreads and Madrasses, carried to the cliff tops, and out to sea, strange primitive rhythms to which the feet of the dancing men stamped in the sand. Now, Tommy came to tell her what Derek had done, and she knew that this year there would be no boats to bless; and that no one would dance.

It was inevitable that she should blame herself, and she suffered bitterly on two counts; first, on behalf of the people for whose trouble she felt herself to be directly responsible; and secondly, on behalf of herself, that she should have loved – and still ache over – a man who could do so foul a thing; that her judgment should have been so false, the desire of her body so fogging her mind. How unfair life was to women, she thought, or how unfair they were to themselves. Tommy could sleep with Georgette and suffer no nerve storms nor spasms; do no one any harm whether he did sleep, or did not. Whereas she, merely by jibbing at her sin like a scared horse at a fence, had injured three hundred ill-fed and inoffensive people who now turned to her brother for help. These were not pretty thoughts to go to bed with, and her pillow knew tears. "Who's been digging up my nuts?" she quoted miserably to herself. And remembered that the book ended – "But no one ever answers."

No one ever would answer. "Who's been digging up my nuts?" was more than ever a rhetorical question, so many words spat out by the spray of a blowhole whose bubbles floated on air. Coconuts hardly counted any more. The matter now was between fresh fish and a stolen cattle; between the rights of a man to his own sand, and the rights of a people needing access to the sea. "Let's make a Polish corridor," Teresa suggested with sarcasm. "It's been so successful in Europe."

"That's roughly what will be done," Tommy said. "And here it may be successful. But it will take a long time to do."

That night there was a spider on the pantry wall carrying its young under its body in a flat case like an exaggerated *cachet faivre*. Three minutes later a cat was scrunching spider and bag. In the garage, infested with brown hopping crickets, lizards pounced on these, giving themselves the appearance of being whiskered, with insects' feelers protruding from one side of their mouths and legs from the other. When Tilly died someone wrote from England – "But I suppose grim things happen everywhere," as though they had hitherto supposed that St. Celia was immune from horror. Why, if one separated blades of grass one found grim things happening; or if one looked at pond water through a microscope. Yet one was brought up to believe, or one believed by instinct, that men were less cruel than insects or germs; and as one grew older, and horrible truths were made obvious everywhere, these were the harder to bear because of the cotton wool that was put upon one's eyes at birth. And the cotton wool stayed stuck a long time for one's personal acquaintances. Nations were wicked, and people in newspapers; but not till you met tooth and claw in your own friends was your sight really clear, and your faith broken.

These were her first reactions. Then hope rose in her again, and the instinct of her childhood. "I don't believe it," she said, confronted by those pathetic signatures, by those crosses marked against names a scribe had written. "There's been some mistake. Derek can't know what he's doing."

"I shall have to see him," Tommy said, "though I shan't relish the interview."

Then it seemed to Teresa that she should see him too, or even first. "Surely I can do something," she said. "I'll write and ask him to come here." There was hope in her heart on more than one score. Might not this business be a bridge to span a gulf? She had no right to think of cats and lizards until she had heard an explanation from his own mouth.

Then she realized that she couldn't write. There was nothing, however innocently worded, that couldn't be misinterpreted – no, rightly interpreted – by his wife. Convention forbade her to issue invitations to him alone, and there was no way by which a message could be safely delivered. She had thought of saying, the phrase leaping ready-made into her brain – "this thing that has been between us is too big to be let die of a silence." But she knew that she must never write that, lest an alien eye see it.

"Let's go together," Tommy said. But she refused, saying: "My asking couldn't be done with you there. I can't leave this to chance. I'll go and look for him." Derek had left her crying by the sea's edge, and since then there had been no word from him, no message save this one gesture of enmity, the closing of the beach.

"Perhaps you're flattering yourself," Tommy said to comfort her. "He probably closed the beach to save his half dozen coconuts, not to spite you."

"No one could be as petty as that," she said. And Tommy had to agree.

He took her to Neva, and left her there under the white cedar tree whose blossoms spiralled to the ground like miniature parachutes. On all that mile-long strand there was no sign of man's existence. No naked figure cast his net into the sea. No raft broke the smooth monotony of sand. No square sails reeled and dipped under the wind beyond the reef. Only a small octopus propelled itself forward along the beach, humping its squat body above its outspread tentacles; a little helpless monster at that size; one black spot on a white universe of sand.

Tommy went on to Blanchard to see Doctor Crewe about the petition; and Teresa, walking on the Ville Rousse road, met Harvey and asked him where Derek might be. The overseer had been hunting wild pig in the heights, and a sow had been chased by his dog on to the rocks and had leapt into the sea. If there had been a boat on the beach he might have collected his meat.

"These are hard times," he said, looking shrewdly at Teresa. "If you could help us, Miss Craddock?"

Harvey's position, she thought, must be hard indeed. He was the mashed egg in the sandwich, the gag between the teeth. A stronger man might have flung his job at his master's head, but he had many children to feed, and a sick wife. Perhaps – with his friends looking their questions, drawing aside from him as being Morell's tool – his present position was the greater martyrdom. The courage of the noncombatant is an impressive thing.

"The Boss," Harvey told her, "is by the sugar plantation at the West End." It was a mile's walk, but she found him there.

It didn't seem real to Derek that she should have come. Slim and graceful and dressed in green, she was the living spirit of his cane-field, something that he had loved and dreamt of come to life in the sunshine, the illusion of a moment that must die as a dream dies. Could he have kept his vision, maintained his fantasy, the course of island history might have been different. But Teresa was too essentially female to be kept on an ideal plain. She was hot and flushed after her walk. The heightened colour of her cheeks, the perspiration on lip and brow, the warm smell of her body, these went to Derek's head like drink so that he longed to throw her down on to the damp ground and take her so, crushing her into the soil among cane roots. Desire had become an obsession, and here was the woman he wanted, no myth of the cane-fields but a breathing hot-blooded creature whose lips had once met his in ecstasy. Then, with a shiver, and it was as though the sun had gone in and the earth grown cold, he stopped being primitive, became a product of civilization again. And took off his hat.

Teresa, seeing the look on his face, remembered that someone had said that he had the eyes of a fanatic. He had thinned in the few weeks since she had seen him; his eyes were more deeply sunk into his skull; his mouth tighter. A lump in her throat made speaking almost impossible, and they stood in silence where once they had talked about flowering trees and peasants' gardens. Now, Derek had his cane-fields where he wanted them. But merely planting sugar couldn't make St. Celia look like Parham Island. Here there were no mangrove swamps; no burnt brown hills lost in a purple shadow; no iron rails to carry cut canes to a silver-chimneyed factory. Derek would never get sugar from his canes, only juice out of which rum would be made. And the canes themselves had refused to submit to the uniform monotony of more conventional fields, but were sprawling out of line in an unrestrained St. Celian fashion that made them strangely ornamental, so that not even Teresa could deny them beauty, nor fail to appreciate how the cutting of the trees had opened up new vistas. Now she could see Ville Rousse from a new angle, the houses and the towered church huddled between the forest, and a cliff that was not russet but fiercely red, below which the sea lay, blue as a peacock's breast, and flecked with white.

"It's almost Italian," she said nervously, because this was not a meeting that you could begin with – How do you do? "It might be a coloured postcard of the Ligurian coast."

He wasn't helpful; said nothing; only stared at her.

"Are you very busy?" she went on. Eyes of women workers were peeping at them through thin leaves. Children stood in the road. A little world ceased whirling for a moment to watch these two. "I was wondering whether we could go down on to the red platform and talk? I'll trust you not to throw me over."

"You're brave, Teresa. My temper is evil nowadays. Sometimes I wish I'd thrown you over long ago."

"Well, if you have to," she said, "make a good shot at the sea. I'd hate to be picked up in squashed pieces. So messy for the pickers."

They came through the fringe of bushes that was still standing between the cane-fields and the cliff. Two hundred feet below them the sea beat sullenly on to crumbled rocks long since fallen to coral insects and made one with sea growths, with brittle mushrooms, with fans, and with grey groping fingers of coral that were like cactus plants. Here and there on top of the cliff were bunches of silver-lined leaves carrying ragged flowers; and in tiny gullies ferns grew, having a golden powder on their backs.

It wasn't easy to begin. "Derek," she said, "let me hear your side of it. They're saying such hard things of you. I won't believe them until you tell me yourself."

"What are they saying?"

"That you won't let the people get fish. That you made that silly old Biggar impose savage fines on the Nolettes for doing something they had a right to do, that they'd always done."

"The fines were justified, Teresa. The men were found guilty of wilful trespass. I had given them warning."

But she said: "A fortnight's warning, wasn't it? Two weeks isn't enough to get a new idea into these people's heads."

"Then let us hope three pounds will be. That was Biggar's object and intention. And, forgive me for knowing my own business best, but the Nolettes had no right to do what they were doing. The foreshore is mine."

It was horrible that he should be so cold, so businesslike, not meeting her anywhere. "But surely," she said, "there are things like rights of way, and easements." She had heard them mentioned often enough in the last few days. "Neva Beach has been used for centuries."

"If there is a right of way, which I deny, let the Nolettes prove it. The proceeds from my stolen cattle should help to finance an appeal."

"Oh, Derek," she cried out, "the Nolettes didn't steal your cattle."

"I have very good reason to think they did."

"But that's ridiculous," she maintained. "They couldn't have. Why, I've known the whole family for years."

"The privilege of your acquaintance, my dear, does not necessarily confer honesty upon a man."

She could have cried out in her rage: "Nor kindness, nor pity, nor justice either, so it would seem." She was sick with anger; thankful that physical weakness made it impossible for her to throw people over cliffs, else the temptation to do so might have been too strong. Then she remembered that she had come here on behalf of others. She would gain nothing by losing her temper. The hurt bewildered faces of Robert and his friends came between her and her anger; faces of women who must now feed their children on roots only, without oil or fish; faces of men who had fought the sea for a living, and who now baited hooks for an evil creature called cong; or made wicker fish-traps that waves and rocks mashed up. And some stood idle, with leisure to foment trouble, even to steal. No one disputed that the closing of the beach would increase thieving.

"Oh, Derek," she begged, "don't be so hard and so cruel." She would keep her temper, would abase herself to the uttermost, if by so doing she could help the people, help Tommy. She would even remind him of what, with every word he spoke, became more and more a cause of deep shame to her. "I loved you so much, Derek," she said. "Don't break up the idea I had of you; an idea that was splendid and good."

He said: "Your love didn't amount to much, whereas my bitterness is strong."

"Then don't let it be strong. Bitterness is a thing that is more dangerous to give than to receive. It is twice cursed. It curses him that gives and him that takes." She might have been talking to the sea and the sky and the clay under her for all the good that she was doing; but she went on: "Bitterness is a cumulative poison. I know, I've suffered from it in my time. And one hate generates another." Empty words flung to the wind and brushed aside. She felt as waves must feel, beating at coral reefs, and in desperation made a more direct appeal. "Do please cancel that order," she said, "about closing the beach. You'll cause such endless trouble unless you do."

"Trouble to your brother, do you mean? It seems that he has time to take trouble; time to interfere in other people's business. Many points of view, Teresa, are considerably affected by the possession of time and money. I have felt from the beginning that if the loss of produce had ever touched your income you might have been more sympathetic to my difficulties."

A hit. A very palpable hit. How could you know what you would do if you came down to a level where the value of a few coconuts mattered. A halfpenny apiece was the most you could pay for them. Actually an exporter got about three shillings a hundred. So a dozen stolen nuts represented sixpence at most. And Teresa knew that if she were ever in such straits that the loss of sixpence would be important she would be capable of anything, even of stealing nuts. But the Morells were not in the sixpenny class; were sufficiently well off to make the raising of the coconut question merely academic. Cattle thieving, of course, even of such a little cattle, was in a different category. And yet was it? If theft were a crime it was as wrong to take copper as gold. All of which notions swept down over her like the waves of the sea, and her mind felt buffeted as her body would be if it fell a prey to waves. But she had come to this place to persuade Derek, not to philosophize.

"People do steal from us," she said. "Avocado pears are taken from the valley, and grafted mangoes and tomatoes. The villagers seem to consider breadfruit and bread-nuts to be theirs alone. We get them ourselves only by favour. I admit that I've been angry over the tomatoes. Of the other things we have enough and to spare. But when you take as much trouble about anything as Henry and I do about growing vegetables, it is hard to have them vanish overnight. But we haven't put barbed wire across the valley to prevent people passing through to their gardens. We should have no right to do so even if we wanted to. Surely there must be a little live and let live in this world; not all this standing on rights."

"A little take and let take, you seem to mean. But our cases are dissimilar. Your pocket is not affected."

"Oh, Derek, be honest with me, neither is yours. And if it were, you are too big and too generous to carry on this petty persecution of a foolish and uneducated people who live on the verge of starvation; for whom there is no work. I thought once that I had come to know you rather well. Three months ago you wouldn't have done this. The fine part of you has got warped, and if it's my fault I'm sorry beyond words."

"It is your fault, Teresa. Your change of heart changed mine."

"But, Derek, that shouldn't be. Your goodness isn't thistle-down, to be scattered by my – inabilities." She jumped up from where she had been sitting, brushed the clay off her skirt, came close to him. "Derek," she implored, and hated to beg from him, "Derek, give up this madness. For your own sake give it up, if not for mine." And she thought that she saw him waver; believed that her power over him was not quite dead, although her affection might be. He had said things already that morning that it would be hard to forgive.

"You have no right to ask that of me, Teresa."

She said to him: "Hasn't a friend the right to ask anything?"

"A friend hasn't, but a mistress might."

She was never sure whether he had meant it that way; whether he had really offered her a cold-blooded bargain, like the villain of a melodrama. She knew that the scenery against which they were playing their little act was painted in colours so garish that no sophisticated theatre would have allowed them. But not in her wildest dreams could she have visualized such a crude denouement to the plot. The situation dated right back into the eighties, could not surely have been heard on any reputable stage for half a century. So it happened that, as once before when talking with Derek on a cliff top, she finished off the scene as a screaming farce; for there are some occasions which call only for laughter or tears, and it was in her nature to prefer laughter. Striking an attitude, she said: "Derek, there is only one answer. Death rather than dishonour." And, still laughing, ran down the dark path to the road, remembering the proximity of precipices, and not at all sure that if Derek objected to farce he might not turn the play into a tragedy, casting her as the victim. Even so he caught up with her, and, in the safe shelter of cane leaves, forced another scene on her, begging and imploring her pity; apologizing and threatening in the same sentence, till she silenced him at last with: "It's no use, Derek. We don't talk the same language any more. It's over."

She started to walk away down the road, but he followed her, saying: "At least get into the car. You can't walk all the way to Woodstock at that pace." Last time they had parted, he had left her crying on the turf and had stalked away, a more effective piece of

216

drama than driving her in his Ford, so that she sat beside him with a strong sense of anticlimax; and he hardened into an even greater bitterness because she had laughed.

And in her heart she went on laughing because, although she had failed to do anything for the people of Ville Rousse, she felt she had accomplished much for herself; and her elation was due to a sense of freedom, for Derek no longer represented a heartache, nor even something to be ashamed of. He had become a joke. Love blunts one's sense of humour. Hers was now sharpened again, and she was more light-hearted than she had been since Tilly's death. So that when Tommy, who was waiting beside the white cedar tree, saw her face he thought she had succeeded in her mission; but he changed his mind when he saw Derek's.

"I haven't been able to make our friend see things quite as we do," she said, jumping out of the Ford. "But I'm sure that if he thinks things over – "

"Thinking won't alter my opinion, Craddock. I mean to insist on my rights." And when a man says that it is no use arguing, because fundamentally the phrase means nothing; it being doubtful whether we have the right to anything in this world except our own secrets.

So the petition, after long delays and many re-draftings, was laid before the Council; lawyers debated the advisability of the Nolettes lodging an appeal; Nine Power Conferences were held on Brussels carpets; and the affair dragged on into infinity, echoing from one mountain top to another, percolating into by-streets, and being discussed by the very waves of the seashore, and by lizards on veranda rails.

XXXIV

Some took one side in the contention and some the other. "You have no choice," Geoffrey Hylton said, echoing Golightly's advice. But Maurice Collins, that hearty man, approved of Morell's action, having a slogan to the effect that niggers should be kept in their place; without quite appreciating that keeping them hungry brought them out of their place, making them rampage like irate ants, demanding that right to live to which every creature seems to think itself entitled, although other species may say: "*Je n'en vois pas la necessité.*" Die-hard estate owners rejoiced in their hearts, hoping that from now on their own coconuts might be sacred; and there were others, who had no interest in the matter, who thought that perhaps Tommy had been interfering; until Derek – angered beyond bearing by the petition, and the number of names it – began to victimize those who had signed it, and thus crystallized public opinion against him. For, after all, the basis of democracy is that everyone should have the right to ask for justice, even if justice be in the end withheld. Derek denied work to any whose names had appeared on the petition; which hoisted him with his own petard because everyone had signed it and he needed labour. He decreed that in future he would not lend carts or chains or nails; and threatened to forbid the people to cut lumber, or to collect firewood on the estate, refusing them also the use of mangoes, or breadfruit, or the pigeon peas grown as cover crops. Above all, because he, too, had signed, he cancelled the priest's ration of milk.

Father Dolet was an old man, not very strong. He needed the milk. Sometimes it was hard even for a priest to understand human motives. He couldn't know that Derek was hitting wildly, blindly, at a woman who had offered him love, and had then taken it away again with laughter.

The Administrator and Mrs. Grace came to Ça Ira for their farewell visit to the Grande Anse Section. They had expressed no public opinion on the foreshore rights question, knowing that the ultimate solution would come before their successors. But people of the Collins kind – and he should have known, having spent a lifetime currying favour with Government House – took it for granted that they would be on the Morells' side, the other savouring of Socialism; of the right of subject peoples to assert themselves; of scum to rise to the surface. But the matter of the priest's milk shocked Mrs. Grace and biassed her husband's opinion. "Which is typically false reasoning," Teresa said, having already given Father Dolet a cow out of her own pocket, buying it from a Ville Rousse family and thus circulating a little cash. "Penalize the Church and the rich squeal. Whereas mere peasants can be let starve for lack of fish, or be told to eat meat instead."

It was easier than it had been to eat at Ça Ira. Susannah was less Anglican in her outlook; let butter run away with her instead of baking powder. Norah had been to Capesterre, and had spent ten days drinking but she still suffered from fever – that synonymous term – although Albert throve determinedly on his arrowroot diet to prove Teresa wrong in her recommendation of milk. Every week Rosalie brought up the wash from the river with a sniff in her nose and a curl on her lips. "You have a man for fish," she had said to Norah. Norah had scored by finding a cheaper commodity for her *tu quoque*. Every thud of the flat iron was like the stamp of a foot, a declaration of defiance.

Colonel Grace, C.M.G., might have given rise to the original Englishman-in-the-jungle story. He made dinner jackets obligatory even in the country, stubbornly wearing one in the heat of summer; and Tommy, who kept his evening clothes in Capesterre, had to send for them and wear them at dinner for the duration of His Honour's visit. Mrs. Toulouse, manageress of the boarding-house the Craddocks patronized in town, missed the launch with the suitcase and nearly caused international complications; although on Saturday evening she was able to telephone with a due sense of the urgency of the situation – "A special boat leaves at five o'clock tomorrow morning. The Captain promises to deliver your coat."

On Sunday at nine, when expectation had reached fever point; when Tommy had convinced himself either that the launch had sunk, or that the captain had fled with his precious booty to Guadeloupe, and was at that moment attending High Mass in the best cut dinner jacket in the Antilles, a message was delivered to the effect that the suit had reached Grande Anse and was being sent up by donkey. Teresa picked some fallen coconut branches and strewed them across the road. "This has a Biblical flavour," she said. "Your fine raiment shall enter our courts with praise."

At noon the captain of the launch himself telephoned to know whether the suitcase had been delivered. The whole island hung upon the answer – what is there to do on a Sunday morning but listen in? – and when it came in the affirmative a sigh of relief was breathed over a dozen wires, and the girl at the Grande Anse Exchange let the good news escape into the street where it blew gaily away with the dust, reaching the furthest houses under the breadfruit trees and even the sloops in the harbour. But Tommy hung the jacket on a coat-hanger in a draught, and looked at it with deep disfavour.

Mr. Golightly took charge of the reception in Grande Anse, although, thanks to an officious telephone message, the population had wilted slightly by the time its services were required. Some of it had even melted away. Knowing that he was well ahead of time the Colonel had anchored his launch for an hour in a quiet bay and had gone to sleep, letting the mechanic catch fish and Mrs. Grace manicure her finger nails. Meanwhile, someone in Colibri telephoned that His Honour had passed. Frantically scurrying, the people swarmed on to the jetty; and waited in vain, mocked by a grilling sun and an empty sea. Not till a rescue party had been organized was the launch seen rounding Point Lèze; rounding it at exactly the scheduled hour. Then were noses powdered again, and positions taken up.

This was the first time Teresa had seen Janet since hostilities had been declared. "There's something about the air in the Grande Anse Section," old Mrs. Cummins said who had lived sixty years in the colony. "It makes people quarrel." But hitherto

Teresa had never quarrelled with anyone, would have thought it bad form. So she tried to speak naturally to Janet, who was standing beside Mr. Biggar.

"I'm always afraid when I see a crowd on this jetty that it'll do what Tommy's bone manure did, and break the structure's back. It would be fun for the Administrator to find us all struggling in the sea."

Janet's smile was as refreshing as a bucket of snow would have been, and colder than any plunge into the ocean. Obviously, she would not think it bad form to quarrel, but, on the other hand, desirable. Impelled, however, by the sheer magnitude of such an undertaking, Teresa resolved to appeal to her better nature, feeling that she should leave no stone unturned, and not knowing then, but only guessing, how far Janet was behind Derek in the matter of foreshore rights. She said: "Oughtn't we to get together, Mrs. Morell, to persuade your husband to let fish be brought into Neva Bay again? If necessary it could be sold under supervision. We – you and I, I mean – mustn't let women suffer more than they have to already for the sins and follies of men." And when that line failed she hinted a warning. "If the people are driven to despair they might do foolish things. At the other end of the island there was a house burned once."

She should have known that with a woman of Janet's type that note would strike no answering chord. "My husband will not be afraid," said that little grey compressed woman, "he is in the right." Whereupon Teresa turned away hopelessly, saying: "Right? That word can be made to mean anything. This would be a better world if there were less talk of right in it, and more of love."

It didn't seem to be a hot day at all any more, but grey and cold. She could see Mr. Biggar thinking: "Really, there is no knowing what Miss Craddock will do or say next. Fancy mentioning love on the Grande Anse jetty, with the Administrator and Mrs. Grace climbing out of the launch, and the town band playing 'God Save the King'." At least, most of them playing it.

Mr. Golightly pulled his speech out of his pocket; discovered that he had no spectacles; delved further to produce them. Hatless in the presence of royalty, perspiration dripped into his eyes, blurring his glasses. He interrupted himself to find a

221

handkerchief and replaced it, absent-mindedly but effectively, upon his head. His daughter, tearful in white muslin, presented a bouquet to Mrs. Grace, and the Boy Scouts paraded in good order. It was only unfortunate that the Union Jack flying on the post office should have been upside down, and that His Honour should have noticed it.

That night Tommy had to swelter in his dark clothes, but Teresa was able to take off everything and put on again only deep cream beach pyjamas, very decolté. Tommy took one look at her, and said: "Another injustice to men."

"Meaning?"

"That I've got to be hot and you cool."

"Sorry," she laughed, "my mistake. I thought you were going to say something quite different." There was no one but Tommy to choke her with compliments any more, and he needed driving to them.

He said: "I know you did, darling, and I will. The effect is ravishing."

Ravishing. And there was no one to be ravished but her brother, and Mr. Biggar, whose knees were dimpled, and an apparently impervious administrator. Mr. Golightly had been asked to dinner, but had told Tommy that the gas on his stomach compelled him to refuse all invitations. Teresa went back to her mirror and asked herself – was her beauty to be wasted forever, must she get herself to a nunnery, because she had failed love in its last demands; because the gates of Hell had opened to burn up passion, and the breath of its fires left her sapless as dried grass? Or was it that she had failed love, because its chosen object had been unworthy? Had her body known the truth that her mind had rejected? Might there still be a right man somewhere in the world; hope that some day the phoenix would come to life again and her loveliness be worth while? Derek had spoilt her for the business of living un-noticed; but, looking at her reddened lips, her coiled hair, she thought ashamedly – does one deck oneself only for one sacrifice? Sex was surely not the only excuse for beauty. If the picture that she made pleased her brother and her guests, even herself, then it had served its purpose.

Mrs. Grace appreciated the picture more than she might have

222

done had the vice-regal period not been drawing to a close. She took pleasure in expensive clothes, but would not have cared to see this one copied in Capesterre.

"Everyone else," she said with a thin laugh, "puts on stockings for my benefit."

"I haven't any stockings," Teresa said, "nor anything to keep them up with." And, kicking off a shoe to display toenails as scarlet as her lips, she caressed Isabel's back with her bare foot, forgetting what she had said long ago at sight of Derek's ankles, that lower ends spoil everyone.

Isabel was a snobbish person, having no faith in Teresa's discrimination. She would stalk through the village with insufferable arrogance, or from the window of the car growl to right and to left, proclaiming herself the white man's dog and exacting due deference. Even her husband was kept in his place – all her life she was faithful to one dog – and austerely denied the house. Until suddenly, tonight of all nights, in the middle of dinner, she must needs introduce him into the Administrator's presence, a lean white hound with bull-terrier blood in him; flea-bitten, dribbling, rather horrible to see.

Tommy said, having ejected him: "He must have come to present a petition. He's the leader of a deputation demanding compulsory meat rations for dogs, or the right to all fish heads." But the Colonel was not amused.

"There's no good blood in the island," he said, "no sense of breeding." His pale eyes appreciated the foot that had been caressing Isabel, but felt it might have found better material to work on.

Next morning His Honour went up the Hillstone Valley to make a road report. There was a scheme under consideration for opening up the island. And some said: "Let us have roads to attract tourists." And others: "Let us have roads that the peasants may get their produce to the coast." But some said: "Let us have no roads at all, for the peasants can get out their produce by bridle paths, and tourists are economically unsound and make parasites to batten on them, whereas the money could be better spent in other directions." To the Administrator it mattered in no way at all, for he would never see the island again, nor care, after his departure, if it were networked with concrete highways, or left in pristine innocence with only Carib traces to pierce the forest. But he must advise or dissuade the Development Fund; and while their little world waited for his report, Teresa thought of Narden the road surveyor, who lived with his men in the forest; their shelter an ajoupa made of stakes and palm branches; their beds consisting of saplings mattressed with dry leaves; their kitchen three rounded stones with logs between. "If it keeps on raining," Narden had said once – Teresa had met that man at many times and in many places, but never without his umbrella – "our house is dry. But if the sun shines, shrivelling the palm branches, afterwards it leaks like a basket."

The Colonel's expedition met at Blanchard where the motorable road ended. At Woodstock there was a pile of mile-stones lying in the gutter. They had not been set up when the road was in the making, and now the chain stakes had disappeared, and no one knew where they should stand. Vines had bound them to each other, and moss was obliterating their figures. Tommy said: "I wish you would look at Neva Beach, Sir. If you saw it, so long and so empty, you would appreciate the injustice that is being done."

"You mean – I'd weep like anything to see such quantities of sand. No, no, Craddock, this is a question of right and wrong, not of administration. I have no tears left for weeping."

Tommy looked at him sharply. Was the man becoming human on his last lap? Quoting from Alice, and producing a cynical statement that might mean anything.

Mrs. Grace had declined to accompany the expedition, and Teresa, to her everlasting regret, had perforce to remain with her. They two sat together under the saman trees; and while Teresa put in last pieces into her patchwork she thought how heavily it was laden, not only with memories of her dead life, but with this last year's dreams and hopes and disappointments. "One shouldn't take things too seriously," she said aloud. "It's a mistake women make."

"What are you taking too seriously?" her guest asked, peering through spectacles at her *petit point*. "This matter of fish?"

Teresa said: "This matter of fish is symptomatic of the world's condition. My blood has boiled on behalf of Abyssinians, of loyalist Spaniards, of Chinese. Now, it's frothing about the people of Ville Rousse. For or against nations we individuals can do nothing. Therefore, isn't it all the more our duty to strive for the tiny bit of justice that we *can* see, and perhaps control?" So, long ago, her mother had fought for the rights of women. So, now, must her daughter fight for the rights of negro fisher-men; must fight, although the enemy had been her Beloved.

"I have suffered in my heart for so many causes," said the Administrator's wife, "tilted at so many windmills. Now, duty compels my neutrality. My judgment is atrophied and my soul is dead. I take nothing seriously, except my needlework and my food."

"That's roughly what I said at the beginning," and Teresa sighed. "I'm taking this too seriously. Some day I shall have achieved your detachment and be the happier for it. But not yet." Mrs. Grace didn't appreciate how serious this matter was for Teresa. She couldn't know that it was her fault.

Meanwhile the Colonel – correctly but considering the neighbourhood sensationally – attired in rat-catcher, had been given the best horse. A corporal of police preceded him on a stallion. The rest of the field, mounted on sorry nags and sorrier saddles, were hopelessly outclassed, the Colonel proceeding at a sharp canter, which was against local rules.

> "His horse, who never in that sort
> Had handled been before
> What thing had got upon his back
> Did wonder more and more."

Three miles up the valley was supposed to be the limit of equine achievement, but the corporal's stallion – so he averred afterwards – was too excited to stop, and the Administrator knew the way no better than to follow. For the last half hour they rode over roots and mud-holes, on the edge of a precipice where to turn was impossible. Tree-ferns and balisiers brushed the faces of the riders as though to sweep them into the river, river roaring below them over boulders, or collecting itself into deep green pools in whose shadows fish lay. "All in the valley of death rode the six hundred," Tommy murmured. "Knock off a couple of noughts and you have the situation in a nutshell."

He and the doctor, who rode dreamily indifferent to the landscape, secure on some astral plane of his own imagination, came last to the little house among coffee trees where the corporal's horse had condescended to stop. Here the walls of the two rooms were papered with pictures of society beauties cut out of illustrated papers. Rags and old clothing covered a four-poster bed, and there was a red lamp burning in front of a statue of the Virgin, beside which a douche-can was hanging. A Carib woman washed clothes among the stones of a trickling tributary.

"You arrive," the Administrator said sweetly, "as we propose to leave." He didn't realize that he had the better horse; thought, with justification, that he was the better rider.

On the way back, where the valley widened and where with every flood the river took another bite out of its own banks, threatening one month to force the track up on to the mountainside, and in the next leaving bare a useless beach of rounded pebbles where good soil should have been, they met an old withered woman carrying a bundle of sticks. Tommy remembered how once before he had met her in that valley, and he knew that – all ragged as she was – she owned the land in that place. Then she had stood before him in the path, demanding his name and business; having learnt which she had given a shrill cackle. "I think you are the police," she said, "and I drop a keg of mountain dew in the road." A hundred yards back Tommy had noticed the smell and seen broken glass. "But here I have another keg," and, fumbling in the bushes, had produced a Gordon's gin bottle full of a very foul brown liquid that masqueraded as rum. Now, in pursuit of the Administrator, Tommy thought how gratefully he would have accepted a nip of mountain dew, but there was none on offer for the crone carried only sticks.

The expedition was in sad disorder. Some steeds had fainted and rode their riders, while the Colonel and the corporal were dim figures on a far horizon, still cantering among scrubby lime trees where some day rollers would crush metal into mud, and oil from Trinidad be poured out of drums to make a road.

Next day the corporal telephoned: "The Government must get me a new horse, Sir. For mine is altogether discolated."

"And when he next doth ride abroad," Teresa said, peevish at having missed the party, "may I be there to see." But a fortnight later the Graces left St. Celia in a cloud of pretty speeches, and, shaking the dust of it from their feet, straightway forgot the island; and were themselves forgotten.

XXXV

Every summer Tommy and Teresa stayed with Geoffrey Hylton at his house in the mountains. Water fell seventy feet to an ice-blue pool fretted by broken waves; and below the pool, black sodden logs and grotesque roots were caught among sulphur-coloured stones to make a dam, under which crabs skulked, and on top of which ferns had rooted and little orchids. From the lip of the fall there was a bitter wind blowing, and a thin blinding spray filling the green twilight of immense trees. On one side of the river, high above the bed of the stream, was a clearing, where – catching a sunlight the pool had never known – bananas grew, sheltered alike from the cold spray and from the shadow of the forest; and among them guavas and breadfruits and citrus trees, round and about which, as though appropriately to sweeten them, sugar was planted, with here and there to lend flavour, a pepper vine or a vanilla. At the top of the clearing, left unfelled by who knows what accident, by what design, three dead tree-ferns stood like the crosses of a Calvary, their gaunt branches naked against the sky.

"The other day," Teresa said, "I heard a tourist boast: 'I've seen bananas *growing.*'" Watching the play of sunlight on broad leaves; stroking with her fingers a coarse petal that was purple on one side and on the other crimson, she swung her mind back to the first time she had been able to say that. A long while ago it was, and a long way away, in an East Indian valley that didn't exist any more, since a mountain called the Mother opened her sides and buried it under stones and lava, leaving nothing of that place save the memory of a dead sentiment that had only tropical glamour for its unstable foundation. Sometimes she wondered – being now

blasé about bananas and impervious to glamour – whether famili-
arity did not take altogether too much of the kick out of life,
whether the pleasure of despising a tourist was quite equal to the
thrill of still being one.

Sitting in the Herrick River – where spray blew coldly off the
waterfall, and the note of a siffleur montagne echoed among the
rocks like a mournful slate pencil – she consoled herself with the
realization that her own ignorance could offer everlastingly brave
new worlds to conquer. For who was she to despise a tourist, who
could not look at a bunch on a banana tree and tell at a glance
whether it had seven hands, or eight, or nine; who could hardly
be trusted to distinguish a Sucrier from a Cavendish, a Gros
Michel from a Portorique; who could patter only the bare jargon
of a trade that half the island lived on. Listening to the scraps of
talk that were bubbling over yellow stones – ("the Canadian
market is used to the Gros Michel. It's an expensive thing to
change public taste." Or, "the day that Panama disease is wiped
out, the profit in bananas will be gone. They'll be too easy.") – her
mind hovered, like a hummingbird over an orchid, upon that
long-ago island where death had lurked in the rivers and where
even among fruit trees one thought of poisoned arrows invisibly
sped. In those days, and in that place, bananas were not grown for
export, but to be eaten by little black Melanesian people, who,
only if there was trade tobacco to be used as currency, would sell
their surplus to the white officials in the town. Whereas here,
handled tenderly as babies might be, bunches were headed by
narrow root-tangled paths to the open road; were then trucked on
lorries; and at last swung in their thousands on to a white steamer
lying, improbable as a dream, in a blue bay under mountains.
Here, it was only the rejects that could be purchased for eating,
melancholy discredited bananas, half wrapped in a trash of their
own leaves, wisps of which blew through the little sleepy town
that wakened when a boat came in, and afterwards settled again
like a dog disturbed by a fly.

It was pleasant to be for a little while in a new world; to view
the sea from a different and a distant angle; to have those
tantalising unattainable mountains so close that thunder seemed
to be a tangible concrete thing flung from one peak to another, a

terror rolling into the valley as though gathering to itself stones and rubble among which to lie silent; so leaving room in the air for the tiny squeaking of bats; for the noises of mice gnawing, and of distant rain that was like the sighing of waves on sand. At dawn Teresa saw light breaking in diamond-shaped silver patches between the crossed stems of coffee bushes, or between the branches of rubber trees spread like a spider's web against the sky. Once there were ants drinking from a drop of water on a board, their tight completed circle making a buttonholed eyelet of the one drop. And on the road to the river wasps burrowed in the ground, throwing out earth with their hind legs to pile up microscopic mountains of dust.

Harrigan the yard man lived in a trash house under mango trees, their young leaves staring redly out of black-green foliage. On the door of the house there was a message written with a burnt stick. "The one on the cloth is for Mrs. Lewis, the next one for Serena," and Teresa never knew what the words meant, but there, every year, they were; having once been comprehensible to someone but now meaningless as Carib carvings on stones.

"Please, Sir," Harrigan asked, "to give me a dose of Epsom Salts." Which, it transpired, was not for himself but for his light o' love in the village; and on being told that there were none, he said: "It is no matter. She arx me already last week. Now, she can wait until next."

"What did you do with the garment I left here last year?" Teresa asked, having discarded pink silk panties and knowing that Harrigan had purloined them. Often she had wondered which of the Colibri belles were flaunting them.

"I wear them in bed," Harrigan said, adding: "When I am in bed I read the Bible." And showed them his book with an ace of spades marking his place in the Old Testament, and a joker that in the New.

At the back of the waterfall there were other clearings, clearings snatched from a forest whose rotting giants lay in a tangle among grapefruit trees, or else soared in isolation – oozing white tears of resin – with the roots of parasites wound about their bodies like thread on a reel of cotton, Here, the words blown by the wind to the pink-clouded mountain tops were "budding" and "grafting", "Washington Navels", and "Marsh's Seedless". We're aiming at a small fruit," Geoffrey said. "Ships and hotels don't want a crate that'll feed eighty only, and not a hundred and fifty." And again: "I've waited five years to find out that the Agricultural Department made a mistake and sent me seeded grapefruit instead of seedless."

Fruit after fruit was sliced open, squeezed of its juice, tasted and flung aside; some revealing clustering pips where only green flesh should have been; others condemned as woody, too thick-skinned, too acid; and these lay in the long grass looking like the refuse of a party, blackened already by swarming ants and become a refuge for worms. But the trees that had failed in their function, trees that, through no fault of their own, had borne seeded fruit instead of seedless, would not be altogether wasted; would, in the end, justify their five years' enjoyment of God's sunshine, of His rain. For their branches would be lopped off and the stumps bound with tape, behind which the bud of a navel orange would be inserted, so that what was one tree would become another, and would bear marketable fruit, sweet green oranges, where were now acid grapefruit and unwanted pips.

Beyond the last outposts of the forest – "Each brooding unit of which," Teresa said, "must look upon these alien fruits and wonder when will be its turn to be sacrificed, when it, too, will lie prostrate in the interests of Canadian consumers" – they saw the sea shimmering fifteen hundred feet below them; shimmering under a yellow sunset against which stood three dead tree-ferns that, from this angle, were no longer the crosses of a Calvary, but dead tree-ferns merely, left unfelled to grow vanilla on, or perhaps yams.

"Did you know," she said suddenly, for the beauty of the view turned her thoughts to sadness and so inevitably to Derek, "that the Morells have been getting anonymous letters, threatening them?"

Hylton said: "They've asked for trouble. Maybe they'll get it."

"God send they don't," Tommy said. "If Neva were burnt it would swing public opinion in their favour."

It didn't seem fair that one should have to remember trouble in this peaceful place among mountains where three friends were. Smoking cigarettes through the long green holder, Teresa watched and listened to these two men of different races and different upbringing, whose minds were nevertheless in harmony; and wondered why, if love had to kindle unsuitable flames, the lightning had not fallen upon her friend rather than on a stranger. To love a coloured man would, she supposed, be asking for trouble as surely as the Morells were asking for it. Even with love in one's hands would one ever be let slip behind the curtain, know what lay under the mask? And yet, greater sorrow had been brought about by her desire for a white man who had turned out to be a person not of her own creed or understanding. People thought too much of colour in this world. It wasn't colour that mattered, but only mental outlook.

Now and again there was a splutter of rain on the roof – as though the clouds showered down peppercorns – drowning for a moment the talk of the two men ("count bunches", "limes budded on sour orange", "cold storage plants") – drowning the roar of the river and the booming of tree frogs. But when the rain passed away it left the moonlight as it found it, spread like white butter on the flat broad leaves of the banana trees.

XXXVI

At Ça Ira there was more trouble lying in wait for Teresa behind the pois-doux trees. She had vowed that in future she would cling to no one but Isabel, who gave all and asked nothing. Now Isabel was dead, having faced her greatest adventure alone, with never a bark nor a groan to tell where she had died. While they were away puppies had been born to her – ("She's always having them," Teresa had said once to Derek) – and on the evening of their return she crawled out of the night to meet them, crying as though ashamed of what she had done, flattening herself on the ground with her tail wagging feebly and not as usual like a metronome or a winnowing fan. Next morning at dawn, wedged under the house among seasoning boards, she fed the puppies for the last time, her brown eyes pleading with Teresa for something she could not give, speaking a message that she could not understand. And from that hour was never seen or heard of, going out alone into the bush to find the darkness of death.

That night the wailing of the puppies was like the crying of sea-birds, louder to Teresa's ears than the beat of the sea, and more piercing than the shrilling of insects. Scrabbling, scrambling, in a blind world bounded by four sides of a kerosene box; knocking their blunt pink noses against unknown substances; catching their claws in the woollen meshes of a bathing suit she had given them as blanket, they cried their hunger to an empty world. She lit a spirit lamp in the pantry, nursing the blue flame. Warming milk in a saucepan she poured it into a bottle that Norah had lent her, and one after another picked the little cold creatures from their helpless fumbling, and stopped their crying with sustenance. Already they knew the smell of warm rubber as twenty-four hours ago they had known their mother. Pink mouths gaped to show square tongues; round heads were pressed back upon Teresa's own breast; little splat paws clutched at the glass as though by purchase to strengthen their sucking, and she could feel the warm liquid trickling into tummies that swelled under her hand until milk foamed at their mouths and spilled through their nostrils. But their bodies were still cold against her heart, and she wondered whether they had cried from chill as well as from hunger. Lighting the stove again, she filled a soft hot water bottle that, wrapped in a towel, made a warm platform over which they crawled suspiciously, doubtfully, delightedly; until, wedged between the bottle and the box side, they sank into a deep sleep, giving only the twitch of a tail, the wrinkling of a snout, to show her that they still lived.

Sleepless herself, Teresa looked back over five years of a devotion, a companionship, an utter faithfulness, that she would remember until she, too, went out into the darkness. Already the cats, sensing death instinctively, had taken possession of the room that was never theirs, sprawling on sofas and moving leisurely where once they had scuttled. Never again, and tears flowed with the knowledge, would Teresa see her beloved chasing chickens, and being in turn routed by an irate mother hen; pursuing piglets by the river's bank; and lizards that she was never quick enough to catch. She remembered the night they saw a ghost together, a grey shape rushing by in the twilight, and Isabel, still a baby, crying piteously with terror, her heart thumping as she was picked up. Once she had fallen into a crack in a red cliff, one of those frightening gullies that during heavy rain run liquid mud and stain the sea orange, from which she was – at Teresa's own personal peril – plucked from among orchids and golden-backed ferns. And once, for no reason, she had rushed at a woman, bruising her leg, who, an hour later, came to the house demanding as cure for her hurt a hair of the dog to put on the sore place, quite literally a hair of the dog that bit her, and was hardly satisfied with the witch hazel Teresa offered instead.

The saddest words in the language can be – never again. She knew that never again would Isabel tease crabs, or nip a donkey's heels, or scare a stranger; never again sit with crossed paws smiling at the moon, nor stalk through the village arrogantly, proclaiming herself the white man's dog. All these things she remembered, sleepless in the night with the puppies beside her. And knew that only if these lived would the pain in her heart be stilled a little, and this charred and desolate year have more to show for itself than a piece of patchwork, now finished. If a woman loved a man and bore his child, then something was left to her, even though love were dead. Was not Norah, having Albert, happier than she, whose arms were empty, empty save for two blind puppies left to her care with a pleading message that she had been too dense to understand.

But, in a week's time, the puppies were dead also; dead of chill, or of indigestion, or of being orphans. "They don't die easy," Henry had said once of another litter. Now he had two brown bodies to bury, bodies with white noses and white tails. And Teresa's arms were empty indeed and her heart bitter because one year had taken so many things from her – dogs, and a cook, and a mushroom growth of love; and had given her nothing but a patchwork bedspread with memories of her dead life woven into it.

XXXVII

"Miss T'resa, it beautiful," Norah said, when for the first time it was spread out, finished. "Miss T'resa, I like it good."

She stood in the doorway, wriggling herself against the jamb as she had wriggled when telling Teresa that she was with child. Now Teresa could see that she was pregnant with portentous news, but knew that her gestation must not be hurried, and waited while she opened her mouth and shut it three times, thinking how like a crapaud she was, and wondering again how any man had dared.

"I knowing something," she uttered at last, and stopped, waiting to be questioned further.

"How lucky you are," Teresa said. "Many of us never know anything. But won't you tell me what it is?"

"I knowing," the girl said, "who take Mr. Morell's cattle. Robert did not take it nor Nicholas. Abraham, who is married to their sister, take it. That same Abraham who sell diamonds in Capesterre for five pounds."

Teresa stared at her open-mouthed. Norah had indeed been delivered. "He and men from St. Patrick's, they stealing the cattle, but the cattle he strong and he kick a hole in the boat, so that the men must put back and find another vessel, Abraham thrusting his hat into the hole and swimming alongside to keep it there. Therefore they take Robert's boat, and because it is a small cattle they can tie its legs and sail it through the night to St. Patrick's Bay, and there sell it."

So Derek's bull had not gone to Guadeloupe, nor perhaps his coconuts either. "In St. Patrick's," Joseph the overseer had said, "we live in darkness. God send us a road that we may see light."

Teresa remembered the Big House looking down on to the Atlantic, whose breakers swept out of the sunrise into the bay. Shutters creaked in the wind and floorboards rotted. From out of their darkness the men of St. Patrick's had put this thing upon the people of Ville Rousse; and Robert and Nicholas, whose mother had been a witch, were accused of what their sister's husband had done.

"Do many know this?" Teresa asked. And Norah answered: "Only Nicholas know, for next day he bring the boat back to Neva with fish. And he tell me."

It would seem that Norah had her lover again. This was not a thing that a man would tell to his sister's enemy if she were not his mistress. Nicholas was the man who had dared. Yet, the girl did not look well or happy, was still coughing. "You did right to tell me," Teresa said, "but for the moment tell no one else." And then she asked: "Norah, is your fever no better? Can the doctor do nothing?"

"No, Miss, he can do nothing."

"But you still go to the clinic?"

"Not any more. The doctor, he tell me I must sleep with an open window."

"But, Norah, of course you must. I thought you did." It was a thing she had prided herself on, that her servants were so far emancipated.

"Once I did," Norah said, "but not now. If I do the dead hand of Tilly will reach out to me. For at night the dead walk."

The dead hand of Tilly. Susannah had said: "Tilly will seek to return to her room, for the dead are very cold." This was the same dead hand that had come between herself and Derek; that had brought trouble to the people of Ville Rousse and had caused suspicion to fall on the heads of Robert and Nicholas. Now, it was putting a dread finger on Norah, spoiling her health. Was it over Nicholas that the two girls had fought, she wondered; and must the quarrel last beyond the grave into eternity? Did a dead hand come between Norah and Nicholas in their ecstasy, dividing, frightening them, so that the man babbled his secrets?

"Abraham is gone to the French country," Norah said. "He safe now."

Teresa went into the garden to look for Tommy, wondering how this information could best be used. And she thought how heavy the air was, laden with sunshine, and how still were the sea and the trees that seemed to be lifeless under this hurricane season heat, as though the threat of thunder or cyclone had magicked them into immobility. Tommy was speaking to Henry, Henry who was in trouble because his keeper had gone mad and would have to be sent away. "I sad," he said, "for I work hard to make her happy." But she had tried to kill him, first with knives and axes which he had hidden away. Then she had thrown cups and glasses at him, but these he had not hidden because they were so little dangerous. "To do that," he said, "would have hurt her feelings. But now I have no cups and no keeper."

The Craddocks knew by now that the Government would do nothing; that the fight for Neva Beach must be fought out in a court of law. Little things direct the destinies of men. Maurice Collins had not forgiven Hylton for a remark made in the Cintra bar, and Hylton was the Craddocks' friend. "I thought that was how you made something out of a trip," Geoffrey had said, "charging up a deck chair to your expenses' account." The fat man had influence on the official half of the Council, and had thrown his immense weight on to the Morells' side.

"An Englishman's home is his castle," he mouthed. And Teresa made a picture of Derek all alone on his long beach building sand castles; or alternatively, ramparts of sand to keep out a sea that had no respect for his rights, but now and then stole a whole tree from him, or shifted the estuary of the river. Collins might claim to keep niggers in their place, but no one could control the sea. And even niggers were not easily kept, but signed petitions and talked of easements, and wrote anonymous letters almost as though they were human beings.

Tommy deplored the letters. He said: "The forces of evil must be suppressed by the steamroller of our own integrity," having warned Corbin long ago that he would adopt that glorious phrase as his own. He practised it as he shaved, declaiming the words to his own reflection. The Government would do nothing, but he had a good case at law to prove that by usage from time immemorial the public had acquired a prescriptive right to beach their boats at Neva. But the ways of the law were long and tortuous, and the expenses would have to be met out of his own pocket.

"You're with me in this, Teresa?" he asked. "If we're together nothing matters, but a house divided against itself – "

"I'm with you, Tommy," she answered. "I made a fool of myself. No one but you knows how big a fool. But that's over." Their two shadows, one tall and thin and the other fat, were lost in the bigger shadow of the saman trees, and the setting sun poured molten gold on to the still sea. If they should win this case, she thought, and free the people, then the dead hand of Tilly would be dead indeed, and would trouble them no more. But she shivered a little as night fell, because she knew that the future was very long and the law slow.

XXXVIII

Derek heard from Jessaman his gardener that Isabel was dead. "Deceased Partridge lose a dog in the same way," he said. "It go out into the Bush and die alone." Derek remembered how fond Teresa had been of the dog, and a wave of tenderness swept over him, a feeling that was the more tender because he had a mistress now, a peasant girl in Woodstock, and was no longer the sex-hungry person who had nearly flung Teresa down among cane stalks. "I'll go to her," he said to himself on impulse, "and tell her I'm sorry about the dog. So, perhaps, we shall be friends again" – he had forgotten that he had rejected friendship – "and Craddock will withdraw this foolish lawsuit."

He came to her as once before by the Souffrière valley. But that first time had been on a day of rain and storm, and he had come over the divide to find the grey sea smirched by the wind. Rivers had roared in his ears, and he had seen trees bent at right angles. Where paths should have been there was liquid mud. Now, although it was the season of storms, heat lay on the land and trees were dry and brittle. The smell of sulphur filled the old crater, for there was no wind to blow it down the valley, and the sky was brazenly blue with the peaks purple against it.

He found Teresa by the Ça Ira River, for she had been bathing in the pool that they called the Big God Nquong's, and had a towel over her arm and her hair hanging in two long plaits. "Why has he come?" she wondered. And her soul skipped like a little hill at the thought that this might be a visit of surrender; but she greeted him as though she had seen him only that morning.

"Soon it will be titiree time," she said, "and the rocks will be black with young fish moving up from the sea. They will squirm up the waterfalls like wriggling worms; and some will get lost in backwaters, and some be left high and dry to rot and to stink."

Together they walked in the shadow of cocoa trees, talking of Isabel. And she told him of Ma Nolette's spirit that sat in that place making the cows run dry, so that no one would pasture his cattle in that part of the valley; but she did not mention the name of the ghost, for Nolette would have been a contentious word between them. She did not know why he had come, but she feared to throw firebrands into the dry wood of their memories lest a flame be kindled. Here there were nutmeg trees, under whose yellowing leaves fruit hung, looking like green unripe peaches; and in a cut segment of bamboo two tiny tree frogs lay in water with nothing more of themselves showing than frightened eyes.

"There was village drama this morning," Teresa said. "Français the carpenter came to telephone for the corporal. 'An old woman,' he said, 'is abusing my wife. I not wishing to persecute her because she is too old, but I ask the corporal to come and tell her to cease.'"

"And did he come?" Derek said, but hardly seemed to listen to the answer. He was more uncomfortable than she at this meeting; for the spirit of the past weighed on both their consciences, but most heavily on his.

Tommy had gone to Grande Anse, and Norah brought tea for them on the veranda. So they broke bread together, bread in the form of cake into which Susannah's baking powder had not run away. Below them on the lawn there were a dozen ground lizards looking for mole crickets. And Henry passed with his gun, threatening a chicken hawk, and saying: "When I have a pain in my shoulder then I know that I hit. But once in fifteen times I miss."

Derek and Teresa were together again, but there was no life in their meeting, which was a thing cold and unprofitable as yesterday's pudding. This man had become to her like a quinine pill from which all sugar has been sucked, leaving bitterness only. "It isn't the island I'm going to love," he had whispered, "but you," words now meaning so little that she thought a flying fish had said them, or was it a turtle? And hope that he might persuade the

Craddocks to drop the case withered and died in Derek. When he got up to go he had still given no reason for his coming, save to condole about Isabel; and Teresa's soul had stopped skipping because she realized that this had been no visit of surrender. Nevertheless, she would wrestle with him for the last time, although feeling had so hardened in her that her heart belied the soft words spoken.

"Derek," she said, and the world held its breath while she pleaded, even the birds falling silent. "Derek, for the sake of what was once beautiful between us, grant me this one thing before it is too late. Let the people beach their boats on Neva again." And as he stiffened with refusal, she put out her hand to stop his words and said: "If I were to prove to you that your cattle was not stolen by Ville Rousse people, nor perhaps your coconuts either, would not that make a difference?" But he shook his head.

"Who stole the cattle is beside the point," he said. "The fact remains that the beach was used. I stand on my rights, and having begun this I must go on." She saw now that he was obstinate, not on account of anything that she had been or done, but for obstinacy's sake, bolstering his pride in his possessions with the conviction that no one could take from him one tithe of his rights nor one iota of his hold over the lives of others. "If I gave in now," he said, "they would think that I was afraid, and nothing that I have would be safe any more."

The world went on with its breathing; birds sang again, and a donkey brayed. She remembered Laertes, the donkey at Surinam, begging for bread on the stoep where were Sanders and Andrew and Luther and John, and Prudence the washerwoman saying: "Pelican live by fish alone, but we must rent land to grow bread." "It isn't like this on our island," Teresa had maintained, "it isn't like this at all." Yet, here was the very spirit of Parham, brought over and fostered by one man. And who knew where it would lead them, or what the end would be?

Derek went away from her down the hill. And as she watched him go she saw the tortuous processes of the law winding away into the future like a white dusty road, leading him on to his own defeat. A year ago, dreaming of this man, she had picked up a fragment of stuff brought from St. Pierre in Martinique; had remembered black-red wine served at sunset, and a bearded, chattering priest straying like a goat among ruins. "*Et, pfui*," the priest had said with a flick of the fingers, "*tout était fini.*"

"*Et, pfui*," Teresa said, flicking cigarette ash on to the lawn, "that thing is finished." Love lay in ruins, but creepers covered the sore places; soon grass would grow in the streets, and what might have been a proud city would be altogether forgotten. Far out at sea there was a steamer passing, its smoke hanging motionless on the still air. From the forest behind her doves were calling. Henry locked up the tool-shed and said good night.

"This evening I must go early," he said. "I have the promise of a nice cover for my cow."

OTHER CARIBBEAN MODERN CLASSICS

Now in print:

Wayne Brown, *On The Coast*
ISBN 9781845231507, pp. 115, £8.99
Jan Carew, *Black Midas*
ISBN 9781845230951, pp.272 £8.99
Jan Carew, *The Wild Coast*
ISBN 9781845231101, pp. 240; £8.99
Austin Clarke, *Amongst Thistles and Thorns*
ISBN 9781845231477, pp.208; £8.99
Austin Clarke, *Survivors of the Crossing*
ISBN 9781845231668, pp. 208; £9.99
Neville Dawes, *The Last Enchantment*
ISBN 9781845231170, pp. 332; £9.99
Wilson Harris, *Heartland*
ISBN 9781845230968, pp. 104; £7.99
Wilson Harris, *The Eye of the Scarecrow*
ISBN 9781845231644, pp. 118, £7.99
George Lamming, *Of Age and Innocence*
ISBN 9781845231453, pp. 436, £14.99
Earl Lovelace, *While Gods Are Falling*
ISBN 9781845231484, pp. 258; £10.99
Una Marson, *Selected Poems*
ISBN 9781845231682, pp. 184; £9.99
Edgar Mittelholzer, *Corentyne Thunder*
ISBN 9781845231118, pp. 242; £8.99
Edgar Mittelholzer, *A Morning at the Office*
ISBN 9781845230661, pp.210; £9.99
Edgar Mittelholzer, *Shadows Move Among Them*
ISBN 9781845230913, pp. 358; £12.99
Edgar Mittelholzer, *The Life and Death of Sylvia*
ISBN 9781845231200, pp. 366; £12.99
Andrew Salkey, *Escape to an Autumn Pavement*
ISBN 9781845230982, pp. 220; £8.99
Andrew Salkey, *Hurricane*
ISBN 9781845231804, pp. 101, £6.99

Andrew Salkey, *Earthquake*
ISBN 9781845231828, pp. 103, £6.99
Andrew Salkey, *Drought*
ISBN 9781845231835, pp. 121, £6.99
Andrew Salkey, *Riot*
ISBN 9781845231811, pp. 174, £7.99
Denis Williams, *Other Leopards*
ISBN 9781845230678, pp. 216; £8.99
Denis Williams, *The Third Temptation*
ISBN 9781845231163, pp. 108; £8.99

Titles thereafter include...

George Campbell, *First Poems*
O.R. Dathorne, *The Scholar Man*
O.R. Dathorne, *Dumplings in the Soup*
Neville Dawes, *Interim*
Wilson Harris, *The Sleepers of Roraima*
Wilson Harris, *Tumatumari*
Wilson Harris, *Ascent to Omai*
Wilson Harris, *The Age of the Rainmakers*
Marion Patrick Jones, *Panbeat*
Marion Patrick Jones, *Jouvert Morning*
George Lamming, *Water with Berries*
Roger Mais, *The Hills Were Joyful Together*
Roger Mais, *Black Lightning*
Edgar Mittelholzer, *Children of Kaywana*
Edgar Mittelholzer, *The Harrowing of Hubertus*
Edgar Mittelholzer, *Kaywana Blood*
Edgar Mittelholzer, *My Bones and My Flute*
Edgar Mittelholzer, *A Swarthy Boy*
Orlando Patterson, *The Children of Sisyphus*
Orlando Patterson, *An Absence of Ruins*
V.S. Reid, *New Day*
V.S. Reid, *The Leopard* (North America only)
Garth St. Omer, *A Room on the Hill*
Garth St. Omer, *Shades of Grey*
Andrew Salkey, *The Late Emancipation of Jerry Stover*
and more…

All Peepal Tree titles are available from the website
www.peepaltreepress.com
with a money back guarantee, secure credit card ordering
and fast delivery throughout the world at cost or less.

Contact us at:
Peepal Tree Press, 17 King's Avenue, Leeds LS6 1QS, UK
Tel: +44 (0) 113 2451703
E-mail: contact@peepaltreepress.com